SIREN

Michelle Briddock

Copyright © 2022 Michelle Briddock

All rights reserved

The characters and events portrayed in this book are fictitious. Any similarity to real persons, living or dead, is coincidental and not intended by the author.

No part of this book may be reproduced, or stored in a retrieval system, or transmitted in any form or by any means, electronic, mechanical, photocopying, recording, or otherwise, without express written permission of the publisher.

Cover Design: Cat at TRC Designs

ISBN: 9798835887521

To my family, whom I love and adore very much.

(Please don't read the sex bits!)

CONTENTS

Title Page
Copyright
Dedication
A NOTE FROM THE AUTHOR
Playlist
Prologue — 1
Chapter One — 2
Chapter Two — 10
Chapter Three — 13
Chapter Four — 20
Chapter Five — 23
Chapter Six — 29
Chapter Seven — 33
Chapter Eight — 37
Chapter Nine — 43
Chapter Ten — 49
Chapter Eleven — 56
Chapter Twelve — 64
Chapter Thirteen — 68
Chapter Fourteen — 71
Chapter Fifteen — 76

Chapter Sixteen	81
Chapter Seventeen	85
Chapter Eighteen	90
Chapter Nineteen	94
Chapter Twenty	97
Chapter Twenty One	100
Chapter Twenty Two	107
Chapter Twenty Three	110
Chapter Twenty Four	118
Chapter Twenty Five	122
Chapter Twenty Six	126
Chapter Twenty Seven	131
Chapter Twenty Eight	134
Chapter Twenty Nine	139
Chapter Thirty	143
Chapter Thirty One	147
Chapter Thirty Two	151
Chapter Thirty Three	160
Chapter Thirty Four	165
Chapter Thirty Five	170
Chapter Thirty Six	177
Chapter Thirty Seven	181
Chapter Thirty Eight	186
Chapter Thirty Nine	192
Chapter Forty	198
Chapter Forty One	203
Chapter Forty Two	208
Chapter Forty Three	217

Chapter Forty Four	223
Chapter Forty Five	227
Chapter Forty Six	234
Chapter Forty Seven	240
Chapter Forty Eight	243
Chapter Forty Nine	248
Chapter Fifty	251
Chapter Fifty One	256
Chapter Fifty Two	264
Chapter Fifty Three	268
Chapter Fifty Four	271
Epilogue	273
Acknowledgement	277
About The Author	279

A NOTE FROM THE AUTHOR

◆ ◆ ◆

I just wanted to take this chance to say that I hope you love reading Siren just as much as I loved writing it.

Siren is a DARK contemporary romance which features various triggers that could be upsetting to some.

While I don't want to spoil the experience for the reader, please be aware that this book contains explicit sexual content and violent scenes that some readers may find disturbing.

PLAYLIST

A list of talented artists who provided inspiration along the way.

- Demons - Imagine Dragons
- Mad Hatter - Melanie Martinez
- Dancing with your ghost - Sasha Alex Sloan
- WONDERLAND - Neoni
- Numb - Linkin Park
- Pretty Toxic Revolver - Machine Gun Kelly
- Million Eyes - Loic Nottet
- Castle - Halsey
- The Fear - The Score
- Wicked Game - Inferno
- Carry your throne - Jon Bellion
- First Fuck - 6LACK
- Human - Taylor Holder
- In The Shadows - The Rasmus
- Mermaid - Skott
- Twisted - MISSIO
- Legends are made - Sam Tinnesz

PROLOGUE

Lexi

Some people fear death.
They fear what's beyond it.
They fear their ugliest sins stalking from the darkness, entwining around their souls like vines, ready to drag them to the fiery pits of hell, where they'll burn and scream for all eternity.
I'm not afraid of death.
I'm not afraid of hell.
I already live there.

CHAPTER ONE

Lexi

My head is pounding already and I haven't even opened my eyes yet.

I'm already dreading the eight hour lecture ahead of me but yearning for that shit all the same. Anything to be out of this dump they call a house.

I can't even put my impending headaches down to alcohol consumption or a good night prior as that's just not the case anymore.

I checked the time, six fifty seven AM. I need to get a move on.

Running my fingers under my pillow, I feel for the small kitchen knife I keep tucked away safely there. I feel its smooth wooden handle before the pads of my finger tips graze the cold metal attached. *Right where it should be. Good.*

I rise from my bed, tucking my bare feet into my fluffy, black peep toe slippers and slowly head to my bedroom door, placing an ear against the wooden panel. Silence.

I exhale a sigh of relief. I haven't slept through the night in months, or even more than a few hours at that.
Living in this house is like living in your worst nightmare.

The noises through the night, the banging, the crying, even the silence at times can be so terrifying that I have a sturdy silver bolt on my door. You'd think this would make me feel safer, and I have to admit that to a certain extent I guess it does, but still not enough to help me dare to sleep at night.

I hurry to my en suite and turn on the shower.
Mum hasn't paid the electricity bill again so it looks like it's another cold one for me.

Taking a deep breath, I step into the chilling spray of the icy water. My skin immediately prickles at the sensation and my pierced nipples harden as the water cascades through my long, dark auburn hair and down my slightly concave stomach and toned thighs.

I wash as quickly as I possibly can, immersing myself in the scent of my peaches and cream body wash before grabbing my towel, brushing my teeth and heading back into the bedroom.

My room isn't much to look at. It has little in the way of furniture. An old, second hand bed and a small, chipped pine bedside table, some old battered drawers and a wardrobe which apart from the fact it doesn't match anything in the room, is also littered with fist holes. One so big, you can actually see a sleeve of one of my tattered, old denim jackets stored behind it. However, at least the room is clean and tidy unlike the rest of the place.

I grab my black distressed jeans from the wardrobe and the black sweater I picked up at a thrift shop, *it's more low cut than I would have liked, but hey beggars can't be choosers,* and pull them on quickly.

I run a brush through my long locks which fall to my lower back and let it air dry while grabbing my tote bag, ready to go.

I stare at myself in the mirror. Slight dark circles are beginning to form under my eyes like shadows tainting my porcelain skin. One blue eye sparkling like a sapphire and one brown eye, the colour of molten chocolate stare back at me. Heterochromia is the actual name for it. I'm not sure why it happened to me, genetics' I guess, but it's the first thing that people notice about me when they meet me. That and my flaming red hair.

Over the years my looks have helped out in one way or

another. I've done a little modelling here and there for a few pennies but nothing too major. Unfortunately my looks have also attracted the attention of the scum who visit my house on a regular basis. Another reason for the safety lock on my door.

Unbolting the door slowly, I peer out before making my exit. No one appears to be awake. *Thank God.*

Reaching the staircase, I walk down the stairs quickly observing a couple of heavily sedated people sleeping in my hallway at the bottom.

See, I've lived with my mum my whole life. Just me and her, in this house, but it's safe to say I never had a normal, regular childhood.

My mum has been a heroin addict for as long as I can remember. My house is constantly littered with needles and syringes along with God knows how many alcohol bottles, but that's not even the worst of it.

My mother soon realised that her part time job at our local supermarket wasn't going to fund her increasing habit so she chose a career path she knew would be better for gaining her cash quickly. Prostitution.

I don't actually know how many men have passed through the front door of my home since I was a small toddler and to be honest I don't even want to think about it.

I've seen more in my nineteen years than most see in a lifetime and everytime I would cry and beg my mother to stop what she was doing, she'd smile at me through those glazed eyes, dark and sunken into her gaunt, deathly pale face and tell me she loved me but that I was asking too much of her.

I threatened to leave more times than I could count, but each time she'd cry and beg on her knees for me to stay, and that little girl inside me, desperate for a mothers love would succumb and here I stayed in this shithole of a home.

I did at one point, when I was about thirteen, consider looking for my biological father. It was around the time that the dynamic at home had started to worsen, beginning with one of my mothers clients taking my virginity while she was passed out on the sofa naked. The memory branded into my mind.

The pain. The blood. The shame.

Something died inside me that night. After that, men took from me regularly and I learned the hard way to bury my emotions and harden myself to the outside world, but none of that applied when it came to her.

My mum had an affair with a married man when she was sixteen, and after telling him that she was pregnant, he cut off contact, throwing money at her for an abortion and practically disappearing off the face of the Earth. My mum may be a lot of things but she was still my mother, and unlike my dad, she never gave up on me. I think that's the main reason I've stayed so long.

Walking into the kitchen, I opened the fridge. I'd started buying food for us now, as giving my mum money and hoping she'd use it on rent or shopping was pretty much a waste of time. I'd usually return from school or work to see her high or even comatose with her latest piece of shit sat nearby watching.

I grabbed the small tub of pasta I'd prepared the previous night and turned to head out of the door.

Suddenly a wide, heavy arm slammed against the fridge door right beside my head, caging me in on one side. I didn't even know he was in the house but the stench of his breath, whiskey and rotting meat invaded my nostrils like toxic gas.

He pressed his large body against me, smiling down at my slender five six, from his six foot stance.

"What the fuck do you want Anton?"

Anton had been my mum's partner, albeit pimp for about six months now.

He's in his late forties and often hangs around the house with a bottle of beer in hand and a sinister scowl on his face. The screams and crying have become worse through the night since he arrived.

He's dressed in his usual stain covered vest and boxers, his sandy blonde hairline receding further and further as the days go by.

He stares down at me with a cold, calculating expression,

licking his tongue over his upper yellowing teeth. *God he's ugly.*

His eyes filled with a hunger and lust that makes my stomach churn with nausea as his gaze skims lower over my breasts and small waist.

He grunts in appreciation. "When are you going to make me some money sugar?" He slurs, lifting the finger of the hand not caging me in to stroke down the side of my throat and onto my chest. "You know these tits will bring me a good price now."

He roughly cups my breast, squeezing hard. "And that tight little pussy..."

I push against his chest as hard as I can.

"Get the fuck off me, asshole," I shout.
He steps back, momentarily caught off guard with a smirk on his face as I head to the table, grabbing my bag and throwing the small pasta container inside.

"Tell mom, I'll sort the electricity later."

As I go to walk to the door, a hand grips my wrist, pulling me backwards and twisting it behind my back, pushing it upwards towards the nape of my neck.
The pain lances through my shoulder like a lightning bolt as a squeal escapes my throat.

Suddenly Antons heavy body slams me down, bending over the kitchen table, knocking the air from my lungs. His free hand, forcing its way up my sweater and into my bra as I thrash around frantically trying to get away.

He pinches my nipple as hard as he can and I cry out with the pain. Feeling his disgusting, warm breath by my ear as he pants, his erection pushing into my ass. *Thank God I'm wearing jeans.*

"You're going to get what's coming to you, you disrespectful little bitch, and then you're going to work for me like the good little slut that you are. Just like your whore of a mother"

Saliva sprays across the side of my cheek as he speaks and continues groping while I squirm.

"Let me go, you piece of shit...stop!"

Anger is burning in my chest as I continue to struggle against his vice-like hold and I wished to God I could reach my knife, still

sitting pretty under my pillow upstairs.
When will I learn to keep that shit on me at all times.

All of a sudden with a cracking sound, Anton releases me, staggering back clutching the back of his head, the sudden feeling of distance between us a welcome relief.

"Get the fuck away from her, you disgusting cunt."

I hear the words before I turn to see her face.

Five foot six like me, curvy body and a mass of dark curls flowing wildly besides the beautiful olive tone of her face.

She drops the chair she's just wrapped around Antons skull to the floor beside her.

Sim has always been my best friend, mostly because we both grew up on this estate and both our mothers are junkie whores, except Sim's mama has it together a lot more than mine does.

Glancing at my gorgeous heroine with a relieved smile, which she reciprocates, I don't think I've ever felt as happy to have given her a spare key to this cesspit as I do now.

"You bitch!!!!" Anton is howling, clutching the back of his head, attempting to stop the bleeding from the small laceration caused by the chair. It definitely could have been worse. I wish it had been worse.

"You could have killed me!"

Sim smirks in his direction.

"Yeah well shame I didn't, you old pervert."

With that I stride towards Anton, grabbing his broad shoulders before raising my knee and slamming it as hard as I can into his groin as he lets out another sickening scream.

"Don't ever fucking touch me again!" I spit, turning away from his sorry ass.

Sim grabs my arm as I reach for my bag and leads me towards the door.

"Come on Lex, let's get out of here."

I follow Sim out through the front door, taking one last look at Anton, seeing the true coward he is, still wailing in pain.

My lips can't help but curve up into a smile.

"Lex seriously, why do you stay there? It's worse than my place and that's saying something."

Sim loops her arm through mine giving my bicep a comforting squeeze as we walk the few blocks to the Blackbridge university campus where we are currently studying our English literature degree together.

Sim has always wanted to travel so she's hoping this degree will get her into travel journalism where she can tour the world.

Me, however, am hoping this degree is going to be the start of my career as a contemporary romance author.

"I can't just leave, Sim you know this, my mom wouldn't last two minutes on her own. She needs me," I replied. I'm not even sure if I believe my own words anymore.

"She needs fucking rehab babe," says Sim, reaching into the pocket of her leather biker jacket to pull out a cigarette.

I sigh. "Yeah and I'm gonna get her the help, I am. I've been saving for a while now, I have a stash in a jam jar under my bed and as soon as I've got enough I'm gonna pay for her to have the best treatment. We're going to finally make things better."

Sim looks at me confused. "Uh ha," she replies. "And what about what just happened a minute ago? We gonna talk about that?"

My eyes drop to the floor.

Anton has always been leery and suggestive but that's the first time he's actually been so *handsy.*

"I can handle him, don't worry he's just a creep."

Sim nods although I know what she's thinking. That I'm fucked in the head. *She's probably right.*

"Well I'll give ya something, you're a better daughter than me Lex. My mums bad enough but if she was only slightly as bad as yours I'd be bailing."

I nod. Deep down I know she's right but right now I'm eager to change the subject. I pull out my phone.

"Hey, have you seen Landon Bryce's insta?"

Sims' face brightens and I instantly know the subject has

changed from my dire home life, to the absolute brain dead playboy that graces our lectures. One that Sim has been pining for, for the best part of a year.

I smile. I know Sim means well but I'm stuck between a rock and a hard place right now and she knows that.

It was only going to be a matter of time before things were going to get better. *I hoped.*

CHAPTER TWO

Alaric

"I'm s..s...sorry okay, I get it, I fucked up."

I let out a frustrated sigh as I stared at the man laid out before me. Thick rope shackles his arms and legs to each corner of the table as his squirms like the stuck pig that he is, pulling against his restraints, thrashing in desperation.

"Fucked up?" I can hardly quell the exasperated laugh struggling in my throat. "Fucked up, my dear Mikey is an understatement. How many times have I told you specifically not to sell drugs in my club? And yet here we are, yet again because Demitri has found some junkie kid peddling pills on the territory where he doesn't belong."

My anger is beginning to rise. I can feel the heat in my chest from just looking at this poor excuse for a human. His eyes blackened by my own fist and his middle fingers on each hand severed at the knuckle. *That one was Axel's handywork.*

"Then why is the little asshole not tied to this table?"
What an actual piece of shit this cretin is.

I hold the growing storm in my chest threatening to implode and impale the fucker on the end of my knife already, as I walk over to where Mikey, the 'big shot' drug dealer as I've been told he likes to call himself, is splayed out. He's dressed in only his white vest, hanging loosely over his lanky frame, splattered with his blood and his ripped boxers covered in piss that he so kindly gifted us during Axel's creative streak with his fingers.

"Now why would that be fair Mikey boy? I mean he's just some little, runty kid doing anything for a fix but you, you're the scum bag sending him in here to make money on my turf, from my customers and Mikey, that just doesn't sit well with me, and it definitely doesn't give La Tanière a good image now does it?"

Mikey looks at me with a vacant expression.

"Now this might seem a little dramatic to you. I mean, your petty little drug business is hardly something that I want to be dealing with right now, but see this isn't the first time you've been warned, is it Mikey boy? and you just. Don't. Learn."

At that, my brother Axel takes the cloth from the adjacent table and drapes it over Mikey's head.

He begins to scream at this point, begging and crying but I'm done listening.

I grab the large glass jug I got from the upstairs bar area and dip it into the bucket of ice water under the table, lifting it over his head *careful not to waste any,* tipping it slightly until a steady stream is gliding from the jug directly onto the cloth covering his face, seeping through fast into his mouth and blocking his airways.

His strangled screams turn to gurgles as he thrashes helplessly against the rope at his wrists.
His breathing hitches and his whole body jerks. I turn to Axel, a satisfied smirk on his face.

As the jug empties and the stream ceases, he removes the soaking cloth from Mikeys face as he coughs and gasps, his breathing shaky and I swear he's going to piss himself again.

He tries to lift his head but Axel grips him by the hair, smashing his skull back down onto the table.

"Now Mickey boy, what have we learned today?"

"I...I...I promise no more coming to the club, no more..."
His coughing cuts him off mid sentence.

"Oh I know there will be no more Mikey, because after several warnings to no avail, people are going to start thinking the Mackenzie brothers are going soft."

I wink at him, the fear burning in his bloodshot eyes. "And we can't be having that, can we?"

With that, Axel draws his meat cleaver from behind Mikeys head, jamming the blade through the underside of his chin, the hook retreating from his shocked mouth as his eyes almost pop from his skull.

He gurgles as crimson liquid spills from his mouth and the wound beneath his chin.

I wait, staring down at him until the gargling ceases. Then silence.

I dust down the jacket of my tailored Armani suit and turn to Axel, his white t-shirt painted in Mikeys blood.

"Get changed," I order to him. "We got stuff to get sorted with Cass before we open tonight."

"Sure thing boss."

Axel salutes as I gesture with two fingers to Jax and Demetri, our security by the door.

"Get this mess cleaned up."

Jax nods. "Boss," he replies.

I've got more important things I need to be dealing with before La Tanière opens its doors tonight.

CHAPTER THREE

Lexi

Getting into uni was probably my greatest accomplishment so far but recently lectures have been a drag.

My focus was dwindling from the course and I wasn't finding the same enjoyment in it as I used to. I guess I could thank my lack of rest for lack of concentration but to be honest my heart just hasn't been in my studies for a while now.

Sitting beside Sim, twirling a strand of her shiny, dark hair around her finger, I stared straight ahead at professor Nicols writing on his board. Fucker might as well be talking in Spanish for all the difference it's making to me this morning.

Landon Bryce sits right in front of our table gazing forward while Zack Ashton sits beside him, turning his head in our direction.

I attempt to keep from catching his eye but as I look over he winks at me, lifting his hand as if he's gripping a cock and motioning towards his mouth using his tongue as a blowjob reference.

He smirks before mouthing "fuck me slut," silently and turning back towards the front with a chuckle.

My home life is pretty much public knowledge to some degree. The tutors don't know to what extent but it's known to the students that my mum is a crack whore.

The end of lectures could not come quick enough.

"Hey I'm heading over to Mals coffee for an hour, wanna come?" Sim smiles at me, grabbing her books and tossing them into her large, blue satchel.

"Sure, to be honest anything to keep me out of the house would be great right now," I sigh, picking up the remainder of my text books and stacking them inside my black tote.

"You gonna take me up on my offer Lex? I'd show you a good time baby," Zack calls as we head to exit the room.

"Drop dead."

"Ignore him." Sim motions forward, following behind me, trying not to look back.

I turn briefly to see him smirking, his blonde floppy hair grazing his eyes. He'd probably be pretty good looking if he wasn't such a creep.

"Come on, what's wrong baby?"
This guys just not gonna give it up!

"No one wants to shag you pencil dick," I yell back. Sim and Landon burst out laughing as the expression on Zack's face goes from smug to simmering rage in two point five seconds.

I hear him cursing at me and Sim as we leave the room, not bothering to look back.

I've been coming to Mals coffee for as long as I can remember.

It's a beautiful, rustic little place just right by the university campus and you always get the most lovely staff in there. Plus they know my order of a vanilla latte with extra syrup pretty much by heart now. So I barely ever have to ask unless it's the temporary weekend staff working the shift.

Luckily today it's Judy, Mal the owner's wife so she makes sure she has my order and a mocha for Sim ready within minutes as she sees us walk in.

"Thanks Judy." I give her a warm smile.

"On the house darlin'," she replies, rubbing her hands on her little pink apron.

"Thank you."

I blow her a kiss of gratitude and carry our drinks to the table that Sim has found for us.

Sim flops into the soft, cushioned sofa chair with a loud sigh.

"Urgh heaven." Her eyes begin to roll back into her head. "Today was torture."

I smile and bring my cup to my mouth, the silky smooth texture of the liquid warming my insides and bringing a much needed calm.

"You can say that again, my focus is lacking Sim, I'm not even sure if I want to carry on with the course."

Sim raises her head from the neck rest, glaring at me.

"Wow Lex, what else are you gonna do? I mean eventually you're gonna wanna get a career. You can't keep going with the circus lessons, they pay fucking pittance."

She takes a large gulp of her steaming mocha.

I laugh. "They're not circus lessons, they're silk aerial classes and anyway I don't do it for the money I do it cos I love the kids."

My evening job, teaching young teens silk aerial has been my escape for the past two years. It's where I've always felt the most calm and free when the chaos of home had become too much for me. The feel of the cool silk against my skin, the rosin clinging to the heel of my palms and the total bliss of all my problems seeping from my body as I freefall. I never use safety nets, which I think is part of the thrill for me, knowing at any moment I could plunge to my death with not a care in the world about it.

"Sure I get it," Sim continues sipping from her oversized mug. "I guess I would just miss your skinny ass on the course. I mean who would perve over Landon with me everyday? But I get it, I mean you don't get that hot body from nowhere," she smirks.

I roll my eyes before smirking back.

"For starters, I don't perve over Landon, you do and also you know better than anyone that being skinny is down to the fact I'm constantly wondering where my next meal is coming from."

"So Kathryn still not any better?"

Sim knows my mother is a lost cause, hell even I know it but it's just not in my DNA to fucking leave, no matter what it's doing to my sanity or my soul.

"Private health care will help. I know it. I just gotta save a bit more and then we're outta there."

Sim gives me a sympathetic look.

"Well here take this." She hands me, one hundred and fifty pounds from her purse.

"Sim I can't take this, it's your wages."

"It's a small amount and it's fine, working the bar at Lou's gets me loads of tips." She smiles, pushing together her boobs to enhance her already ridiculously large cleavage. I laugh as she winks at me. This chick is my lifeline, I honestly don't know what I would do without her.

Tucking the notes safely into the zip pocket of my tote, we go back to chatting about life in general.

Now sometimes in life you meet people with a presence. One so potent that they command the attention of a room, cloaking it all in a suffocating darkness that terrifies you because you can't escape it and terrifies you even more because you don't want to.

That presence has just walked right through Mal's door.

Roughly six foot five of pure, unadulterated sin.

He walks towards the counter dressed head to toe in fitted, biker leathers that do nothing to hide the show of lean yet rock solid muscle that coats his frame.

His raven hair is messy and unkempt thanks to the biker helmet he holds under his left arm, and his short stubble casts a five o clock shadow across his perfectly cut jawline.

I see a hint of what appears to be a neck covered in ink, peaking above the collar of his zipped up jacket. He shrugs his hair from his face and I can see his eyes are a light grey, so menacing I feel like his very stare is piercing my soul as he glances over.

His lips curving up into a slight smile when he sees us looking over. It's so faint but it's there.

Sims' jaw is on the floor.

"I have died and gone to heaven, have you ever seen anyone so fucking hot in your entire life?"

Is that a trick question?

I look away from him, back to her direction. "I mean yeah he's attractive."

Sim looks at me like I have three fucking heads.

"Attractive? That there is a god, Alexandra."

I wince at the use of my full name. Sim continues staring towards the coffee shop counter as said hot god orders his beverage.

"Axel Mackenzie." I hear Judys voice as she saunters from behind the counter and embraces the lather clad stranger. Her tiny five foot frame looking almost comedic in comparison to his height. "Long time no see."

"Judy Fey, still doing Mals dirty work I see." His voice is deep, masculine with a seductive tone like melted chocolate.

Judy giggles, swatting his chest. "What can I get for you sugar?"

Axel considers the menu. "Just an espresso for me, long night ahead at the club."

Judy nods, firing up the coffee machine.

"Ahhh La Tanière, how is your uncle?"

"Oh you know Elliot, no keeping him down."

The two continue their discussion as I turn back to Sim doing my best not to get caught eavesdropping.

"What's La Tanière?"

Sim looks at me with a shocked expression.

"Are you fucking kidding me? Bird, La Tanière is only the most controversial, infamous nightclub on the outskirts of Blackbridge. It's French for The Lair. Think *Moulin Rouge* on crack and you'll only be half way there. The acts are meant to be insane, like real dangerous shit with no precautions. Heard it's wild and the waiting list to get in is months long, Jesus girl, have you been living under a rock?"

No, just a crack den.

My interest peaks. "Wow, sounds pretty cool."

"Also apparently the acts are all freaks and when I say freaks I don't mean the weird kind." Sim snickers behind her cup.

I glance over to see Axel, *now we know his name,* and see him looking directly at us again. Maybe he's wondering why the gorgeous but clearly insane brunette is still gawking at him. Sim is doing nothing to hide how much she's salivating right now.

"I've heard they fuck each other and it's not just behind the scenes."

My eyes don't leave Axel's impossibly handsome face until I hear the words.

"We should go tonight."

My head whips back to Sim, "what?"

"We should go tonight, to La Tanière."

She's bouncing in her seat like a Goddamn toddler waiting for ice cream.

"I need to smash that," she looks directly at Axel, who's grabbing his coffee to leave.

"I thought you said the guest list was months long?"

"It is but I have an idea."

Sim pushes up her cleavage, pulling her long glossy curls over her shoulder and stands up before gliding over towards our handsome stranger, catching his arm before he leaves. I can't quite make out the words exchanging between them but the hungry glint in Sims eyes looks predatory as she touches Axel's bicep while speaking, looking directly into his eyes.

A few minutes later she's heading back to the table as he heads out of the door.

"We. Are. In!" Sim shrieks, flapping her arms in front of her in an excited gesture.

"How?" my brows knit together in confusion.

"Oh come on Lex, we're two hot women offering to come into his club."

"His club?"

"Yeah he co-owns it or some shit and said we just needed to tell the door that we're on Axel's list and we'll get in no problem." She beams with all her perfectly straight, white teeth on show.

I nod. It doesn't surprise me that Sim got an invitation to an exclusive place just by batting her full, fucking goddess eyelashes at a guy. Men are crazy for her.

"So we going?" Sim holds her breath as she waits for my answer.

"Urgh fine."

"Yes, yes, yes." Sim is shaking my shoulders, pulling me into an ecstatic hug. I smile, hugging her back. I love her …and her brain dead schemes.

CHAPTER FOUR

Alaric

Heading to the office I straighten my tie. Pulling the arms of my suit jacket further to cover the tattoo sleeves on both of my arms.

My Uncle Elliot prefers a more suited and booted look, especially where his club is concerned.

Axel tends to have a lot more of his ink on show, especially the ones covering his neck and gets away with mostly hanging out in casual gear, but he's not the one who will be taking over La Tanière as top dog when Elliot retires. That will be me.

Most of the staff are tatted to fuck as well, seems to be a running theme around here.

Speaking of Axel where the fuck was he?
I told the fucker to make sure the acts were ready for opening tonight and I haven't seen him anywhere near the office since.

I walk in to see uncle Elliot at his desk, cigar in his mouth and a glass of bourbon in his hand, staring down at paperwork on his desk.

The years had been kind to him until lately when his fifty eight years of age were starting to really show on his face.

His completely shaved head always seemed to make him look younger which he credited to the lack of grey hair but time was definitely catching up to him.

He looks up as I enter the room. I don't think I've ever seen my uncle in anything short of the immaculate designer suits he owns, one of which he's wearing right now.

"Alaric." He removes the cigar from his plump lips.

"Elliot." I reply, tilting my head as I close the door.

"We good for tonight?"

"Of course uncle, Cass has sorted the girls with a new routine and we've replaced Jazz as the new white rabbit in the AIW act."

Speaking of the devil, Cassidie Sloan, our creative director walks into the room.

She saunters in like she owns the fucking joint, her dyed red bob swaying wildly at her shoulders and her tight, black suit dress pulled taut around her surgically enhanced chest and arse.

Cassidie is in her early forties and has worked at La Tanière for the last two years.

She's hot in a cougar kind of way and the way she looks at me and my brother like she wants to fuck the darkness out of us, despite the fact I'm thirty one and Axel is twenty nine, makes my cock twitch but I'd never touch the bitch. She thinks too highly of herself and I swear the only reason Elliot puts up with her shitcunt attitude is because she keeps the acts in line, helps them with their training and rides his fucking face as and when he wants it.

He thinks I don't know but I've heard the fucking grunting from the office when they're having their 'meetings.' Plus she turns a blind eye to the extra curricular activities that go on behind the scenes at the club but I suppose so do the rest of the staff. They have to go to work here or they'd be out on their ear and none of them could afford that.

See, our acts at La Tanière all have something in common. They're all survivors of some kind of hell that Elliot pulled them from. Whether it be abuse or addiction, they all came from a life of shit so Elliot brought them here, got Cassidie to train them up and utilise their talents, gave them homes in the building right inside the club courtyard and built this place to become the most famous place in the country never mind just in Blackbridge.

"So I take it everything was sorted with our friend Mikey?" Elliot looks to me for confirmation.

I lift the clear orb paperweight from his desk inspecting it between my fingers. "It was."

I hear Cass scoff behind me. "And where is he now?"

"Taken care of," I bite, without turning to face her. "Jax and Demetri have cleaned up."

Elliot nods. "Good, a message needed to be made clear there."

He collects the paper work together and secures it with a paper clip before placing it inside his desk drawer and securing it with the padlock.

"And how is everything for tonight Cass? Al here tells me the girls have a new routine."

Cass flashes her immaculate, veneered smile.

"They do, the burlesque will be talked about for months after tonight. Leela and Ashleigh are ready for it. The whole team is set to go."

"Good stuff." Elliot stands from the desk. "Where's Axel?"

"The wanderer returns."

Axel strides through the door, takeaway coffee cup in hand.

"And where have you been?" I sneer.

He laughs, bringing the cup to his mouth.

"Taking a break brother, you should try it sometime. Torture and murder can really make a fucker grumpy."

Cass raises her eyebrows.

Before I can reply, Elliot jumps in.

"He's here now, let's get this show on the road."

Grabbing my glock and shoving it into the holster at my hip, I head for another night of work.

CHAPTER FIVE

Lexi

Searching through the battered sections of my wardrobe, I pull out some dresses on hangers and throw them onto my bed where Sim is sitting, her feet tucked under her ass cradling a bottle of vodka.

Sim always looks effortlessly gorgeous.

Her full figure, hugged to perfection in a black silk mini dress with spaghetti straps. She'd casually thrown over her black leather cropped jacket and teamed the sexy dress with some studded ankle boots. Her long, dark brown hair cascading down her back in loose curls.

"I don't know which one to go with." I glance at the two dresses I hold in each hand.

"The green one, definitely the green one."

I hold the dark moss-green wrap dress up to my body, staring at my reflection in the mirror.

I feel like everyday I'm in this hellhole, I'm losing myself piece by piece. I can see it in my eyes.

"Green it is."

I wiggle out of my towel and pull the green, silken dress over my black g-string and up over my breasts. I'm thankful for my perky tits tonight, as this dress is strapless so there's no way I'm going to be able to wear a bra.

I flat iron my long, red hair until it's poker straight and sleek and do my makeup heavy and flawless with red lips and a smokey eye that makes the heterochromia even more prominent.

I add a fine gold necklace and then turn to face Sim.

"Urgh you sexy bitch, remind me why I don't hate you again?"

I laugh, "because you're my fucking best friend and I can't function without you."

"This is correct. Now drink."

She throws me the vodka bottle. One thing about Sim is she drinks like a goddamn fish.

When I bring it to my lips, I swig at the clear liquid neat from the bottle, feeling the warming sting as it travels down my throat.

After finishing half the bottle of vodka between us, Sim and I grab our clutch bags, my black blazer and head for the door.

A taxi rank is stationed within a short walking distance of my house so we head over there and grab the first cab to La Tanière.

The extravagant club is easy to spot even before the taxi reaches its front doors.

The building is huge, almost looking like an old cathedral but made from fine red brick. Drapes of black satin hang from the dome shaped windows and spotlights glide from the floor over the front of the enormous structure.

Guests queue behind black ropes in a single file line outside the large, red wooden doors where the security stands.

Sim barges her way to the front, much to the disgust of people appearing to wait patiently.

"We need to get to the back," I attempt to whisper in her ear as she pulls me through.

"Nope. We don't actually. Trust me babe."

When we reach the front of the line, we're greeted with two burly bouncers in black suits, wired up. The bigger of the two holds out his arm to halt us to a stop.

"Name?"

"Sim Delaney and Lexi Power, we're Axels VIPs."

The bouncer raises an eyebrow and looks to his colleague before checking the list. Something in his smile tells me that we're not the first girls to claim we're guests of the owner.

"Figures," he sighs, confirming our names on the list. "Go on in."

Sim shines him a cheeky smile before heading inside. The other bouncer, the shorter of the two, throws us a wink as we enter.

'Legends are made' by *Sam Tinnesz* is playing as we walk through the entrance hallway and a woman in a purple top hat, waistcoat and hot pants takes our jackets.

The place is amazing.

A large bar covers the far back wall and a huge dance floor leads towards a massive stage shrouded in crimson curtains.

The DJ stands on a balcony. The man is ripped with long, sandy hair swept back into a man bun with the sides shaved short and a long shaggy beard.

He's wearing just a dark blue denim waistcoat with his jeans and you can see the intricate ink that covers his arms. He shouts through the tannoy and the crowd roars as steam is released from the ground.

I can barely hear Sim over the noise as she motions towards the bar for a drink.

Before we get there, a hand comes out in front of us. I notice it's the smaller bouncer from the front door.

"As VIPs of Mr Mackenzie, you have a private booth to the right of the club. Unfortunately he is prior engaged this evening and will not be down to greet his guests, however you have a bottle of champagne waiting. On the house."

Sim and I looked at each other in surprise before letting the bouncer escort us to the booth.

Round, black velvet sofas surround the glass table in the middle which holds an ice bucket with champagne lodged inside.

I look up to see another balcony high above the VIP section

overlooking everything. That must be where the owners come from their offices to oversee the running of the club.

"Please call for one of our waitresses if you require anything at all," the bouncer says before leaving us at the table.

I pick up the champagne flute as Sim lifts the bottle of *Laurent Perrier* from the ice bucket and pops the cork. She catches the escaping fizz in her mouth before topping up both our flutes.

"Cheers girl." I smile, raising my glass.

"Here's to friendship, sisterhood and tequila."

I laugh as we down our glasses.

The club must be at full capacity half an hour later as I observe the private booths filling up with all sorts of people. Mostly older men in business suits. Plus a few with girls wearing next to nothing, pretty much like us. I begin to suspect we may not be Axels only female VIPs but I don't care, the booze is flowing and *'Demons'* by *Imagine dragons,* my favourite song is playing.

I drag Sim to the front of our table and we begin dancing. I hold her hand in the air as she turns me around, gripping my hips and grinding against my ass in our typical drunken girl dance show.

We're dancing for around five, maybe ten minutes when I can't explain the strange feeling that comes over me, sending shivers down my spine.

I can feel the goosebumps begin to prickle over my whole body as I get the sensation that someone is watching me.

Looking up towards the balcony I see him.
Standing in the shadows, looking straight at me.

At first I think it's Axel as he looks very similar to the handsome stranger we met in the coffee shop earlier today, but there's something different about him.

He's half encased in darkness but I can still see the black suit stretched over a broad chest.

His raven hair is shorter on the sides and longer on top and he shares the same light stubble on his perfectly chiselled jaw. The same as Axel only with a lot more of a clean cut appearance.

His features are masculine yet borderline beautiful but those eyes... I can't make out the colour from here but I can feel the ice in them further enhancing the shivers that are spreading through my whole body and making heat rage throughout my core and pool between my legs.

There's something sinister within his glare. Like a God of the underworld. Hades in human form. He feels like danger and even though the shy part of me is saying to sit back down, the devil in me is saying to continue grinding against Sim, giving him a show.

I decide to go with the latter, looking up to see if I can gauge a reaction.

His face is poker straight and emotionless and I can't tell if I'm having any effect on him at all.

Sim pulls me back towards her as I laugh and look back one last time to see he's disappeared without a trace.

"Look," Sim calls. "The show is starting."

The music drops to a lower volume before gradually phasing out, as a haunting melody fills the room.

I'm grateful to Sim for securing the booth now as we have the perfect view of the stage from here.

A loud boom draws gasps from the crowd as flames ignite upon two six foot torches either side of the platform. The heavy curtains begin to open to reveal the stage set up to imitate an Alice in Wonderland theme. Thick smoke clouds the view as it rises from the holes in the stage floor.

A ballerina dressed in a skimpy white rabbit costume and intricate silver mask covering her eyes, pirouettes over the platform as the performance starts.

The whole show is mesmerising with dancers and incredible scenery until a strikingly beautiful girl with a platinum blonde pixie crop, dressed in a revealing Alice costume with blue tutu reveals herself from within a large tulip.

The top half of her costume is completely missing with just two blue, jewelled tassels hiding her nipples on her large, perfectly round tits. Her face is painted like a cracked doll with a fake smile. It's haunting, yet alluring and sexy as hell all at the same.

She begins to command the stage as *'Mad Hatter'* by *Melanie Martinez* begins to play.

Jeers and wolf whistles echo from the crowd as she suddenly begins to bend backwards until her feet are still flat to the floor but her stomach is laid to the stage beneath her ass.

"Oh my god she's a contortionist," screams Sim, staring at the stage in awe.

"Jeeez that bitch got moves."

"Yeah, imagine what she's like in the sack," Sim laughs, downing more of her champagne and joining in with the heckles.

I have to admit, the girl can bend. That's some weird ass shit right there but she pulls it off flawlessly.

When the act is finished, the stage curtains begin to close slowly again to the roaring crowd as everyone continues to applaud and some throw money towards the stage.

The Dj starts the music back up again and everyone gathers back on the dance floor.

I'm beginning to feel the effects of the champagne by now but I don't give a shit, being here with Sim is so much better than being at home, facing Anton or my mother and even though I had to dip into my cash supply to come out tonight, I've started to realise I'm in desperate need of some fun in my life.

I'm nineteen years old and it's about time I started living like it.

CHAPTER SIX

Alaric

The night is almost coming to an end and judging by how manic the bar has been all evening and how packed out the club is I'd say it's been another success.

I adjust the wire in my ear and start my patrol back around the club for the final time, making sure I make my way over to the VIP area first to see if she's still there.

I have no idea who she is but according to Jax who showed her to her table, she and her little brunette mate were invited here by my brother.

Typical really considering all that fucker does is think with his dick.

I haven't seen Axel for the majority of the night, not since I went to his office and saw him balls deep in some waitress.
I swear we only just hired her!

Fuck, If things end up like they did with the last bitch he fucked, we're going to have to get rid of her before her probation is up. Axel always seems to attract the cling ons.

I stare down from the balcony as I see her dancing again with her friend. I could tell when our eyes met earlier that she wanted me to watch her as she drunkenly gyrated over the brunette with that tight little body, in that fucking insane green dress that hides basically nothing.

Her long red hair drops to her ass and I imagine wrapping it around my fist while she's on her hands and knees.
Fuck! My cock strains against the zipper of my suit trousers desperate to be freed.

I sit on the chair near to me to continue watching her.

"How's your night going?"

A seductive voice sounds from behind me, as a slender arm slivers over my shoulder and I know exactly who it is before I've even turned around to see her face.

"Sapphire, don't you have work to do?" I turn and look up to see Sapphire, our Alice in Wonderland contortionist standing above me, a glass of rose in hand.

She's changed from her performance attire and is dressed in a simple, pink robe. Her broken doll makeup, now completely wiped away.

"Nope, all finished for the night, Cass has said I'm no longer needed as back up for any acts so I'm off for the night, just wondered if you'd like any company?"

She pulls the tie at the front of the robe to reveal her completely naked body beneath.
I glance over her body before looking back at her face.

"No." I bring my glass of whiskey to my lips.

She pouts, her bottom lip curling over before sliding a manicured hand into my jacket.

"That's not what you said last night."

I look up into her ocean blue eyes and then look back towards the beauty still below me.

She's sitting back down in the booth now talking to her friend, oblivious to my gaze.

The good thing about this balcony is that even though guests can see us up here, the shadows cover most of what they can see so we can see them a lot more clearly than they can see us.

Without a single word I take Sapphire's hand in mine, setting her wine glass on the table and leading her down in front of me, tugging her arm down roughly until she's on her knees between my thighs.

She looks up at me with her doe eyes and soft lips but my gaze can't be lifted from the red head below.

I unzip my trousers until my insanely stiff cock springs free. I take it in my hand, pumping along the shaft twice.

With the other hand, I grab the back of Sapphs pixie cropped hair, just enough to grab a handful, and force myself into her mouth with one hard thrust, breaking the resistance as I slide down her throat.

She gags and I don't even give her time to adjust before I'm moving in and out, fucking her face, her full, pink lips close firmly around my large width.

She raises a hand to pump me at the same time as I push her head down more forcefully onto my cock.

As she sucks and pumps my dick desperately, I watch the little siren below begin to collect her belongings, she must be ready to leave.

There's an air of innocence to her and I start to wonder how pretty she would bleed under the tip of my knife while she comes.

I feel like I could just, so easily, storm down there and fuck the innocence right out of her on that table in front of everyone. Hell, it wouldn't even look out of place in this joint, but instead I imagine it's her mouth I'm fucking as Sapph continues to swallow me down.

A couple more trusts and I spill myself down the back of her throat with a low growl, cum mixes with the saliva dripping from my dick as she swallows it all down like the good little slut she is and then licks off the rest. *God this girl can suck.*

She smiles at me as I shove my cock back into my trousers. I'm guessing she's hoping this will continue after the club closes tonight but I'm just not in the mood.

I'm really particular about the girls I fuck and to be honest fucking Sapphire has been a moderate release from the stress of our business but I'm getting bored of her and even though she claims she knows this arrangement has always been physical, I get the sense that she's hoping it's going to become more. It isn't.

"Go home Sapphire."

I don't even look at her as I speak but I sense the smile drop from her face.

"But…"

"Now." I snarl.

"Boss." Her expression hard as she re-ties her robe and heads back down across the balcony leaving me to my thoughts and my whiskey.

I look back down towards the booth and the little siren is gone.

CHAPTER SEVEN

Lexi

"Can't believe we shiddent shee that hot guy."

Sim is slurring her words in the back of the taxi, leaning her whole body towards the door.

I laugh, my head a toxic mix of all the different alcohol we consumed. *Shit I'm gonna feel it in the morning.*

Sim throws her arms around me. "Come back to mine, I want to know you're okay."

I smile at my drunk friend, returning her warm hug.

"I can't, I need to check on mum but I'll call you tomorrow. Promise."

"Fiinnneee!" Sim pouts but I know she still loves me. She's the sister I always should have had.

The taxi stops outside my front door and I hug and kiss Sim goodbye before handing some cash over to the driver.

I check my phone. Three AM.

I head up to my door, almost tripping on the steps leading up to it, and fiddle with my set of keys that I barely managed to pull from my clutch bag.

I made it through the door, the darkness encasing everything.

I didn't want to wake mum so I decided to use my phone to help me make my way to the bedroom.

I climb the stairs, trying to be as quiet as possible until I pass by her bedroom. I slowly crank the door, wondering if I'll encounter Anton tonight or if he's out. Luckily I noticed my mum laid in the bed alone with the covers pulled up to her chin.

I go over to check on her, as a sleeping drug addict always makes me wary due to the fact that I keep picturing her overdosing and choking on her own vomit.

As I reach the bed I hear her snoring softly.

I shake her shoulder lightly but she's dead to the world. Lifting the covers, I notice the bruising around the crease of her arm and small droplets of blood on the bed sheets. She's clearly been injecting that shit into her veins again today.

I lower the covers and creep out of her bedroom, closing her door silently. At least she's alive.

I let out a sigh of relief as I turned towards my room.

Just as I opened the door, the pungent scent of stale beer hit me before he did as the heavy back of a hand smashed against my face sending me flying backwards into my door.

My eye felt like it was going to explode and the metallic tang of blood I could taste on my tongue from my split lip.

As I tried to regain composure, I felt a fist being driven into my face and I was knocked to the floor.

"You stupid bitch." Anton towered over me in his wife beater and dirty stained trousers. "You and your little slut friend think that you can humiliate me? You're gonna get what you deserve now you little slag."

He grabs me by the collar of my blazer forcing me to stand, but with the impact of his punch and the amount of alcohol I've consumed, I'm struggling to stay on my feet. My legs are like jelly.

As he lifts me to face him, I swing my head back and thrash it forward with as much force as I can muster. My forehead connects with his nose in a sickening crunch.

"FUCCCCKK!" he screams, staggering backwards and releasing me, clutching his bloodied nose, which I'm pretty confident is broken.

I turn and bolt for the door but before I can, a hand lunges towards me fisting in my hair, dragging me backwards and slamming me face down onto my bed. My head is pounding and my body fatigued as he shoves my face into my pillow so hard I can barely breathe.

I try to calm myself, slow my breathing but my body is in fight or flight mode and the panic has set in as I thrash underneath his heavy body. My hearing has dulled and all I can make out are the disgusting names he's screaming in my ear as he presses all his weight into me.

The stench of body odour invades my nostrils and I'm fighting an overwhelming urge to vomit as acid is rising in my throat, and that's when I hear it. The horrifying clink of his buckle opening.

At first I think he's going to remove his belt and beat me with it. I'm hoping that's what he's planning because the alternative is too much for me to even consider, but it's then that I realise that that isn't his intention at all as one hand continues to fist in my hair and the other forcefully pulls my dress up high over my ass.

He grabs my g-string and tears it off in one swift motion, tossing it to the floor and kicking my legs further apart with his foot.

I cry out, as without warning he reaches between my legs and slams two fingers inside me, deep and hard. My muscles clench against the unwanted intrusion.

"So tight," he pants heavily in my ear. "But that's not what I'm interested in tonight. I don't want you to enjoy this, I want you to know what happens when a whore like you thinks she can make me look like a mug, I wanna see you bleed."

Tears begin to fall down my cheeks, soaking the pillow as I continue to scream and sob.

Suddenly I feel his dick, hard and ready slide down the crack of my ass and I pray to god to strike this man dead right now or strike me dead first as right now I don't even want to live anymore, but it never happens. He's still breathing and unfortunately so am I. He drops his trousers to his ankles and slams his dick into my ass, so roughly to the hilt, an animalistic scream that I didn't even realise was my own comes roaring from my throat.

"Fuck that feels amazing," he groans above me before retracting and pushing back inside me.

Each thrust felt like daggers tearing me apart from the inside out and at that point I was sure every shattered piece of my soul had left my body.

When he'd finished he pushed off me, pulling up his trousers.

I laid motionless and silent on my bed as I waited for him to leave my room. But he didn't.

Through clouded vision blurred with tears, I could see his large form tear away at the things beneath my bed until he came across the jam jar stuffed with notes that I had been saving for my mum's rehab.

"Call this a little payment for my troubles," he scoffed, pocketing the cash before turning back to me.

He grabbed the back of my hair again, lifting me from the bed. The will to fight had ceased and I let him control my movements as he released my hair, shoving me to the floor.

As I fell, he stood above me with a foot either side of my body and bent down until he was sitting on my chest. I whimpered quietly at the agony my body was in.

"Goodbye Lex." I heard him say and with several blows to the head, I went from feeling everything to feeling nothing at all as it all went black.

CHAPTER EIGHT

Alaric

"I've been informed of a potential competitor, I'm sending Rio to take a look later."

Elliot sat back in his chair, addressing the room.

It was only six AM and the bastard was already talking shop, hence the reason he'd requested to have breakfast in his office with me and my brother.

It had literally been three hours since the club cleared out and I was still in last night's suit, my hair ruffled and messy. There really was no rest for the wicked in this place.

I picked up my espresso, knocking it back quickly in one large gulp.

"Like we've ever had to worry before," I say, tilting the small, empty shot cup back and forth between my thumb and index finger.

We've had many so-called competitors over the years. There is always going to be competition when it comes to bars and nightclubs but La Tanière is, and will always be the best and most exclusive club there is around.

Elliot leans forward. His elbows resting on his desk, staring straight at me.

"This one is different, Colt seems to think something is off and you know that fucker has a sixth sense."

Colt is the Mackenzie's informant and has worked for Elliot for years. He's also one of the ones Elliot has taken in over time and he's loyal as a fucking pit bull.

He's the best at digging up dirt on anything and anyone so having him on our side is a massive advantage, and if Colt thinks something seems off then it usually is.

"And why is that?" I ask, mirroring Elliot's position as I roll up the sleeves of my unbuttoned white shirt and lean forward to rest my forearms on my knees, narrowing my eyes slightly.

"I'm not sure yet but the club is due to open in a week or so. Maybe we could invite the new owner over for a little drink. Scope out his intentions for the new place especially as it's set to open just around the corner from us."

I smile. "Don't tell me you're going soft in your old age uncle?"

Elliot chuckles his deep throaty laugh. The sound of a man enslaved to his cigars for way too fucking long.

"It won't be tea and biscuits we'll be offering if there is anything suspicious going on, mark my words boy."

I hear a quiet laugh from Axel standing behind me.
He leans against the back of the sofa in the corner of the room, cleaning his nails with his knife.

"There's actually a more urgent reason I've brought you here this morning," said Elliot. His expression turned from amused to sinister in a blink. "Another one of the girls has gone missing."
I look up in shock at what I'm hearing.

"What do you mean another one?"

"I mean Alaric, that Trinity, one of the dancers has gone missing. The little, blonde skinny thing, she's the third this month…"

"I know she's the fucking third this month and we need to be finding out what the fuck is going on. I need to speak with Colt and Sully."

I could feel the unease stirring in my gut.

Altogether five of the women working for La Tanière had gone missing in the last two months.

They were all young and all beautiful. Most of them from

the burlesque show we put on at the club, and they've been vanishing without a fucking trace. Just gone, into thin air.

These were girls that wouldn't just take off. They had a home and a job here with the club and when Axel had gone to check out their apartments at the complex where all the staff were living, the Hive, he found that all of their belongings were still there. Nothing taken or even touched so it makes no sense at all.

"Sully is on a hit, we need to hire more security for the Hive." I run my fingers through my already tousled hair.

"We need to tighten up everywhere until we figure out what's going on."

The door to the office swung open with a loud crash, as Jax bounded through.

"Boss, we got another one. Side of the road. She's in a pretty bad way."

I sprinted from the office down the stairs with Axel on my heels til we reached one of the rooms in the back of the club.

The king sized bed in the middle of the room was surrounded by Cassidie and some of the staff, all looking towards where the flame haired girl lay.

There was no mistaking that it was her. The girl I had seen last night dancing with the brunette.

Her beautiful face was swollen and bruised with blood leaking from her ears and mouth. Darkness tarred most of her flawless cream skin, where she had been gripped and held with force.

The green dress I saw her in just hours before was ripped and bloodied and covered in dirt. Thick mud mattered into her long silky hair.

I looked briefly at her thighs, the dried blood, smeared, marking her.

The rage in my chest began to stir and I felt fire in my veins that I had never experienced before. Someone had done this to her. I didn't even know who this girl was, I'd seen her less than an hour and yet I knew one thing... The person responsible for this was going to die. Doing this to a woman did not sit fucking well with me.

"I recognise her, it's the girl from Mals," Axel spoke from my side. I didn't even ask what he was talking about.

I turned to Jax. "Talk!"

"We were on our way out, me and Demitri took the back road down to Larian way and she was there, dumped on the side of the road like trash. Colt is looking into where she came from but she was barely breathing, boss."

I walked over slowly to the bed. Our resident doctor Natalia was sitting on the edge of the bed with her.

"How bad is it?" I ask under my breath, not even realising I'd been holding it this whole time.

"Pretty bad Al, she's been beaten to an inch of her life. Luckily most of the injuries appear to be surface level but I'm really concerned about the head trauma. Whoever did this to her clearly thought she was dead when they dumped her on the road, that's one crazy bastard to just leave her in the open like that and…"

"And what?"

"I've examined her fully, and… she was raped, and I mean brutally."

My stomach twisted as I fought the acid rising in my chest, my fist twitching by my side as the need to kill was stronger than ever.

"Will she survive?" I didn't know why I was asking, why I even cared.

Elliot had taken in women as well as men that had been harmed in the most horrific of ways and I never saw it as anything at all. Just another day at the office but now… now I felt overwhelming rage which I put down to the fact that this girl must be twenty at the fucking most. What sick cunt would think that was okay?!

Natalia looked up at me.

"She will, I'll give her some fluids and we'll stitch up her lacerations but she will heal. She's just gonna need time."

I nodded. "Get her cleaned up and make her comfortable."

"Will do."

I knew I could trust her with Natalia. She was the best doctor we could find, and she'd seen it all.

Working for us had its perks but it also had its downsides especially the work we did behind the cover of La Tanière.

Natalia dealt with it all but she was especially fond of taking care of the recruits for the club.

There had been many times she'd been called in the middle of the night to help with some kid that had been brought in beaten or overdosed, drugged up to their fucking eyeballs.

Natalia was a gem and one that we wouldn't risk losing hence why we hired her ex-military husband Zayn to work alongside her, working as security at the Hive. Natalia had made it clear she wouldn't have him in any other position we were offering. She valued his life too much. Guess I'm yet to know what the hell it feels like to be in love, but from what I've seen of it so far in life, it's some bullshit that I'd rather avoid.

Cass kept checking in on the red head throughout the day.

Natalia had done an incredible job of cleaning her up and now she was left to sleep.

I needed a retreat from the frustration I was feeling due to the information I'd received today about the missing girls, so I decided to head down to the basement to see who we had lined up for a little questioning today.

My best friend and employee Rio had already told me he had someone bound and gagged down there. Someone linked to our latest contract.

Luckily no more idiot drug dealers. I was ready to let out a little frustration with my blow torch.

"Let's play brother." Axel seemed just as keen as I was. Holding his bag of *toys* as he called them.

"It's needed after today," I scoff.

On the way down, Elliot and Colt were crossing the landing in front of us.

"We have details on the girl," said Elliot, pointing to the file in

Colts hand.

Colt ran his fingers through his long blonde hair, pushing it away from his face, before opening the Manila folded.

"Alexandra Mercedes Power, nineteen years old, goes by the name of Lexi. Attends Blackbridge university. Close acquaintances with a miss Simone Delaney. Lives in a crack den not too far from where she was found, with her mother Kathryn Power, a known prostitute and heroin addict. Sounds like a real shithole, not even the kind of place rats would live in."

"She'll be staying here." Elliot takes hold of the folder and begins flicking through.

"Here?" The word falls from my mouth.

"According to what we've discovered about her, she's skilled in aerial acrobatics and she can't go back to the place she came from. She'll be a great little addition to the team."

I grind my teeth at his words. "Don't you think we should talk about this?"

The girl is hot to look at and I'll take great pleasure in tearing the cunt who did this to her limb from limb, but taking her on? We have a fucking business to run behind the scenes, it seems old uncle Elliot is forgetting about that.

"We will, with the girl, in a week or so," he replies, "When she's strong enough. Maybe then we can find the bastard who did this to her."

He starts to walk away.

"Cass will see to it that she is given a permanent place at the Hive but until then…" he turns and the fucking smug look on his face says it all.

"She stays with you!"

Oh fuck no.

CHAPTER NINE

Lexi

When I was little I used to imagine what heaven was like.
I think it was after hearing so many people tell my mother that if she carried on the way she was, then she was going to be going there real soon.

Back then I didn't understand what they were saying or what they meant.

I imagined heaven to be like a huge playground, filled with fluffy clouds and cotton candy and everyone was happy and loved. One thing I didn't imagine heaven to be like was a large white room with a giant, four poster bed with black silk sheets, which is exactly what I had just opened my eyes to see.

My head felt like an atomic bomb had detonated inside it and my vision clouded as I squinted hard, trying to get my eyes to adjust to the sight.

My memory was hazy but one thing I remembered was Anton's fists flying at my face over and over and thinking this is it, this is the day I'm going to die.

Opening my eyes, surrounded by the comfort of the sleek, cool sheets that felt like water against my skin, did make me wonder whether I had died the night of the attack. However I'm pretty sure you don't feel this much pain in heaven so I'm guessing I'm probably still alive unfortunately. But where the fuck was I?

I gently turned my head to scan the room.

It was luxurious with a simple design. Everything was white besides the black bed sheets and the whole room was encased in light, flowing freely through the floor to ceiling windows that overlooked a city. *The city I lived in I hoped.*

Sasha Alex Sloans 'Dancing with your ghost' played gently through the speakers around the room as I tried again to turn my head slightly.

Footsteps caught my attention as they walked towards where I was laying on the bed.

A young girl, no older than about seventeen stood beside the bed, holding a jug of water.

"You're awake," she beamed.
Her pretty, jade green eyes lit up as she looked down at me.
She placed the jug on the bedside table.

"I just went to get you some water, just in case. Good job I did, wasn't it?"

I tried to lift myself carefully up onto my elbows to get into a sitting position.

"Careful now," the girl protested, quickly putting her small arms around my back to help me sit up.

"Thank you." I finally managed to muster the words although they came out with more of a croak than anything else. *Jeez my throat was dry.*

"Who are you?" I asked, as she sat down next to me on the bed.

"I'm Morgan, Morgan Nightingale. Nice to meet you Alexandra."
I raised my eyebrows in surprise at her knowing my name.

"How do you know who I am and where the hell am I?"

I continued to stare at Morgan. She was so beautiful, flawless cream skin and long, light brown hair almost as long as mine. Her little white tank top held on loosely to her petite frame. She reminded me of a little porcelain doll.

"I know who you are because Miss Cassidie told me, and you're at the private quarters of Mr Alaric and Mr Axel. I've been asked to help out. Get you anything you might need while you're recovering."

"Mr Alaric and Mr..."

"Axel." Morgan interrupts. "The owners of La Tanière."

My stomach drops and I'm pretty sure in that moment that my heart stops for a second.

Axel? La Tanière? Oh Jesus it's the guy from Mals, and Alaric? Surely that can't be...

"Thank you Morgan, I'll take it from here."

A deep, masculine voice radiated through the room and I already knew it was him before I saw him.

His tall frame came into view from behind the corner.

Morgan stood without saying a word and gave me a kind smile.

"Thank you," I say again quietly as she nods and walks toward the door.

He begins to walk towards the bed.

He's taller than he looked the night at the club on the balcony and I can make out his face clearly for the first time and he is nothing short of breathtaking, I'll give him that.

His pale grey eyes penetrating and soul destroying.

He looks less polished than he did the night of the club, *God knows when that even was,* wearing a dark, navy blue hoodie and dark blue jeans with biker boots undone with the laces tucked in.

This man is sin personified.

My chest tightens. I must look like pure shit.

"Hello Alexandra. My name is Alaric Mackenzie. I'm the co-owner of La Tanière. I believe you've already heard of my brother Axel?"

I gaze up at him before swallowing hard.

"It's Lexi and how long have I been here? How did I even get here?" I ask.

"I'm sure you have lots of questions and they will all be answered in due course. For now, all you need to know is that you were attacked and found by my security who brought you back to the club. You've been unconscious for a couple of days. We were concerned about your head injuries so the fact that you're asking questions is a good sign. This is my home, my guest room."

He runs a hand over the short, dark stubble on his chin.

I look down to see I'm wearing a plain black oversized t-shirt which clearly isn't mine. My cheeks heat at the assumption.

"Don't worry it was Morgan who changed you," he said as if reading my mind. "Your dress was disposed of."

I nod. I don't even know what to say, I'm in too much pain to even think.

"One thing we do need to know though is if you remember your attacker?"

I scoff, "remember him?"

My quiet, sarcastic laugh to myself clearly surprises him as his thick, dark eyebrows rise.

"Look I really think I need to be leaving now, I need to check on my mother she's...not well, thank you for helping me but I should get going." I attempt to throw a leg out of the sheets.

"Stay," he barks.

I halt in surprise.

"Excuse me?"

Who does this guy think he is?

"You won't be going anywhere. At least not until your new quarters are ready for you"

He sits down on the large, cream chair by the bed. His elbows resting in his thighs.

"New quarters?" My eyebrows knit together in confusion

"That's what I said," he answers, looking straight at me.

Heat flares between my legs. *Fuck you stupid vagina, just because he's pretty. He's still a fucking man and they all take and hurt and destroy. This one's no fucking different.*

I force back a laugh escaping my throat.

"I don't know what this is," I gesture between the two of us, "but I'm going to go now, I need to get home."

"Your home is here now, like I said at least until you move into the apartment that is being set up for you. Then you'll live there and work at La Tanière. I hear you're quite the acrobat."

"Silk aerial," I protest.

How the hell does he know about that?

"Well whatever it is, you'll perform it for the club and this will be your life now."

I peer at him as if he's lost his mind, he must have. Is this guy for fucking real?

"My life now?" I laugh and it bloody hurts all over. "Look mister, I don't know what you've been smoking and I'm really grateful for your help and everything, believe me I am, but as I said I'm leaving right now."

"And as I said, you're not going anywhere," he growls. My eyes widened in surprise at his sudden change in tone.

"What are you gonna do about it? Kidnap me?" I laugh.

His eyes narrow and he leans into me until his hands are on the bed and he's inches from my face.

"If that's what it takes princess, then mark my words I will." He moves in closer. His voice lowered to almost a whisper. "See I know all about your mother being, how do you put it?... not well and I'm pretty sure her track record of drug abuse as well as petty theft and...". He hesitates, "supplying minors."

My eyes darted to his.

"That was her boyfriend and I did all I could to keep those kids away from our home."

I can feel a pulse beginning to pound within my temples.

I was as surprised as anyone to find out my mother of all people had begun to supply dodgy heroin to the kids of our estate and I fucking tried to stop it. Most of the time only to be met with the fist of whatever pimp she had lurking around.

"Oh I'm sure you did." Alaric smiles, and I can feel the taunt in his voice. "But the cops aren't going to really care that you *tried* now are they? When they're alerted to her little crack den. They'll haul her ass in a cell quicker than you can say mummy issues. It's just another junkie whore off the street to them."

Who the fuck did this prick think he was?

"She's not a junkie whore. She needs help." Tears pricked the corners of my eyes as I fought back my emotions. I wouldn't cry in front of this bastard.

"Then stay here, work for us and she'll get the help she needs. That much I can promise you." He smiles and I want to smack it straight from his smug face.

"Blackmail, great!" I throw up my hands, landing them back by my side on the bed. I exhale loudly.
I'll do this for my mother. I'll do what I need to do.

"Fine, it doesn't look like I have much choice does it?!"

He smiles, standing back to his feet and looking down at me.

"I'll send Morgan with food for you, looks like you could use a little meat on your bones."

I look down over my slender frame, bringing the covers higher to cover myself more.
I see him smile at my movement.

"Now lastly..." he slides his fingers under my chin, lifting my face to meet his gaze and grazes the pad of his thumb over my bottom lip.

Chills erupt over my skin at his touch and I see the fury instantly arise in his eyes as he looks at me.

"Who did this to you?"

CHAPTER TEN

Alaric

I knew it was him.
I knew it was the mothers fucking boyfriend.
Scum of the earth, I could tell from what I read about him in Colts findings. At least we wouldn't have to go far to get this sorted.

"So when do we pay step daddy a little visit?" Axel asked, taking his shot on the pool table against Rio, as Sully and I stood, leaning against the bar.

Sometimes I needed to get away from La Tanière and the little run-down pool bar down the street was just the place to do it.

It made a change for the four of us to actually be out together as it seemed rare these days that we were all free at the same time.

"When he least expects it," I answered, lifting the beer bottle to my mouth.

"I'd finish the mother off as well, seems like a waste of good oxygen."

Rio never was one to mince his words and I loved that about him.

We'd been best friends since high school and even though we couldn't look much more different, me with my clean cut look and him with his rugged beard and dark man bun, we were one and the same on the inside.

Other than Rio, and Axel, the only other person I was close to besides Elliot was Sully.

Sully never took work as seriously as the rest of us did. He was the joker of the group. His dark ginger hair shaved shorter at the sides and longer on top. Not that different from mine besides the colour.

I always joked that he was the prettiest ginger I'd ever seen, though none of us had any problem when it came to getting women.

Chicks fell at our feet at La Tanière. We could have a different pussy on our cocks every night if we wanted. Axel and Sully often did. Although Sully was greedy and would often take two or three back to his apartment at the end of the night. Staff included.

He was fucking our two best burlesque dancers, Leela and Ashleigh last week. The fucker is always dripping in pussy. Must be the dick piercing.

Rio has a bit of a thing for Sapphire but she always made it clear it was me she wanted.

She was easy on the eye and good in bed but there was just nothing there apart from the pussy and she's easy as fuck. I like to work for my reward.

I turn back to Rio who's still waiting for my reaction to his comment.

"The mother stays alive. I'll deal with her later."

Rio nods, shooting the black ball straight into the pocket, ending the game, much to Axel's annoyance.

"Fancy a game big bro?" Axel challenges.

I stand taking the que from Sully.

"So when can I fuck the little redhead?" Axel laughs, breaking the set of balls to begin the game.

Irritation flows through my veins as I grip the que so hard my knuckles turn white.

"Keep your fucking hands away from the staff," I sneer.

He looks at me with raised eyebrows.

"Jealous brother?" He teases.

I shake my head in annoyance.

"Elliots going to have your balls if you carry on fucking the staff and I'm not stepping in to save you."

Axel laughs out loud, throwing back his head.

"Maybe give it a go sometime, might relieve some of that tension sunshine."

He smirks as I run the pad of my thumb across my bottom lip.

"I have more important things to deal with right now."

"Ahh yes, but still playing on your mind though isn't she?"

I ignore his jibe as he lets out another fucking infuriating laugh. I will murder the little fucker one day. He wasn't far wrong though, having Lexi around so close was playing on my mind a lot more than it should.

I didn't like sharing my space with anyone, never mind some chick we didn't even know, but Elliot seemed adamant he wanted her to join the team and I trusted his judgement.

Thrashing Axel at pool was child's play and soon we were heading back to the club.

My phone vibrated, receiving a message from Elliot. He'd called for a meeting with myself, Axel and Colt. Apparently today was the day we would meet the owner of La Tanières potential competitor.

Back at the club, Elliot was perched in one of the large leather booths with Colt by his side.

I arrived with Axel in tow, still skulking about being annihilated at the pool game.

"So the new club is to be called Scarlet!" begins Colt, scrolling through his phone casually. "I believe the owner we will be meeting today is a Mr Darien Steele, we don't know much about him yet, he's proving a little more tricky to chase up than usual but I'll have something on him by the end of the day."

Elliot brings his glass to his lips.

"The fact he's harder to track is alarm bells in itself but we'll hopefully know more when they arrive."

My eyebrows lift slightly at Elliot's words.

"You think they may have something to do with *the business*?" I ask.

He looks at me like he knows exactly which business I'm referring to.

"I'm not sure but I won't be leaving anything to chance. We need answers and we need them today."

The unease in the room is palpable and you could cut the tension with a knife. Something definitely feels off about this meeting.

The doors to the club open slowly and Jax and Demitri enter with two other security guards on their heels, security guards that are definitely not a part of our pack, followed by a small entourage of men in pristine, black suits.

In the middle stands a tall, dark haired man. His sharp features and the fucking ridiculously expensive suit scream power and money.

I've seen fuckers like him before and they're like vipers, but they've never been a match for me, Elliot or Axel. The guy can try I suppose.

"Gentlemen." He holds out his hand as I stand before the booth, ready to greet him.

I stare at his outstretched hand, my palm not leaving my side. He smiles when he sees I won't be shaking his hand.

"My name is Darien Steele, myself and my business partner will be opening our club Scarlet in the next week, and we wanted to make you aware as we know this is your territory and we wanted to assure you our business is somewhat... *different* to yours, so we won't be getting under your feet."

"Alaric Mackenzie," I finally answered. "And what do you mean by different? In what way is your club... *different* to ours?"

He looks at me straight in the eyes, his irises so dark, it creates the illusion of one giant pupil. A black hole of nothing.

"Well for starters we are an exclusive club, as in we accept members only and membership is significantly high in cost. It's a... private gentleman's club if you will."

I nod, so basically strippers. That was nothing new in this area of Blackbridge.

"I see, well it's good to know there will be no problems on your side."

He smirks and I already know I don't trust this guy, theres something shady as fuck about him.

"So when will we have the pleasure of meeting your business partner?" Elliot asks from the booth.

I turn to see his narrowed eyes staring at Darien in suspicion. He clearly feels the same way that I do.

"Well I'm glad you asked actually as he's just got here."

With that, the doors open again to reveal another man. If Darien looked sinister then this guy was the grim reaper.

He looked about Elliott and Darien's age, late fifties but with dark hair in loose curls on top of his head.

His body looked ripped under the white shirt he wore as though he was no stranger to the gym, but the one thing I noticed more than anything else was the large, angry looking scar that travelled from the corner of his right eyebrow, right down to the middle of his right cheek, gliding straight through his right eye.

His left eye was the clearest blue but the right was replaced with what I presumed was a glass eye, with a white iris. It reminded me of the little siren with her multi-coloured eyes.

Heat flooded to my groin at the thought of her and I had to remind myself where I was.

The scar looked raised as if it had been performed by a blunt blade.

His eye met mine and he stared at me, burning a hole to my very core.

Elliot rose from where he was seated and moved forward to where I was standing.

I turned to look at him but was shocked by the vacant expression on his face.

His skin had gone completely white like he'd seen a ghost. A look I never thought I'd ever see on the face of my uncle.

"Vincenzo De La Hoy."

Elliot's words slipped from his mouth in a strangled rasp.

"Elliot Mackenzie."

An evil smile tilted the lips of the man before me.

I'd seen it a million times before, this fucker was bad news but how the hell did he know my uncle?

Elliot coughed, clearing his throat. "It's been a long time."

"That it has, that it really has. I see you've met Darien, my new partner, aren't you going to introduce me to... what are they? Your nephews?"

He turns his attention back to me.

"Who the fuck are you?" I blurt out before Elliot gets the chance to speak.

"Alaric!" Elliot calls, silencing me. "This is Vinnie, he was... an old business partner of mine. We lost touch a long time ago."

He turns back to Vinnie. "I'm surprised to see you after all this time."

Vinnie laughs and the sound echoes around the room, booming from the walls.

"Yes so it seems, I thought you would be welcoming the sight of your old *business partner.*" He looks briefly towards Darien and then back to Elliot. "Anyway, gentleman, I just thought I would show my face, manners and all that, but unfortunately this was a flying visit. We have Scarlet opening in a week and I'm sure we'll be seeing a lot more of each other in the upcoming future, so for now I'll say goodbye. Elliot, Alaric and..." he pauses as he looks at my brother now sitting beside Colt. "Axel Mackenzie."

A dark shadow flashes across his good eye, it's only there for a second but I saw it. The whole thing is definitely off.

With that, he turns and leaves the building with Darien. The entourage following close behind.

The doors slam shut leaving the four of us in silence.

"Care to fucking explain?" I glare at Elliot, who looks at me with pure murder in his eyes.

"Like I said, we were in business together. Planned to open a club like La Tanière years ago but it never went ahead. He skipped town after some dodgy dealings and I never heard from him again. That's all there is to it. We need info on Darien Steele and soon, and we need to find out all we can on Scarlet, Vinnie De La Hoy is not to be trusted."

Elliot picks up his whiskey glass and heads up the winding staircase to his office.

"Do you buy it?" asks Axel, coming to my side. "The old business partner routine? That they just parted ways without any trouble?"

I continue to look in the direction that Elliot had just departed.

"No," I replied, "but that's all we have to go on for now, so Colt, do as he says and get the info we need, ideally by tonight."

Colt hears my orders, nodding as he leaves the booth and exits the room.

I didn't miss the look in Elliot's eyes when he saw Vinnie De La Hoy for the first time and I also didn't miss the way his hand went instinctively to his hip.

The place where he keeps his gun.

CHAPTER ELEVEN

Lexi

I might still be healing but my body was feeling surprisingly so much better and there's only so much resting a girl can do.

I had to admit I was getting extremely anxious about this whole situation and I've never been one to just sit back and accept things, so today was the day I was finally going to see what the hell goes on here.

I gently climbed out of the bed and walked slowly over to the large en suite bathroom with the waterfall shower.

Climbing inside the cubicle, I welcomed the warm spray of water cascading over my bruised skin.

I flinched at the tender areas around my shoulders, but soon my body was relaxing back into the wall as I let the calming heat of the steam take over my mind and body.

After my shower, I took the time to blow dry my hair straight and have a look through some of the clothes that had been brought to my room by Morgan.

She was such a sweet little thing. I made it my mission to find out more about her.

Putting on some tight, distressed jeans and a black tank top, I was feeling more human than I had in forever.

A knock on the door startled me.

"Come in," I replied.

I was half expecting it to be Alaric, so I was more surprised when an attractive, older woman entered the room. Her dyed red bob swayed at her shoulders.

"Hello Alexandra."

The voice was husky, yet feminine.

"It's...just Lexi, Lexis fine."

My attempt to smile was clearly forced and I felt like this woman could sense that straight away.

"Lexi. You are to be our newest act. I hear you are gifted in silk aerial. My name is Cassidie Sloan. I'm the creative director for La Tanière. I help the acts if they need anything in the way of choreography etcetera."

Her lips curl at the edges but the smile doesn't quite meet her eyes. She's clearly putting it on for show.

"I don't need choreography."

No point beating about the bush. If I have to perform here, I might as well make it easier on myself.

Cassidie nods.

"Very well, we will head over to the back of the club. That is where all the acts prepare for the evening shows."

She holds out her arm to lead the way and I follow closely behind.

The section of the club designed for the rehearsals was like a huge gym.

Several performers were practicing their own routines including burlesque dancers and ballerinas floating around a makeshift stage in the middle of the room.

I walked slowly throughout the building, Cassidie by my side, taking in everything around me.

One person I recognised straight away was the contortionist from the show I saw, that fateful night I had attended the club with Sim. Her body twisted into an awkward looking back bend. She glanced over, narrowing her eyes slightly before going back about her business.

"That's Sapphire," Cassidie pointed out. "She performs the Alice in Wonderland act also known as AIW. It's one of our most popular shows. Then over there you have Leon."

I look to where Cass is pointing to see a tall, slim yet toned figure with sandy blonde hair. He looks to be in his early twenties, wearing tight, lycra leggings and a lycra vest, both in black. His arms, painted with neon stripes.

"He's a blade swallower," she continues.

I raise my eyebrows taking in the guy's slim form.

A blade swallower? Jesus!

Leon looks over, a bright smile on his face and gives me a little wave. I wave back instinctively.

"The dancers over there are Leela and Ashleigh and then you've got Oake."

I glanced over to a corner of the stage where a tall guy stood in all black. His head shaved to the scalp apart from a black Mohawk trailing down the middle.

His face was stunningly beautiful with a double nose piercing and lip piercing, right in the centre of his luscious bottom lip.

He glanced over with a scowl and then continued with whatever it was that he was doing. *Something involving rope or so it would seem as he was wrapping it around his wrist.*

"He's an illusionist," said Cass, continuing on.

Lastly I spotted Morgan.

She was wearing a cream, corseted dress, her long hair draped over her slender shoulders, reading from what appeared to be a song sheet.

"And these will be yours," Cass pointed to the corner of the room where two beautiful, red strips of silk hung from beams on the ceiling.

I walked towards them, grasping the cool, soft material between my fingers and feeling a sudden surge of energy take over my body. I couldn't wait to feel them slide against my body.

The feeling was bittersweet. I was excited to start training again, but I missed the kids I used to teach. Sim was right, the money was terrible but it was my life for so long. I craved it now.

Shit I needed to call Sim, she's gonna be worried sick!

"You'll be known as Siren," says Cass, staring at the silks. "A goddess of the sea. Everyone has a stage name."

Siren? Sure whatever the hell they want. My mum was still fucking things up for me, even now.

I had to stay here, if I ran she'd go down for the dodgy heroin she was selling kids and she wouldn't last two minutes in a prison cell.

Cass left me to my thoughts, heading back up to the offices so I decided to hang around and get a feel for everyone here.

"Lexi," Morgan waved her little arms. "You're up and about, that's great."

I smiled, there was something so innocent and warming about this girl.

"I am, and erm... thanks for the clothes."

She giggled, a blush coating her already naturally pink cheeks.

"No problem. Alaric asked me to get you something and I kinda guessed your style. I wasn't sure but you don't look like the kinda girl who's going to go for the pinks."

I laugh. "Yeah you got that right." Pink is certainly not my colour.

"Come and meet the others."

Morgan grabbed my hand pulling me towards the two dancers, dressed in blue, ruffled mini dresses and fishnet tights.

They both had long wavy hair except one was blonde, this one I discovered was Leela and the other had vibrant pink hair. That would be Ashleigh.

They were both friendly, chatting away about who I was and what my story was all about.

"We grew up together in orphanages," said Leela, pointing between her and Ashleigh. "We were adopted together but when we were fourteen, our adopted parents were killed in a car accident. Elliot brought us here so we didn't end up back in the system and potentially separated. Saved our lives I guess."

I hear a scoff from behind Leela.

"Saved your lives?" It was Sapphire. "What do you know about hardship, you both got adopted young by a good family and as soon as anything happened to them, Elliot was right there to fix all your problems. I got shipped around from foster home to foster home. Nightmare to nightmare and only got out when Elliot caught me being used to ship drugs into his club. You don't know anything about hardship."

Ashleigh rolled her eyes. "Don't worry about her, she's always like that."

"However…"

I didn't realise Sapphire was still a part of the conversation but clearly she had more to say. "Things are better than ever now. I have a great home, I'm the star of one of the most famous nightclubs in the country and I have Alaric so that's all I need."

Her smug grin felt like a punch to the chest at that moment and I shrugged away the feeling of unease. Did she know I was staying at Alaric's apartment? She must do. Were they together?

I didn't know why that seemed to bother me, he was an arrogant prick who blackmailed me into staying here. He could fuck whoever he wanted, I had no interest. It was just pissing me off that my body didn't seem to think the same.

That fucking sharp, angular jaw combined with eyes the colour of passing smoke and my pulse is racing and my palms are sweating.

Seriously Lex, get a grip you slut!

Although I needed to find out if he was keeping his end of the bargain regarding my mum.

I didn't trust that she would get the help he promised but I'd give him the benefit of the doubt…*for now.*

Sapphire heads back to the mats where she was practicing her routine and continues her stretches.

"Ignore her," whispers Morgan. "Her and Alaric are not *together* together." She looks at me, gesturing with her eyes to explain her point.

I shrug my shoulders. "It's fine."

"Come on, I'll introduce you to Leon."

Morgan bounces excitedly towards the guy in the black vest

with the charming smile.

She flings herself into his arms and he catches her effortlessly, her legs wrapping around his waist.

"Hey gorgeous."

Leon places a kiss on Morgan's forehead.

"This is Lexi, she's new here."

Leon turns and smiles again. A perfect set of straight white teeth.

"Hey Lexi, Leon." he gives a small wave.

"Hey, so are you Morgan's boyfriend?"

Both of them burst out laughing.

"Erm no, Morgan's only seventeen, she's like a little sister," he winks at Morgan, who throws him a large grin of her own. "Plus I erm… don't bat for that team if you know what I mean?"

My face heats. "Oh I'm so sorry I didn't…"

Leon laughs, "hey don't worry, you weren't to know, but yeah Oake here has more chance of getting my dick than Morgz."

He smiles over at the moody looking guy with all the piercings who glares in our direction. Fuck if looks could kill!

"Keep your fucking dick to yourself Leon." Oake barks.

"Jesus what's his deal?" I ask.

Leon and Morgan both still smiling tauntingly in Oakes' direction.

"He's always been like that since he arrived. He's had a rough past, at least that's what we heard. He's never spoken to anyone about it, keeps himself to himself," explains Leon.

I nod, noticing the lingering gaze Morgan gives to the stubborn illusionist. She turns back to us before I can question her on it.

"So how did you guys get here?" I ask, sitting down on the bench next to where Leon is training.

"I was found by Elliot. My story, I've heard, is pretty similar to your story," says Leon. "Let's just say being gay wasn't something my brother approved of."

I narrowed my eyes as he lifted his black vest to expose his bare torso.

I gasped at what I saw next.

Thick scars covered his whole chest right down to his navel, like brush strokes on a canvas.

"Leon…" my gaze stayed locked on his chest. An ache forming inside my own.

"It's fine it's in the past" he brushes off my startled gaze.

"But your brother?" My words are barely more than a whisper.

"Homophobia can be found anywhere, even where you'd least expect it."

His audible sigh sounded defeated for a second but then he walked over to Morgan picking her up and spinning her in the air.

"But I found my own family, a better family… one that I wouldn't change for the world."

His words sounded comforting to me and at that moment I had a good idea as to why.

Knowing what these people had been through made me realise that all this time, living in an unsafe house with a mother who, let's face it, couldn't give a shit about me, I wasn't the only one going through this and these people had found each other and, what seemed from the outside, a better life.

"So what's your story?" I asked, turning to face Morgan who was straightening her dress after being spun by Leon.

She smiled, "come on, I wanna show you something."

A small, cool hand grasped my palm and pulled me in the direction of another small room.

The only thing inside it was a tall microphone stand, the mic perched on top and some speakers and amplifiers in different parts of the room.

"This is my world."

Morgan's face beamed brighter than I had seen it before as she looked towards where the microphone stand was situated.

"I'm a singer. I'm known as The Nightingale, you know, cos of my surname and stuff…and I guess nightingales sing pretty nice too."

"Yeah I guess they do."

Morgan walked slowly towards the mic, her tiny fingers clasping around it.

"My dad was a bad man." She spoke without even looking in my direction. "He owed a lot of people a lot of money, but in the end he owed the wrong person."

The look on Morgan's face changed from her usual happy go lucky self to someone entirely different as if she was in a memory, reliving it in front of me in a dream-like state.

"Elliot didn't care about the money, not when he knew what my daddy was doing to me when my mom was sleeping."

Nausea rolled in my gut and I swallowed hard to suppress the bile rising in my throat.

Suddenly something broke within Morgan's mind and she turned to smile at me as if she was back in the room. The glazed expression in her eyes vanishing.

"My dad offered me as payment when he couldn't get the money and Elliot accepted. He brought me to La Tanière, where he told me I'd be safe and I've been singing here ever since. I saw my mom a few weeks later and she said my daddy had disappeared. Just vanished without a trace... guess he didn't wanna hang around anymore."

I narrowed my eyes as I took in the way Morgan brushed off what she'd just told me, about her father just up and leaving. Something told me she knew better.

"Yeah," I finally replied. "Guess he didn't."

CHAPTER TWELVE

Lexi

The next few days I was feeling grateful to have Morgan by my side.

I hadn't seen Alaric and Axel since our conversation about me staying here. Whenever I asked Morgan, she said they were away doing business, *whatever the hell that meant.*

She and Leon had been great at keeping me company, and I finally managed to get a new phone from Cass so that I could text Sim and let her know everything was okay, promising I'd see her soon.

Spending time down in the training gym was like a much needed relief for me. I could feel my body getting stronger whenever I was on the silks.

The death stares from Sapphire were coming in thick and fast whenever I was down there, but I chose to ignore the tension. She was the one who had the problem with me, not the other way around and I'd been informed by Leon that she was overheard bitching about the fact she never got to stay at the apartment with Alaric overnight. Again not my problem.

This girl definitely had a chip on her shoulder and I had no time for any of that.

"The next show, we want you to perform," said Cass approaching in the tightest leather suit dress and knee high boots.

"I haven't had that long to practice," I protested, but was met with a disapproving side eye.

"You've had enough time."

My eye roll was obvious enough for her to see, but she didn't say anything.

Cass was a strange one. It was like being here was through force and she wasn't happy most of the time.

I guess after being blackmailed to stay, I knew how it felt but I was starting to realise that this place wasn't as bad as I first anticipated, and getting to know Leon and Morgan had made it all the better.

I grabbed my phone, plugging it into the small speakers in my training area and flicked through some playlists trying to find something I could practice my routine to. I settled on *'Million Eyes'* by *Loic Nottet*. This would be the best soundtrack for my first performance at La Tanière.

As I circled the floor before climbing the silk, I felt transported back to my place of happiness and for the first time in so long, I felt the freedom that I craved.

Sweaty and exhausted, I headed back to the Mackenzies apartment after three hours on the silks.

I was as ready as I'd ever be for the performance at the club and right now all I needed was a much deserved hot shower.

Opening the front door, I instantly knew for the first time in days that I wasn't alone when the scent of leather and citrus filled my nostrils. A heady mix of masculinity heading straight from the shower.

Closing the door quietly behind me, I crept towards the guest room I'd been staying in.

"Feeling better I see."

Turning slowly, my eyes instantly fixed on Alaric's deep, smoky glare as he stood before me in nothing but a white towel wrapped around his waist.

His dark hair, wet and spiked and droplets of water from the shower beaded across his tanned, muscular chest and abs, that were covered in intricate artwork. Not something you could see clearly in the suits he was always wearing.

His torso was ripped, sculpted like a Greek god. He looked like he belonged on Mount Olympus not in this room.

His lips began to curve upwards as he caught my eyes wondering over his semi naked form.

"See something you like, little siren?"

I flinched at my stage name coming from his mouth, heat radiating from my core and locking between my legs.

I quickly cleared my throat. "I don't think so."
I turned away from him towards my door as I heard his deep laughter.

Aggravation flared in my chest at his arrogance, but as I swung my head back to ask him why he was laughing, he was there, standing right in front of me. His large hands gripped my elbows as he crashed his body into me, slamming me against the wall before grabbing my wrists and pinning them above my head. His towel dropped to the floor.
Oh dear Jesus, this guy is big.

He leaned into my body, his frame as solid as stone.
I tried to keep my eyes focused ahead as I felt the bulge of his exposed erection pressing into my groin.
I wriggled in his grasp.

"Let go of me," I demanded.
He smiled. *Fuck me, he was pretty!*

"I don't want you to touch me, you fucking, arrogant pig. How much more clear do I have to be?"

His penetrating eyes burned straight into mine, and I prayed he wouldn't see what was behind the walls that I had so carefully built.

Still holding my wrists with one hand, his other travelled down the sweat licked skin of my cheek, down my throat and between my cleavage, before slipping over my tight stomach which was exposed in my little, black crop top and gliding straight into my workout leggings.

I bit down hard onto my bottom lip to stifle a whimper attempting to escape my throat. The coppery tang of my blood infused onto my tongue.

Using his fingers, Alaric slid my panties to the side before stroking two fingers through my warm, damp heat, across my clit and bringing them back up, out of my leggings and up to my face so I could see myself glistening on the tips of his fingers. A shiver traveled up the length of my spine.

"See little siren, your mouth says one thing…"
He slides both of his soaking fingers into his mouth, his tongue lapping my arousal from the tips. His eyes never leaving mine. "But your body says something else."

A sharp exhale left my lips and I wasn't even aware I'd been holding my breath.

His mouth, so close to my cheek that I can feel his breath on my face, smell the mint of his mouthwash.

With that he grins, flashing all his perfectly straight, white teeth before releasing me and grabbing his towel from the floor, heading back towards his room.

Frustrated, I entered my room, slamming the door behind me.

How fucking dare he not listen to a word I say, even if my insides were screaming to tear my nails down that chest of steel. The urge to taste his mouth felt like I had been starved all my life. But he was nothing more than a blackmailing asshole and I was done with being a puppet for the amusement of men, even if watching him slip his fingers into his mouth and lick my juices off of him was possibly the hottest thing I had ever seen in my life.

CHAPTER THIRTEEN

Alaric

What the fuck is wrong with me?

Between me and my brother, I've always been the one with more self control, but with her, my dick just takes over.

I've become lustful, irrational, but fuck she's hot, gotta be the hottest girl I've ever seen that's for sure.

Those eyes, one blue and one brown drive me crazy, shame she's such a brat.

Returning to my room, I lay on the bed, propping my head up with one arm behind it, the other down at my groin, clutching my cock in my hand.

I start to pump slow, tight movements along the shaft as I picture the little siren's mouth on me instead.

I'm taken right back to the night on the balcony with Sapphire, picturing Lexi there, sucking me dry instead of her.

Everything about the girl is intoxicating.

Her red hair, her cherry lips, that sweet pussy and the way it dripped for me while I held her against the wall.

God she was wet.

I wanted nothing more than to strip her of those tight little leggings, rip off her panties and sink inside her. Claim her and make her realise that when I want something I get it, no matter how much she puts on that tough little act.

I might have this internal war going on, one side telling me to keep focused on business, especially now we have info on Darien Steele or at least info confirming what a nasty piece of shit he is. Convictions in domestic abuse, drug trafficking, and aggravated assault and that's just the crimes the cops were aware of.

But I can't help this other side, driving me to completely consume the girl sleeping in the room right across the hall from me. She's like some fucking dark hole trying to pull me in to this crushing oblivion and I just want to take control of that sexy, little body and mind.

I pump my rock hard erection as I continue thinking about all the dark and depraved things I'd love to do to her, and it doesn't take long until I'm coming undone in my own hand, liquid heat coursing through my body and thick ropes of cum spurting onto my stomach as I come down from my release.

Fuck

The low groan escapes my lips.

I contemplate going over to the Hive to seek out Sapph but that's just asking for trouble and I can't be dealing with all her issues like always after I fuck her.

I grab a cloth and wipe myself down before grabbing my phone, texting Axel to find out where the fuck he's disappeared to yet again.

Messages pour through from Colt, more info on Darien Steele but for some reason, everything regarding Vinnie De La Hoy is coming up blank and Elliot seems resistant to talk about him despite being convinced he's hiding something regarding Scarlet.

Half an hour later and Axel's back at the apartment, hair ruffled.

"You stink of sex."

He laughs, "I've been busy brother."

I glare at him.

"What happened on the Kettering contract?" I ask.

Axel grabs a bag of dipping chips from the cupboard.

"It's finished. The ring leader was taken down today. Rio saw to it."

I nod. "Fine… and payment?"

"Secured."

I nod again.

One thing about my brother is he's good at his job, the business we run behind La Tanière and so are Rio and Sully. I've got the best team on my side.

Axel pulls off his hoodie. "I'm going for a shower."

"Get a good night's sleep," I tell him. "Tomorrow we're visiting step daddy."

CHAPTER FOURTEEN

Alaric

Sitting tight in my black Cadillac with Axel, Rio and Sully, it's not long before we spot the junkie pimp who beat Lexi half to death and dumped her on the side of the road, hoping she wouldn't survive and no one would know it was him who did it.

I didn't need the boys to come along, I was happy to tear that vile piece of shit limb from limb myself but I know how much the boys love a good session, especially Axel. That fuckers crazier than me when it comes to spilling blood.

We discovered from Lexi that the cretin was named Anton. After a few background checks by Colt, we discovered he was a dirty addict who had used a string of women for drugs, money and prostitution, Lexis mother being the latest.

Most of them had overdosed or gone missing so he just moved on to the next.

Women going missing seemed to be a repeat occurrence at the minute, especially when it came to workers at La Tanière.

I'd upped the security on their homes at the Hive but you couldn't follow your staff twenty four seven. They weren't prisoners, *despite what Lexi assumes.*

However due to the nature of business behind the club, the police were the last people we'd get involved in what was happening.

I'd made it my mission to sort this fucking thing out, I always did and this was going to be no different, but so far any leads to the missing girls were coming up with a dead end.

"There he is."

Axel points over at Anton as he leaves the house and rounds the corner. "There's our guy."

Showtime.

I drove the Cadillac closer and around the corner to the exit of the alleyway Anton had just walked though, ready to greet him at the other end with a nice little surprise.

Stepping out of the car, I walk straight towards him, straightening the front of my suit jacket.

"Anton," I speak, just as I reach where he had exited the alley.

"The fuck do you want?" He snarls, giving me a quick once over, his beady eyes skirting over my suit.

With that Axel is behind him, covering his head with a black sack, shutting off his vision completely.

He thrashes in Axel's hold but my brother holds him like a rag doll. *God this fucker really is embarrassing.*

"We have a little business to discuss, my friend."

Rio opens the boot before Sully grabs Antons legs after zip tying his hands together, hauling him with Axel's assistance, into the boot of my car.

His muffled screams are barely audible through the bag and now the boot, but a few kicks and thrashes can be heard as he fights in vain to free himself.

The four of us jump back into my car and head to the basement of La Tanière where our playtime will begin.

Pulling the sack from Antons head, he squints to clear his vision and process where he is.

I doubt he realises he's in the basement of the most famous club in the country. His arms strung up to the ceiling with ropes tied to his wrists.

I made sure to make the restraints just long enough so he's

stretched onto his tip toes. He's been tied there for about thirty minutes now so his arms should be starting to ache pretty badly.

He looks frantically to each wrist before shooting his eyes between me and my brothers.

"Hello Anton, I don't believe we've met, my name is Alaric Mackenzie."

"Mackenzie?" His face pales at the realisation.

"Oh you have heard of us? I guess our reputation precedes us it would seem, even in the world of a lowlife junkie."

He snarls at my insult. "Why the fuck am I here? You've got the wrong fucking person."

I release a low laugh, dragging my hand through my messy hair.

"See Anton, I don't think we have. Now, not that long ago we had a girl brought into our care. A young girl, only nineteen you see. Long, red hair... ringing any bells yet?"

I see it there, quick as lightning, that flash of fear across his eyes.

"I don't know any redhead."

I grit my teeth so hard, pain lances across my jaw.
My patience is wearing thin.

Without another word I smash my fist into his face, breaking his nose with a loud crack.

He screams in pain.

"Come now Anton, I have no time for your lies."

He begins to whimper, slobber dripping from his mouth and tears leaking from his eyes.

What a fucking joke.

"I'm not lying... I have no idea..." *crack!*
I landed another blow to his face, this time splitting his lip like a burst orange.

"Urgh please," he begs.
I shake off my fist, my knuckles grazed. That one was a bit of a stinger.

"Let me refresh your memory Anton. The girl brought to our care was Lexi Power. The daughter of the woman you are currently fucking with."

Looking at me through glazed eyes, he lets out a pained groan.

"She was beaten pretty badly," I explained, pulling out my blade and ripping open his wife beater in one slice.

"She was also raped, Anton. Now what kind of sick fuck rapes his own girlfriends daughter?"

His breathing has turned erratic as I glide the tip of the knife over his collarbone and bring it down to his chest.

"I didn't rape her," he screams. "The bitch wanted it as much as I did." *And there it is!*

Fury flares across my body in sharp waves and I can hardly see through the red mist, clouding my vision at his words.

I dig the end of the blade into the skin of his chest, the flesh parting like butter.

He squeals but the restraints hold him in place.

I should bring my gun to his head and end this now, but a quick death is too good for him, and I never was one for mercy.

Dragging the knife through his sagging flesh, I carefully carve out the word 'RAPIST' across his chest. His screams like sweet music to my ears and I bask in his agony.

Good thing this fucking basement is soundproof.   One thing you have to remember when you work in our world is make sure your interrogation slash torture room is undetectable.

"I doubt Lexi is the first girl you've done this to, but let me tell you something, she will definitely be the last."

He trembles furiously, blood seeping from the gaping slices on his chest as I stand back to admire my handy work.

"See we like the little siren," says Axel stepping in front of where Anton is hung. "She belongs to us now and we don't take too kindly to anyone who harms what is ours. The only ones allowed to make her bleed are us."

Taking the cigarette from his mouth he pushes the burning end of it into Antons wound.

An animalistic scream pierces the air as the smell of burnt flesh singes my nostrils.

Satisfaction surges through my bones along with arousal at

the image of seeing my little siren's flawless skin painted with her own blood.

I adjust my cock inside my trousers as I catch the smirk from Rio, who clearly knows where my mind has headed.

"Pleasseeee!" Anton begs through laboured breaths. "I'm sorry!"

Axel laughs. "It's too late for sorry."

I nod towards Rio and Sully who grab a leg each, holding him in place, while Axel heads over to a filing cabinet in the corner of the room, returning with a large hammer aiming it straight at the abuser's knee caps.

Antons eyes bulge from their sockets as he realises what is to come.

As I'm met with the sound of cracking bone and the strangled cries of pain, I sit back while my brothers do their work and think about how I can't wait to see the little siren shine her light on her first La Tanière performance.

CHAPTER FIFTEEN

Lexi

"What's the Feast of Fire?"

I lounge out on Leon's sofa, listening to him go on about his excitement for some big event coming up at the club.

"It's only like the party of all parties," answers Morgan, laying on the floor, stuffing more dipping chips into her face.

The three of us decided to take a break from training as we'd spent most of the day in the gym getting ready for my first big night tomorrow, where I would perform at La Tanière for the very first time.

We grabbed some chips and dips and headed up to Leon's apartment in the Hive to chill out.

His apartment was clean and neat with an edgy vibe. Dark purple walls and mirrors and candlesticks that looked like they had been sourced straight from the eighteenth century.

"I can't believe the Mackenzie's never mentioned the Feast of Fire," says Leon, lounging on the other sofa, a bottle of *Budweiser* in his hand. "It's pretty notorious, a party just for staff of La Tanière and sometimes the Mackenzies close friends. There's music, booze, everything. It's awesome."

"Sounds *awesome*."

My sarcasm isn't lost on Leon who throws a cushion at my face.

"It's just an excuse for Leon to get drunk and barf everywhere," says Morgan, looking in his direction.
I smile.

"Oh yeah and what about you miss Morgz?" interrupts Leon, "don't think I didn't notice you fluttering those pretty eyelashes at a certain magician."

Morgan rolls her eyes. "Illusionist actually, and I wasn't fluttering anything at him."

"Oh, is this Oake?" I ask. I sensed the tension in the room and I could tell a million percent when I saw Morgan's lingering gaze at Oake that first time I was in the gym, that she had a thing for him.

"I don't have a thing for Oake," says Morgan, knowing exactly what I'm thinking. "Plus how can we really let our hair down knowing Trinity's out there and no one knows where she is or what's happening to her?"

I'd heard the story circulating down at the gym, of some of the girls going missing and no one had a clue where they were. Trinity from the burlesque squad being one of them.

"Were you close?" I ask.

Tears coated Morgan's beautiful green eyes but she held them back.

"She was one of my first friends when I got here. I was so scared. I knew I was in a better place but I'd never been away from my mom and it terrified me. Trinity took me under her wing, helped me find my confidence with singing. It was her who suggested my stage name be Nightingale, same as my surname." Morgan continued and I could sense the love she had for her friend and the painful loss she felt when she thought about her.

"They'll find her Morgz," says Leon, dropping to the floor and pulling Morgan into his chest with one strong arm. "Al and Axel are two of the best, you know that, no one gets past them eventually. They have to be, in their line of work."

My blood runs cold at his words. "Their line of work?"

Leon and Morgan both look straight at me, a feeling of anxiety growing between us.

"It's not really my place to talk about that stuff, better to speak to Al."

Leon was clearly regretting his words so I decided not to push the matter, *for now*, but it was something I intended to bring up with Alaric when I had the chance.

When that would be however, I had no idea as I had purposely avoided him since our little encounter last night.

The feel of his hard body against me, the warmth of his breath on my cheek, and the sight of his cock.

Jesus, that man was huge. My thighs clench at the mere thought. I'd be torn in half for sure.

His arrogance drove me crazy but it was impossible to look away from him. I'd never seen a human so fucking stunning in my life.

"Have you spoken much to your friend?"

Morgan's comment drags me from my daydream as I snap back to attention.

"Erm... we text, I should probably call her though."

Morgan nods. "Have you been friends for long?"

"Since we were little kids, Sim had a similar upbringing to me. Her parents were addicts too but just not as bad as my mom."

Morgan throws me a sympathetic look. I hate when people have that look of pity, I've never needed it.

I stayed at the house specifically for my mom, despite what went on there. I couldn't just leave her, it was bad enough that I was doing it now and that wasn't even by choice.

I endured what I did for her and I'd do it all again if I thought for one second any of it would make her better.

"You must miss your friend, Sim." says Morgan. "I miss Trinity everyday, we even had keys to each other's apartments, she had this gorgeous sweater, bright pink." She giggles in my direction. "She said I could have it but I never took it at the time, I wish I had now, at least it would have been something that could bring me a bit of comfort."

"Well if you still have the key, maybe go round to her

apartment and get it, it sounds like she wanted you to have it and if it makes you feel closer to her. I take it everything is still there? I've heard they're expecting the girls to come back."

Morgan nods, "yeah all the girls stuff is still there."

"Well what are we waiting for?" I jumped to my feet, grabbing Morgan by the hand. "Let's go get your sweater."

The apartment had a haunting feel as Morgan turns the lock and enters followed closely by myself and Leon.

The room still smells like someone lives here. The potent scent of lavender in the air.

It looks exactly like it would if someone had been here this morning and just left for work or something. Clothes thrown over a chair, a used mug with a lipstick stain still sitting on the kitchen counter.

A shiver ran up my spine as I explored the room slowly.

Morgan ran straight to the bedroom, searching through a mound of sweaters on the messy floor.
I watched as her tiny hands dug to the bottom of the pile.

"Here it is," she shrieked with delight.

As she pulled the sweater up to her chest, a tiny object, no bigger than a bead from a dress dropped from the crumpled piece of clothing.

"What was that?" I asked.

Looking to the floor was when I spotted it. Reaching down and taking its miniature form between my thumb and forefinger, and laying it in my palm.

Leon appeared and both him and Morgan glanced into my hand.

There sat a small, glistening ruby, perfectly cut into the shape of an oval.

"Wow, look at that," gasped Leon. "Think it's real?"

"Could be," I replied, inspecting the tiny jewel. "Looks like it's fallen out of some kind of jewellery."

"That's strange," says Morgan. "Trinity never really wore jewellery, well except for the costume jewellery she had on for the shows."

The three of us stood puzzled for a minute.

"Well I'll keep hold of it until we find out where it's from, don't want it to get lost if it is real."

I placed the ruby into the pocket of my flannel shirt.

Morgan seemed happier now she had her sweater and time was getting on, so we headed our separate ways. Morgan and Leon, back to their apartments and me across the courtyard to the Mackenzies place.

As soon as I was back, I decided to make myself a smoothie with anything I could find in the fridge.

I'd eaten hardly anything all day and my stomach was growling, it was borderline painful.

Switching on the tv, I grabbed the chopping board, a handful of strawberries and a banana.

Before I'd even had a chance to slice through the first piece of fruit, the tail end of a newsflash caught my attention.

'Police are still making enquiries into the death, but believe the man to be in his early forties and associated with drug gangs around the Blackbridge estates.'

Grabbing my phone as the news didn't give much information, I typed a quick search about the report into *google* and there it was in black and white.

Nausea bubbled in my stomach and I felt like the wind had been slammed from my chest. I tightened my lips to stop myself from throwing up.

'Drug dealer found nailed to tree after being castrated with blowtorch. Body believed to be that of local man, ANTON STEPHEN ARCHER.'

Fuck!

CHAPTER SIXTEEN

Alaric

There's nothing you need more after a day of torture than a cold beer and time to unwind, but on entering my apartment with Axel and seeing Lexis expression as she sat on the sofa with her smoothie, I knew a relaxing night was the last thing I was going to be getting.
This chick was pisssd.
 "Lexi baby, hope there's a smoothie for me?"
Axel winks at her and jumps on the other end of the sofa.
 She scoffs at his remark, as he laughs.
 I don't say a word. I have nothing to say.
 I'm assuming the reason she's fucked off is because she's seen the news and is aware her sadistic, abusive step daddy is dead.
 We made no attempt to hide the body. He was used to set an example. A warning, you could call it, to others who harm the way he did.
 I have to say there was something uniquely satisfying about the way he cried when he was nailed to that tree by Sully.
 I wonder if he felt the same way about Lexi, when he took from her what wasn't his to take.
 Axel lifts his feet, dropping them onto Lexis lap, to which she pushes them straight off in disgust.
The boys an idiot.

She jumps out of her seat and comes over to me as I grab my beer from the fridge.

"Are you going to explain what the hell happened today?"

She stands with her tiny hands on her hips, looking fucking insane in those little, silky shorts and tank top pjs, a scowl across her face and I want nothing more than to bend her over and spank her ass raw until she knows never to look at me with that anger again.

"Axel, can you give us a minute?" I look to my brother who is now rolling *his* eyes.

"Fine," he sighs as he walks to the fridge, grabbing a beer and popping the lid off with his teeth before taking a swig and heading to his bedroom.

I remove my tie, unfastening the top couple of buttons on my shirt.

Lexi still stands motionless, staring at me.

"Well?"

I smile at her. "Well what?"

"Are you going to tell me how Anton Archer ended up nailed to a tree... castrated?" Her voice sounded pained, like she was swallowing down acid that had risen in her throat. "And don't tell me you had nothing to do with it because I know you're lying."

I put down my beer bottle on the table.

"I'm not going to tell you I had nothing to do with it, because then I'd be lying. Anton Archer was a piece of shit, scum of the earth, the worst of the worst and he had no reason to keep breathing, so we took care of it."

She looks at me with a hardened expression, her eyes narrowed.

I half expected her to freak out, scream and cry at the fact she was looking into the eyes of a killer, but she didn't. She looked straight at me, defiance in her eyes. *Fuck she looks hot.*

"And do you do that often? Take care of it, when someone does something you don't like?"

Yes

I smile at her. "I always get my own way, little siren, if that's what you mean."

My eyes rake over her body. I see how hard her nipples are beneath her tank top and the thought of taking one in my mouth sends blood rushing to my groin.

"I mean, what is this other business I hear you're involved in? I know whatever it is it can't be fucking legal. Just tell me what the fuck is going on. You killed a guy for fuck sake."

"So much bad language, little siren."

She huffs. "Stop calling me that."

I smirk. "What? You don't like your show name? Pity as I was the one who chose it"

Her pink, pouty lips part in surprise.

"I wanna know the truth," she says so quietly it's almost a whisper.

I nod. "Fine, you wanna know the truth? The truth is yes, we have another business behind the facade of La Tanière. The club is our legitimate business. A place where Elliot was able to save and give a life back to young people who had suffered, but it is also a cover."

I see Lexis' throat move slightly as she swallows.

"For what?"

I inhale deeply. "Contract killing."

Her eyes widened in horror.

"So what the fuck? You're like assassins or something?"

I laugh quietly. "We're hired on a contract by people wanting to get rid of someone, yes. They're bad people Lexi, the world is a better place without them in it."

She exhales slowly and I can see the tiny pulse throbbing in her slender neck.

"Have you killed many people?"

I nod, taking another sip. "Yes."

She sighs as she blinks, her stunningly long eyelashes fanning against the perfect skin of her cheek.

"So I've left a dump of a home, filled with drug addicts so that I can be forced to live a life amongst killers?" Her voice begins to raise as I see the frustration in her eyes start to grow. "Why did you do this to me? Did you really think you were saving me? Putting me into this life. I don't want this, I don't want to be a part of this and I don't want to be near you."

She turns to walk away as I lunge forward, grabbing her arm and turning her to face me.

My hand grasping the back of her neck and pulling her flush against me as I slam my mouth onto hers in a crushing, punishing kiss. Her lips part instinctively as she inhales, letting my tongue slide in and tangle with hers.
God she tastes better than I thought she would.

With one hand still fisted in her hair possessively, tilting her head back to gain better access, I snake the other around her slim waist, pulling her as close into my body as I possibly can.

She groans into my mouth, the sound forcing the adrenaline to charge through my veins and my cock to harden instantly.

Until this moment I never knew I was drowning, sinking beneath the surface, until she came along and breathed air into my lungs.

I'm suddenly jolted from my haze as she pulls away. Her plump, pink lips stung from our kiss, panting heavily.

She closes her eyes, almost pushing back the escaping tear, touching her lips as if to confirm what had just happened was real.

Before I can say anything she turns and walks quickly through her bedroom door, slamming it behind her and leaving me here, wondering when the fuck I start giving a shit?!

CHAPTER SEVENTEEN

Lexi

That had got to be the worst night's sleep I've had in a long time, and that's counting all the sleepless nights I had at home.

So much chaos is swirling around in my head, I think it might implode. They are assassins!

I suspected something was going on behind La Tanière, something seemed off but I expected it to be something like drugs not contract killing!

That's absolutely insane.

What's more, I had to get my head around the fact that Alaric killed *or had killed,* my mum's lowlife boyfriend.

Not that I could give a shit, and I kissed him. I let *him* kiss *me* for God's sake.

What was I thinking? The guy is an arrogant arse and that's before the small detail that he's a fucking killer!

I knew all this but yet I couldn't get the feel of his lips on mine out of my head. The taste of him still lingered on my tongue, it was intoxicating.

I'd replayed that moment a million times since last night and each time resisting an overwhelming urge to reach between my legs.

I jumped from the bed, heading over to the shower and

switching on the fawcett.

The steam from the spray fills the room instantly, in thick clouds as I step out of my silky pj shorts and lift my cami over my head, stepping into the cubicle.

I glide the loofah over my body, as I close my eyes to vivid flashbacks of my kiss with Al.

My breathing picks up gently as I imagine the feel of his warm lips and his light, stubble grazing my jawline. I slide my hand over my flat stomach, down to the apex of my thighs, before slowly slipping a finger between my lips and massaging circles over my clit.

Then I trace my finger down my slit, until I reach my entrance and glide the finger inside myself.

I groan and let my head fall back into the force of the shower spray as I carefully pump my finger inside my throbbing pussy.

Alaric's menacing, grey eyes are all I can see as I begin to imagine his tongue, sweeping my jawline, across my throat and down my sternum, journeying lower.

I pull my finger from inside me before bringing it back to my clit, rubbing the nub vigorously, imagining it was Alaric's tongue flicking over the bundle of sensitive nerves.

I release a loud exhale as my eyes slam shut, my stomach clenches and my core erupts in pleasure as a torturous orgasm flares through me, leaving me panting and sated.

I open my eyes, rinsing away my release that is now coating the inside of my thighs in a sticky, glistening sheen and finishing up in the shower.

I hate this man, so why the fuck does he turn me on so much?

He goes against every single moral code there is and yet all I can think about is how I want his hands on me, his tongue inside me.

What the fuck is wrong with me?

I hate him, he's a full on fucking prick.

I dry off quickly, slipping a black hoodie over a white tank top, teamed with plain, black leggings. My long, red hair twisted up into a messy bun on top of my head and I'm ready for the day.

Walking to the kitchen, I hear the sound of *'First Fuck'* by *6lack* playing from the radio, and am startled by the sight of Axel standing casually by the coffee machine. Topless.

He stands in nothing but dark denim, distressed jeans. His torso, carved to perfection.

My eyes travel down his ink covered chest, across his toned abs and to the deep V disappearing below the low cut of his jeans.

I lift my eyes in time to see a small smirk appear on his mouth, forcing a blush from my cheeks as if I'm some little school girl caught perving on her crush.

He is ridiculously gorgeous though but more in a rugged way compared to Alaric's pretty boy features. You can tell they're related but there's something so completely different about them as well, and *fuck is that a tongue ring?*

"Lex!"

His words pull me from my trance.

"Come to eye fuck me a bit more baby?"

He winks before plastering a smug grin on his face and yep, there it is, I can see Alaric clearly now.

I scoff. "In your dreams motherfucker, I need coffee."

He laughs, handing me the freshly poured mug.

I take it, sipping at the hot, silky liquid. I don't think I've ever needed coffee as much as I do now.

"Manage to sort everything out with Al?" he asks.

"If by sorting out, you mean discovering you and your family are involved in contract killing, and using your club as some guise to conceal your corrupt lifestyle then yeah I'd say we pretty much sorted it out."

Axel's eyes narrow slightly.

"Hey, La Tanière is not some disguise for our *corrupt lifestyle* as you put it. This club is our uncle Elliot's pride and joy, he's spent years helping vulnerable people, getting them back on track. Yeah, we might be considered the villains behind closed doors but let me tell you something, some of the things these people, who we take the hits on, have done, you couldn't even imagine in your worst nightmares. They're evil Lexi. I don't pretend to be a saint, but I don't prey on the innocent."

I swallow hard, trying to find the words to reply to that but coming up bare.

"Your uncle Elliot sounds like a good man."

"Oh he is," says Axel. "He took me and Alaric in when we were babies after our parents died in a car crash. Al was about two and I was only just born, we've been with him ever since."

I gasp. They lost their parents so young. My heart aches for what that must have been like.

"I'm so sorry," I replied.
Axel waves his hand brushing it off.

"Is what it is," he says. "When we were about eleven and nine, Elliot finally found a woman of his own, lovely she was, I kinda remember her. Her name was Chloe. They had a baby girl, Kayla. She was sick. Too sick to live. After her death things were never the same for Elliot and Chloe. Grief destroyed them so she left. Elliot acted like it didn't bother him but something died inside him the day Chloe left."

Wow. A tight feeling surged through my chest. Now I felt like a real dick.

"Sounds like we've all had a bit of a shit time."
I smile as I look into Axel's eyes and in that moment, for the briefest of seconds his gaze changes from sadness to heat and I'm unable to look away.

We keep our eyes fixed on each other until suddenly he drops his gaze, looking down to his cup.
My cheeks redden as I drop my gaze also.

"You know my brother isn't the asshole he makes out to be."
I laugh quietly under my breath.

"Your mothers going to have a much better life in Havencroft than she would in that fucking crack den."

"Havencroft?" I gasp. "But that's like a prestigious rehab, it would cost more than I make in a lifetime to send her there."

"Well good job you don't have to pay for it then isn't it?"
I look at Axel, puzzled by his words.

"My brother asked for the best, and Havencroft is the best.

You won't have to worry about her anymore. She's safe and she's getting all the help she needs."

I realise I'm sitting with my mouth open.

I quickly pick my jaw up from the floor.

He kept his promise. My mom is in a rehab I couldn't even afford if I combined all my savings and then some.

A feeling of relief hit me like a tsunami and it was as if a weight had been lifted off my shoulders.

Why didn't he tell me? Why did he let me think he was this bastard?

I didn't have the answers but I knew one thing. That block of ice where my heart was supposed to be, was actually starting to thaw a little.

CHAPTER EIGHTEEN

Lexi

Was I nervous? Not really.

My life, from a young age, has always revolved around aerial silks.

It was always my escape from home, to go and teach the kids down the road and work out all my anxiety and hidden anger.

The adrenaline surging through my body as I twist myself into the *inverted crucifix,* spinning high in the air without a net or free falling from a *hiplock.*

There was nothing quite like it.

I chose my playlist for my final day of training before the big night tonight, including *'Mermaid'* by *Skott,* which is one of my ultimate, performance favourites.

"Hair and makeup will be arriving at six, we meet in the foyer so don't be late."

I already knew the voice was Cassidie.

The woman was like a dictator, she ruled this gym with an iron fist.

"Sure thing," I replied.

"You get free reign on how you look as long it fits in with the theme of your act of course."

I nod. Cass fiddles with the back of her perfectly straight, red bob as she walks away and I wonder just what colour her natural hair is, as this vibrant red is nowhere close to looking natural at all.

She looks nervous today, the way she keeps flinching and looking around the room. I've never seen her look like that, she's usually so confident but I just put it down to nerves about the show.

She *is* the creative director of all La Tanières entertainment I guess. That must be a whole heap of pressure.

I've just always found the woman strange. I can't put my finger on it but there's something not right there. I've always had a pretty overactive imagination though so I'm guessing it's just me that thinks it but I dunno, she just feels off.

"Let's hope you don't fall on your face today. That'd be a bit embarrassing."

I turn in surprise at the childish jibe and see it's coming from Sapphire.

She stands with a smirk on her face as she runs her hands over her tight, lycra training outfit. It puts my baggy, off the shoulder white T-shirt and *Nike* cycling shorts to shame.

She always looks the epitome of sex and I have to admit as infuriating her little dig is, I can't stop staring at her. She's stunning.

It wouldn't surprise me if Alaric was fucking her. They would look insane together, like something out of a fucking *Dior* perfume commercial.

"Yeah, I guess it would be," I reply. "Luckily I have no intention of doing that."

She walks slowly towards me until she's almost in my comfort zone.

"You know the *Alice in Wonderland* contortion show has been the top act of La Tanière since I got here, and just because you're currently the talk of the club because you're shacked up with Alaric and Axel, doesn't mean your little rope act is gonna be better." Her eyes travel up and down my body as if she's looking at something she's just stepped in.

"I'm no competition to you Sapphire, my act is different and

there's no reason we can't both be great acts at La Tanière."
Lies! I now wanted to kick this bitches ass.

She laughs, "Oh Lexi, you're so naive. How do you expect the high paying customers at the end of the night to choose you over me or someone like Leela or Ashleigh, if your act isn't better than ours? Do your little circus act and leave the real money making to the big girls."

My eyes narrowed and she could clearly see my confusion as her eyes widened and a satisfied smile began to form on her pouty lips.

"Oh you didn't know? Why do you think there's random rooms with beds around the club? We can take customers there at the end of the night and make as many *tips* as we like. The men nearly always choose me though, so don't get too pissed if you don't make any money."

What the fuck? They allow prostitution here? Is that what this is, some kind of elite brothel on top of everything else?

Sapphire winks. "Enjoy your training oh and Lexi ... don't get any ideas about Alaric. We've been fucking for months, other girls have tried to catch his eye but he'll always pick me. Plus he needs a real woman for the things he's into, a little princess like you couldn't handle it."

She scowls, turning on her heel and heading back to her training area, leaving me with even more questions than before.

Frustration was rising in my chest. *Things he's into? What the hell?*

After everything else he didn't tell me, Alaric also failed to mention the fact that his club was a goddamn *brothel*. *He's fucking disgusting,* and all that bullshit about him and Sapphire. I didn't know why that bothered me but for the first time I couldn't deny that it did.

Maybe it was that kiss that was clouding my brain.   Before I even got a chance to finish my training, I grabbed my water bottle and sweat towel and headed up to Alaric's office.

He may be the most unapproachable guy I'd ever met but this prick was going to give me the answers I wanted, and he was going to give them to me right now.

CHAPTER NINETEEN

Alaric

"I don't have time for your bullshit." I leaned forward, staring straight at her. Her cold eyes boring into mine.

"In my opinion, we should keep Sapphire's act for the finale tonight. We don't know how the crowd will react to Lexi yet," she states, her hands sporting vibrant red talons, placed on her hips.

Cass was getting sloppy around the place lately. I didn't appreciate the way she was strolling around like she was the queen, just because she was fucking Elliot. She wasn't his wife, she was some slut he was using and the dumb bitch couldn't see that.

I was the one to decide who would be seen as La Tanières final act and I didn't need opinions from anyone, especially her.

"I've already said the siren act will end the night, are you arguing with me about it?"

Her lip quivers and I can see the look of fear in her eyes, much different from the promiscuous looks she gives my brother and me.

"No… Alaric, of course not," she laughs awkwardly. "I just thought…"

"I don't pay you to think," I rage, slamming both palms down onto the desk and standing until I'm looking down at her from the other side of the table.

"I pay you to train the acts, make them look pretty, nothing else Cassidie, do you understand?"

Her eyes widened in surprise. "Yes of course."

Suddenly my office door is shoved open and the little siren, *speak of the devil,* comes waltzing through.
She looks pissed.
God that's hot, she's so fucking beautiful.
My cock twitches as the memory of our kiss invades my mind.

"Leave us," I say to Cass, who looks every bit the snivelling mess she's trying to hide. She nods and exits my office.

"What can I do for you, little siren?"
She stares at me, fury in her expression and I do all I can to hold back the smirk trying desperately to get out.

"Why do you keep lying to me?"
I sigh, *not this again.*

"Why do you assume I'm lying to you this time?" I ask, genuinely perplexed.

"You pimp out these girls, after the show, men can... can buy them!"

I see her chest rise and fall in ragged movements as she tries to contain her anger.

"We do not pimp out the girls, Alexandra, we give them a safe environment for if it is something they wish to do. We don't encourage it. In fact Elliot was completely against it at one point." *Until Cass, yet again got under his skin.* "Some of our women...and men, have come from that life and wish to retain it and we won't take away that option, however we make sure they're safe and all the money they make is their own, we have nothing to do with it."

She still looks pissed but she asked for the truth and she got it, I won't sugar coat it for her.

"Right so if I wanted to get a few men together after the show tonight, show them a good time, you wouldn't have a problem with it. I can just jump on their dick, the way Sapph..."

My fist instinctively shoots out, grabbing her around her

slender throat, as I turn her and push her against the wall of my office.

"No one touches you, do you understand?"
I hold her firmly in place as I attempt in vain to control my breathing. Murder is raging through me and I'm almost blinded by the vexation I feel at her words.

She stares back at me, those gorgeous two tone eyes hooded and her sweet lips parted slightly letting out a held breath gently and calmly.

"Why?" she spits in defiance.

"Because you're mine!"

She scoffs, turning her head away to the side. My grip tightens around her throat.

"Look at me," I ordered.

She turns her face back, so her eyes are locked on mine once again, and I lean in until the tip of our noses are almost touching and I can taste her soft breaths on my tongue as she exhales.

"You are mine. If anyone even so much as breathes in your direction. I will kill them."

Her eyebrows shoot upwards as she realises I'm not fucking around.

"What about Sapphire? I know she has men…"

"I don't give a fuck about Sapphire," I hiss. "You belong to me, little siren. You will *always* belong to me."

CHAPTER TWENTY

Lexi

Who the fuck does he think he is?! I belong to no one! After he grabbed my throat and slammed me into his office wall, throwing his alphahole ego around, I was one step away from throwing a right hook straight into his perfectly chiselled jaw. Either that or slam my mouth onto his, the way he had with me in his apartment last night. He's driving me insane.

All these feelings are like a whirlpool in my brain and I can't think straight, hell I can hardly breathe when I'm around him. Axel is so different, he's so much calmer with a cheeky side but Alaric... fuck the man is like the devil himself. His outer shell is impenetrable and even though this dark and brooding image is sexy as fuck, I've never felt so infuriated by another human being in my life.

I charge down the stairs, two at a time as I head back to the gym.

"Everything okay?" The deep voice comes from the booth by the bottom of the stairs, cloaked in shadows.

I squint to get a better look into the darkness as a shiny, bald head comes into focus, followed by a pristine suit and glass of some kind of amber coloured liquid which I assume is whiskey.

He exhales a thick cloud of smoke from his mouth and

replaces his cigar between his plump lips.

"Elliot?"

I stare harder as his full form comes into vision.

"I heard a little shouting from my nephews office, I just wanted to be sure everything was above board." His voice is one tone, lacking in emotion and I'm left wondering if he's being sarcastic about the fact that he heard *a little shouting,* as that was a hell of a lot more than a little. The whole club probably heard.

"Erm... everything's fine," *I lie.* "What are you doing sitting down here alone?" *In the dark, like a creeper.*

"Collecting my thoughts," he answers.

His face looks tired and I wonder what his life has been like. Axel already told me about his wife and daughter but I imagine it's more than just that that has created the lines on his face.

I nod. "I guess even the great Elliot Mackenzie needs a break sometime."

He laughs, throwing his head back. "Sit with me child."

I walk over to the booth, dropping down into the leather seating, throwing my bottle and towel down beside me.

Elliot reminds me of the Godfather. He's so intimidating, yet his eyes glow with a kindness most humans lack.

"You're looking a lot better than when you arrived."

I nod, unsure how to take his comment.

"I take it that the La Tanière family are treating you well?"

I sigh. "I can't say they're not I suppose. Morgan and Leon are great and Alaric... well he put my mum into Havencroft, so I'm forever grateful for that."

Elliot begins to rotate his whiskey glass, swirling the mixture. I watch it like a pendulum putting me into a hypnotic trance.

"I'll never understand a mother who wouldn't protect her own child."

I know he's referring to my mum, but there's a sadness in his expression that makes me think he's referring to his own demons.

"Alaric told me about his cousin, your daughter, Kayla."

Elliot nods, taking a long gulp of his drink.

"She was just a baby when we, myself and my partner Chloe lost her. They don't know for sure what caused her death, she was a sickly baby from birth but I would have done anything to protect her, to have her here with me right now."

His grief is almost palpable but instead of feeling awkward, I instinctively place my palm over his large hand to offer comfort, to remind him that sometimes, no matter what we do, sometimes we can't save the ones we love.

His warmth radiates up through my arm. He looks down at the table, at our joined hands.

"I look at you and the other girls here and I wonder who she would have been, what talents she would have possessed. It haunts me everyday. I became the man Chloe didn't need. Throwing myself into work and making so many bad choices."

I refrain from pointing out how being the ringleader of a contract killing organisation is probably one of those bad choices. Each to their own.

"Do you miss her?"

He looks at me and I feel like I've just asked the most ridiculous question in the world but all he does is smile at me tenderly.

"Everyday."

CHAPTER TWENTY ONE

Lexi

The whole club was in chaos, bodies moving back and forth wherever I looked.

I was pretty confident that ninety percent of my lung capacity was filled with glitter as feathers, fishnets and sequins clouded my vision.

It was time to get ready for the show. My first ever show at La Tanière and the nerves had finally started to kick in all of a sudden.

Being a customer at the club, I had never given much thought into how the acts were feeling, but now it was a whole different ball game. It really was a daunting experience.

"You're in my way." Sapphire barged past me, wearing her signature Alice tutu and blue crystal nipple tassels, carefully placed on her perfect breasts.

Cass had given us free reign on our outfits and a rack of costumes, the length of the whole wall, were situated backstage.

I slid my fingers through the clothing. Feeling the silken material against my fingertips. There were all the colours of the rainbow, many of the costumes glistening in the enhanced lighting.

I must have scrolled my way through twenty costumes before I saw it, hanging there like it was waiting for me. It was perfection, and I knew it was the outfit I would be wearing tonight.

I grabbed it from the hanger and headed straight to a changing cubicle to try it on, staring at myself in the mirror. The stunning, gold halter neck leotard with a bandeau front was striking. The tiny sequin detail around the middle made my waist look even slimmer and the short tulle panel on the back flowed as I moved.

"Wow, you look stunning."

Morgan walked up to me in a black satin, floor length, one shoulder *Givenchy* gown. The middle section cut out to reveal her toned stomach. Her beautiful, long hair was cascading down her back in loose waves and the makeup artist Cass had brought in, had created the most seductive smokey eye. She looked every bit the starlet she was.

"Likewise," I replied, heading over to the makeup artist. Morgan followed behind.

I sat in the chair, ready for my glow up.

"What are you going for?" asked Morgan.

I glanced down at my outfit before picking up the metallic gold shimmer.

"I think we'll go with this one," I replied, handing it over.

The makeup artist lifted her brush, dragging it through the glittering powder and dusted it onto my eyelids, lips and across my temples before adding a little to my arms, legs and hands for effect.

My long red hair was swept up into a sleek ponytail.

"I think you're ready, Siren," says Morgan, holding the mirror to show me the completed look.

"Wow." I was startled at how different I felt, never mind looked. For the first time in forever, I felt stronger, empowered. I looked almost ethereal, like something from a fantasy novel.

I stood, just as Leon bounced over and lifted me from behind. He swirled me around as Morgan chuckled. His black leather waistcoat was cold against my skin.

"Look at the little siren," he giggled. "You ready to go, Hot stuff?"

His face was painted in a joker-like style and his hair was gelled into perfected spikes.

I smiled. "Ready as I'll ever be."

Leon grabbed his sword. I glanced at the scars on his bare chest under the waist coat, hidden slightly by something the makeup artist had used.

His eyes quickly met mine as if he knew what I was thinking.

"I bet you're wondering why I chose the knives and swords right? After what happened to me?"

I open my mouth to respond but the words don't come out.

"It's okay, I'm sure many people would, but for me it's all about power, taking charge of the demons that once took charge of me."

My heart sinks at his words but his face shows that he needs no pity. This is a man who has strength beyond belief.

"The one thing that penetrated my nightmares is the one thing I can finally control."

I didn't know it then, but his words would resonate with me a lot more than I could have ever imagined.

"Girls you're up."

Cass stands with a clipboard in a thigh length, neon orange dress. The material is so tight I question whether it's even possible for her to bend down.

She gestures towards the stage and Leela, Ashleigh and the other burlesque girls stride out, one after the other as flames burst onto the torches around the stage.

Bea Millers 'Like That' roars around the room as the show begins and the girls prance around the stage, feathers fanning, like a beautiful muster of peacocks.

After the opening show, the other acts take to the stage one by one.

'Numb' by Linken Park plays as Oake takes to the stage.

His intimidating act is mesmerising as he takes Ashleigh transforming her into a bevy of doves right before your eyes. The crowd gasps as the birds fly around the room before settling on the rafters.

Morgan brushes off a few bits of lint from her dress. After hearing her in rehearsals, I'm excited more than ever to see her perform live. She almost floats onto the stage, her movements feminine and light as she takes the microphone in her right hand.

As the music plays for *Inferno's* version of *'Wicked Game'*, she begins to sing.

The silvery sound is haunting and as I peak beyond the curtains, I can see the whole club is at a standstill. Every single customer has stopped what they're doing to listen to her. It's phenomenal.

I turn to look over at Oake, who I spot staring from the other side of the stage.

He looks at her in the most peculiar way, almost like he's angry with her. That in itself is the most extraordinary thing, as Morgan is the sweetest, most gentle creature I've ever come across. How anyone could even dislike the girl is ludicrous.

As she concluded her song, you could almost hear a pin drop in the room before the whole crowd exploded into cheers.

Morgan's bright smile attracts the whistles and chants from the crowd, as she takes a bow and glides from the stage. I ran up to hug her straight away.

"You killed it," I cry, throwing my arms around her, not caring if I cover her in my shower of gold glitter.

She laughs, brushing it off. "Oh it was nothing," she beams. The girl is too modest. That had got to be one of the best vocals I'd ever heard and from a girl so young. She was destined for great things.

Morgan and I cheered for Leon as he slayed his performance to *MGK 'Pretty Toxic Revolver'*.

He collects his swords as his act comes to an end but instead of coming back towards Morgan and I, he spots Elliot's *lapdog, as*

I call him, Colt, and jogs off in his direction. I don't know much about Colt but I've heard he was the one who dug the dirt on me regarding Anton and my mother. He seems to keep himself to himself from what I've seen, which I'm pretty glad about to be honest, the last thing I want is someone continuing to pry into my life.

As *Neonis 'Wonderland'* plays I know the time is drawing closer to my act. I shrug off the shiver that travels along my spine.

Sapphire balances on a rotating pole upside down, using only her hands before practically bending her body in half to pick up a small bottle labelled *Drink Me* with her feet. She then proceeds to bring the bottle to her lips and drink. *How the fuck do you drink upside down?*

Smoke rises from the dance floor and as I peer out from behind the curtains, the whole crowd appears as one long, obscured mist, and I'm starting to feel grateful that I can't make out people's faces as I prepare to take my place on the stage.

As soon as I go to take a step forward, *'The Fear'* by *The Score* blares from the speakers, engulfing the room in its burgeoning sound. *This isn't my song?*

I whip my head around in confusion to see Alaric. Gone are the designer suits and in their place are a pair of tight black, ripped leathers and a *bare chest.*

I blink to prevent my eyes from popping from their sockets as I take in his god like form. His amazing tattoos on show across his tight six pack. There's so many but I can make out a lion's head on one of his pecs and what looks like a statue of the Greek god Ares beside his rib cage.

His muscular arms frame his torso and I have to remind myself to keep my jaw off of the floor.

I blow out a long breath. *What the fuck is he doing? How did I not know he had an act? He never trains!*

Our eyes meet as he lifts a hand held torch from a bench at the back of the stage and lights it.

I gasp as I realise what he's about to do, bringing my hands up to my cheeks, I try to hide my anxiety.

The corners of his perfectly shaped mouth curve up into a smirk and the black eyeliner he's wearing make his fucking insane grey eyes pop. I stand, frozen to the spot.

As the music continues to blast, Alaric dominates the stage with his presence. Locking eyes with me again, he sprays a fine mist of fuel from his mouth over the open flame of his torch, creating a menacing fireball. I'm pretty sure my heart just vacated my chest and is just casually chilling in my mouth. I look like a gawking idiot.

The act is phenomenal and as it comes to a close, he rolls the torch over his biceps and looks to the ceiling, opening his mouth wide before swallowing the burning end of the torch, extinguishing the fire.

As the crowd goes wild, he exits the stage at the other end, right into the pathway of a smiling Sapphire. I look away, choosing not to react to that one right now.

My newly selected music plays, *'Castle'* by *Halsey* and I've almost forgotten that I'm meant to be performing at all, never mind right now.

The red silks drop from the ceiling as I make my way to the centre of the stage.

I can feel eyes on me although even as I strain my vision, I can't make out the faces in the audience. As I stride to the middle, wolf whistling and jeering threaten to distract my focus, but I inhale deeply, letting the music course through my body, like the very blood in my veins.

I've always been confident in not only my abilities but also in my body so I wasn't phased by the fact I was wearing something so revealing. My long, slim legs and toned arms on show along with a modest cleavage.

One thing about silk aerial was how fit it kept me. No need for daily trips to the gym.

I grip the cool silk in my fingertips and wave it out, creating ripples that mimic the waves of the ocean, before gliding my body around it in a graceful dance, my movements smooth like water.

Grasping the ropes within my palm and sliding the excess material behind me with the sole of my bare foot, I proceed to wrap the silk around my wrists until I feel secure then circle up into a *cross back straddle.*

The low gasps of the crowd fill me with the adrenaline I needed and soon I'm climbing higher up the ropes, twisting the fabric around my ankles and contorting my body into the splits followed by the *Cupid seat.*

As the music continues to flow and the chorus hyping up the crowd, I quickly wrap myself in the silk and twist as fast as my body will allow, dropping my body upside down mid spin.

The crowd gasps in anticipation as the speed of my spinning accelerates, my body defying gravity without so much as a cushion for safety, before gently slowing, leaving me to climb to the very top.

I can feel the tension in the room as I slide the material around my thighs, and as the music comes to an end, I free fall in a dramatic *slack drop,* much to the horrifying screams of my onlookers. My body snaps to a halt just before I hit the floor. Satisfaction fills my core as I smile at the crowd and take a bow.

Cheers erupted throughout the room. I glance either side of the stage to see my team clapping and cheering, all except Alaric and Sapphire who stare at me. Her expression, one of contempt and his of no emotion whatsoever.

I smile at them regardless. This was my moment and I intended to take it.

CHAPTER TWENTY TWO

Alaric

Fuck she was driving me insane!

As much as I tried to fight it, her body called to mine in a way I didn't even know existed and I knew the little siren felt it as strongly as I did.

Last night, she looked fucking unreal. Her perky, but full tits sitting perfectly in that little gold costume she wore, her skin gilded in the lights of the stage.

Fuck I wanted to damage it so fucking badly. I should spank her ass raw for the way she smirked at me at the end of her act, fucking little brat.

Downing my espresso, I attempt to pull my thoughts from the gutter and concentrate on the work in hand.

"I need to make a few calls." Elliot spoke sitting on the small corner sofa in my office, Axel standing to the side of it. "Rio has been sent on a job for the Mcinally boys and won't be back today and Colt…fuck knows where he disappeared to last night but he better show up pronto."

Fuck, I hadn't even realised Colt had done a disappearing act. My brain was fucked.

Elliot smirked in my direction. "You boy, need to stop

thinking about your dick."

A loud chuckle erupts from Axel as I raise my eyebrows in mock surprise.

"Don't think we all can't see how you look at that girl."
His words feel like a blade to my chest.

"I don't know who and what you're talking about."
He lifts his coffee mug to his mouth taking a quick sip.

"You know full well who I'm talking about, Alexandra."

I sighed as I pinched the bridge of my nose. "I won't be discussing her with you."

His smirk widens, the fucker. "She's a beautiful girl."

"What are we focusing on today uncle? Because my sex life isn't up for discussion."

He laughs, shooting me the middle finger.

"Maybe you should fuck her uncle, that sweet pussy might like the *older* man," Axel jibes. My eyes snap in his direction, waves of violent protectiveness cursing over me as he grins.

Elliot chuckles again. "Not for me son, as gorgeous as she is, she's the same age as my Kayla would have been."

His eyes have always displayed sadness, whenever Kayla or Chloe have been mentioned. I may have only been eleven when they came into our lives, but I remembered it like it was yesterday.

The happiness Chloe brought to Elliot, and to me and my brother was irreplaceable. I only saw Kayla a couple of times as she was only earth side for a week, but I know how the love Elliot had for her has ruled his life ever since. No one on the outside would ever know the big, bad wolf had a heart.

Before we had a chance to continue our discussion, Colt strode into the office. He looked like he hadn't slept, his hair ruffled and his shirt unbuttoned at the top.

"Good night?" Axel smirked.

Colt glanced quickly in his direction, not saying a word, before dropping a tattered, paper folder on the sofa next to where Elliot was sitting.

"I've been looking further into Darien Steele, it's taken a few days but his file arrived in my inbox this morning."

Having cops indebted to you always has its advantages.

"As well as some of the charges we already know about, he was suspected a few years back of something else, something that was never proven and he never got done for, due to some issue with missing evidence."

Alarm bells ring like a hurricane in my head.

"And that was what?" Axel asks.

"Sex trafficking."

Why was I not surprised, the asshole looks the type.

"Looks like your old business partner is in with a pretty shady crowd uncle," I smirk.

Elliot places his empty coffee cup down on the table and stands. "I want someone undercover," he says, completely disregarding the comment. "I want someone on the exclusive guest list for Scarlet, and I want to be watching when they go in."

I nod. "It needs to be someone they won't recognise. I'll speak to Rio when he gets back and we'll get to work, as soon as Scarlett opens its doors we'll be there."

"Good," says Elliot, heading over to the door. "We'll be prepared for when they open, but for now Al, I have a hit I need you to oversee. You'll be away for a couple of days, and then we've got more important matters to deal with."

"Oh yeah? and what's that?"

A large grin expands across his mouth.

"The Feast of Fire of course."

CHAPTER TWENTY THREE

Lexi

"What are you wearing for the Feast of Fire?" Morgan stands rummaging through my closet to see what she can find. I've always wanted to be someone who owned lots of pretty clothes, but as the daughter of a drug addicted prostitute, I was hardly dripping in diamonds.

"I'm not sure, have you any idea what you're wearing?"

The night had finally arrived for the Feast of Fire. I hadn't seen Al for a few days, come to think of it, I hadn't seen Axel either but I was feeling pretty confident that they would be making an appearance tonight.

Morgan had come over to get ready and we were having a little girly bonding. Aside from Sim, I'd never really had any close girl friends, so this was definitely welcomed.

Morgan held up a pretty, little, floral jumpsuit with spaghetti straps. It reminded me of a fresh, summer meadow and the leaf decoration across the chest area matched her jade green eyes.

"That is hot stuff Morgz," I smile.

Her cheeks flush their usual pink, as she tucks a strand of her hair behind her ear. *This girl has got to learn to take a compliment.*

"Thanks Lex, I was kinda hoping..." she paused as if reconsidering what she was about to say next.

I smile, "you were kinda hoping a certain someone would notice you tonight?"

She exhales, dragging her palm over her face. "Urgh! Is it that obvious? I'm sick of the shit I always get from Leon."

She sits next to me on the bed, as I take her small hands in mine.

My voice softens. "Yeah it's kinda obvious, but hey, the guys a catch and he knows some pretty cool magic tricks."

Morgan laughs. I'm glad she's finally admitted her feelings for Oake to me. The way they look at each other, I'm surprised nothing has happened yet.

"Now," I say, standing and grabbing my makeup bag, "let's get you looking so smoking, Oake won't be able to take his eyes off you."

She dances over to me at the dressing table and we get to work.

I opted for a bottle green, bandeau maxi dress with thigh high split hem. It complimented my long, red hair perfectly, which I released from my messy bun and let it hang naturally, cascading like a crimson waterfall down my back to my butt.

Morgan slips on the jumpsuit and wears her hair poker straight, it glistens like melting chocolate.

We both go pretty heavy on the makeup tonight. I mean it is a party after all and fuck, it has been a long time since I was at a party. *Fuck Lex, you're nineteen going on ninety.*

As we're finishing up, a knock on the door pulls us from our chatter. As I open the door, I'm greeted with a beautifully wrapped silver shoebox. The black, tulle ribbon wrapped around it, creating the perfect, eye catching finishing touch.

"Oooh what's that?" Morgan shrieks as I bring the box into the room and place it on the bed.

"I don't know, it was just delivered."

"Open it, quick." Morgan is practically bouncing with excitement.

I open the beautifully packaged box carefully to reveal a small card, sitting atop of red tissue paper with the words *'Little Siren'* written upon it. There's no other words, so I drop the card and peel back the tissue paper to reveal the most beautiful pair of pointed toe *Louboutin* heels. Morgan gasps.

"He bought you shoes...like most guys buy jewellery or something but he bought you shoes, that's even better."

I giggle. I love her childlike enthusiasm for just about everything.

"I don't even know who they're from," I say. "It doesn't even say on the note."

Morgan scoffs, "oh come on, of course they're from Alaric."

I stare at the perfect, sleek, red sole before slipping them onto my feet.

"Now you *look* like a siren," Morgan laughs.

I roll my eyes as I look in the floor length mirror in my bedroom. I barely recognised myself these days.

It seemed so long ago that I was dressed in ripped clothes from thrift stores, and now I didn't go more than a day without wearing something new or designer. It still felt surreal.

I had contemplated leaving now that my mum was in rehab but I knew that her funding would get cut if I did. As amazing as this life was becoming, I still felt like I didn't have my freedom.

La Tanière may have offered me a better life, but can anyone truly be happy if they aren't free?

As we leave Alaric's apartment, Jax and Demetri, the security guards walk towards us.

"Miss Morgan and Miss Lexi, we'll be your drivers this evening."

"Drivers?" I question, "To where?"

Morgan giggles beside me, "Jesus you really don't know anything do you?!"

I narrow my eyes at her as we silently follow the two meatheads in front.

Outside the club waits a black, stretch limo.

Jax opens the door and I slide in, Morgan behind me.

"So," I say as I slouch into the ridiculously comfortable leather seats of the car, "you gonna tell me where the hell we're going?"

Morgan leans into me as if she's about to tell me a secret. "The Feast of Fire is always in the same place, silly." She looks at me with a playful glint in her eyes. "Alaric's *home*."

"What the fuck? I thought I was *staying* at Alaric's home? The apartment?"

"Oh you are. Alaric and Axel have the apartment to be close to the club but they have numerous homes, this one being the main one. I guess it's a good idea to have multiple homes when you're... you know... an assassin." She laughs and I'm starting to question the sanity of my new found friend. I guess that would explain why I hadn't seen Alaric or Axel get ready for the Feast of Fire.

Within ten minutes we pulled into a gated location. More security guards sat on the entrance as Jax typed in a code number and drove our limo inside.

The road leading to the house was long and winding and passed various, dramatic statues of Greek gods along the way.

The grounds were huge and immaculate, it would have taken about twenty gardeners to achieve this. *Fuck sake Lex, gardeners? There's the ninety year old again.*

As we arrive at the front of the house, various limos containing so many different people are also driving into the parking bay. I recognise a lot of the guests as staff from La Tanière. Waitresses, hosts and hostesses and performers such as Leela and Ashleigh, arriving in style.

"Where's Leon?" I peer from the window to see if I can spot him.

"No idea, he's been so shady this week. He disappeared the night of the show, and every day this week that I've tried to hang out with him, he's brushed me off saying he's busy. What the fuck Lex, he's never busy."

"Dunno," I shrug. "Maybe he has someone on the outside he wanted to see? A friend maybe?"

Morgan doesn't look convinced. "Leon has no one outside of La Tanière, it's his life, I feel like he's being really secretive as well."

"Well I'm sure he'll tell us when he's ready," I remarked. "Now let's go and have a great time tonight."

Morgan smiles, her uplifted shoulders dropping and I know at that point she's relaxed and ready to have a great time like I am.

The house is huge like an enormous mansion made of long glass panels. Seriously, there is glass everywhere. The house is stunning. Modern and chic.

Demetri opens the door, offering his hand to Morgan as she exits the car, and then to me.

The cool air grazes my bare shoulders as I hitch the cream pashmina further up to cover myself from the light chill.

We climb the few steps to the front of the house and my breath hitches as I see him standing there.

Alaric stands between Elliot, on his left and Axel, on his right. All three of them were wearing matching black designer suits with bright white shirts and black ties.

His raven hair, styled to perfection, made me want to run my fingers through it and rough it up a little.

"Lex, you're staring," Morgan whispers. I snap from my trance.

Alaric walks over to us, kissing Morgan on the cheek before she spots Leon ahead and hurries off, leaving me alone with him. He takes my hand in his, pressing a gentle kiss to my knuckles.

"You look like fucking sin," he hisses under his breath and my stomach somersaults as his hand travels to my lower back ushering me forward.

I smile, "you still look like an asshole."

He chuckles, then drags his tongue over his bottom lip. *Fuck Lex, stop staring.* He looks into my eyes, down to my lips and then back to my eyes again before smirking. I mentally try to steady my breathing.

We head over to greet Elliot and Axel, The latter giving me a wink and the former embracing me in a warm hug.

As we all venture through the doors into the ballroom, *yep this house has an actual ballroom,* music blaring to which I recognise *Missios 'Twisted'* playing.

Fire eaters perform around the edges of the room and two long banquet tables are set out with an array of exotic looking foods from meat to fruits. It looks like something you'd see in the palace of a king.

I start to spot a few faces I recognise. Unfortunately Sapphire being one.

She looks as stunning as always in a baby pink, floor length gown, Bardot style. She's standing with Leela and Ashleigh and a couple of other girls from the burlesque troupe. I walk to the large table, situated in the corner of the room, filled with glasses of *Moet.*

I know they're talking about me, and I don't need a mind reader to know it's not good. The scowl on her face says it all.

As I grab my glass, a feminine hand with red talons grasps the one next to it. Looking up, I'm instantly greeted with the sparkling eyes of Cassidie.

"Lexi, you look beautiful."

I have to pinch myself to actually acknowledge that the woman has just given me a compliment.

"Thank you, so do you," I smile.

To be fair she has an incredible figure for an older woman, obviously enhanced but I gotta give it to her she knew how to work those assets.

The figure hugging, strapless. floor length, black leather dress left nothing to the imagination and gave a kinky, dominatrix vibe.

"How did you find performing at La Tanière?"

The way she pronounces the name sounds like she's trying desperately to perfect a French accent.

"I loved it," I replied. "The silks are home to me, it was great to give people entertainment like that."

Cass smiles, but the gesture, again, doesn't quite meet her eyes. There's something strange about this woman.

"You know, some of the girls here extend that entertainment further into the night."

I bring my champagne glass to my lips and take a large gulp. I know exactly what she means by that.

"Yeah well that's not really my scene." I try to brush off the irritation grating my bones.

"Shame really, you could be raking in that cash if you played your cards right, I know some customers who would pay handsomely for the siren."

Her words feel like a million spiders crawling all over my body. I turn to her, forcing the repulsion to one side and smiling sweetly.

"Well I'm flattered but it's still a no."

"Fair enough." She drains her glass and turns on her heel to walk away, but not before looking back over her shoulder one more time.

"But Lexi, please let me know if you change your mind, it wouldn't be any different to your mothers pimps fucking you, only this time at least you'd get paid."

She smirks before walking away, and it takes every muscle in my body to stop me from grabbing a handful of her split ends, and kicking every bit of silicone out of her plastic body. Instead I down my champagne and proceed to down another.

My blood is heated to the max but soon it lowers to a simmer as I hear the playful giggles of Leon and Morgan. I go to join them at one of the large round tables they're sitting at.

"And where have you been lately?" I point an incriminating finger at Leon, his face turning pink.

"Oh I've already asked that question and he's not budging," giggles Morgan, rolling her eyes.

I laugh. "Probably a secret lover," I joke.

Leon's eyes flash to mine, laced with guilt. I think I may not be too far off with my assumptions.

"Stop being such nosey knebs," Leon jokes. "I've been busy is all, I do have a bit of a life you know."

Morgan looks at me with a doubting expression, before we

both fall into fits of laughter.

"What?" His confused look makes us giggle like school girls even more.

As the party gets into full swing, I become increasingly aware of Alaric's stare from across the room. His body attracts mine like two magnets.

Just when I think he's going to come over to our table and say something, the crowd of people standing between the entrance and the dance floor begin to part one by one, until two men, followed by what appears to be four bodyguards, come into view.

The room falls silent. The atmosphere growing icy as chills erupt all over my body.

I don't even know who these people are, but the one with the scar slashed right over his eye is looking straight at me.

CHAPTER TWENTY FOUR

Alaric

Who the actual fuck invited them?

The tension in the room turned palpable, as Vinnie De La Hoy and Darien Steele waltzed through the crowd like they were the fucking guests of honour.

I watched closely as Vinnies eyes locked on Lexi. Pure, unadulterated rage surged through my body.

"Well, looks like quite the turnout," Darien laughs, scanning the room. "I'm almost offended that you didn't invite your fellow businessmen."

"You have no business here," I scowl.

Elliot stretching out a hand and laying it on my shoulder, no doubt he knows the anger is brewing.

"What do you want, Vinnie?" Elliot asks calmly.

His gaze bypasses Darien, and goes straight to his former business partner.

"To join in the celebrations Elliot, you and I were always one for a good party now, weren't we my friend?"

Elliot's expression shifts and the Elliot, we at La Tanière see, transformed into the Elliot who hasn't thought twice about putting a bullet into someone's brain for the right price.

Head held high, he strolls over to where the pair are standing and faces Vinnie, their noses almost touching. Like two vipers raised and ready to attack.

"We are not friends and you are not welcome here, now leave!"

The tone of Elliot's voice laced with a threatening edge.

Vinnie laughs loudly, throwing back his head.

"Well see that's a damn shame, I've missed so much of your life since our last encounter. Your growing businesses, your nephews and… your child."

Elliot's body freezes. I see the clench in his jaw. "How do you know about my child?"

Vinnie smiles. "Kayla wasn't it? you know Elliot, it's such a pity you and I couldn't have put our differences aside and moved on. Such a shame what happened to poor Kayla, and to your partner Chloe of course, nothing worse than a mother losing her child."

"You walk a fine line Vicenzo," Elliot warned.

Vinnie smirked, turning towards the crowd.

"You know, I used to have a child once. The light of my life, my whole world, but unfortunately they were taken from me, thanks to their whore mother. I was never the same." A cruel smile creeps up on Vinnies lips.

"You need to leave…now," says Elliot, his voice so low it's almost a whisper.

"Oh but I wanted to see your newest act, I've heard so much about her, the Siren isn't it?"

He turns to look straight at Lexi, who begins to look behind her as if unsure the bastard is speaking about her. I lunge forward on impulse, until my brother grabs my arm, stopping me from progressing.

"Come forward," says Darien.

Lexi steps away from Leon and Morgan and walks towards where the men are standing.

"Wow, you truly are as magnificent as they say." Vinnie lifts his hand, taking a strand of her shiny, red hair between his fingers and bringing it to his nose, inhaling deeply.

"Mmm." His eyes flash a sinister heat and I can no longer stay in place, despite Axel's protest.

In an instant I'm standing before him, my fist grasping the collar of his expensive designer shirt.

One of the bodyguards accompanying him reaches to his hip where I spot a sliver of a gun. Vinnie instantly throws up his hand, as if telling him to back down.

"Do not touch her," I growl as his eyes widen in surprise and then narrow as he takes me in, a smug smile on his face.

"Well, well, well," he says, his eyes still narrowed as if he's just figured out a piece of a puzzle. "Isn't this interesting."

I ignore his taunts as he glares between myself and Lexi, slowly turning his head back and forth. My grip tightens.

"My uncle has already told you, you're not welcome here. Now you can either get the fuck out, or I'll make you, your bitch," I point towards Darien, "and your lapdogs, get the fuck out myself."

I'm done with his bullshit. Something is definitely not right and Elliot clearly doesn't want them here.

I know my uncle and he's always been the strongest man I've ever seen grace this earth, fuck he was one of the top assassins in the country, even had the cops eating out of his hand, but lately he looks spooked.   He's made no secret about the fact he's not as fit and healthy as he was, but he could still beat seven bells out of Vinnie De La Hoy, and something told me he was holding back. I just couldn't put my finger on why.

"We will leave...Darien," Vinnie releases himself from my hold, straightening his shirt and jacket.
"We'll be seeing each other soon."
He nods to Elliot and looks to my brother, who is still standing within the crowd.

The entourage begin to move out, until Vinnie turns back to face me.

"Oh I almost forgot..." He pulls a small, black box from his pocket. "A gift for the Siren, I hope we see each other again soon."

He walks over to Lexi, handing her the box. She looks at it before looking back up to Vinnies face, her expression blank like she doesn't know what to say.

All I can think about is pressing my blade into his jugular and slicing him open like a lemon.

"Until next time, sweet Alexandra."

Without another word he smiles at her, and turns to follow Darien and their guards as they head towards the door.

CHAPTER TWENTY FIVE

Lexi

I hold the box in my hand, as I watch Vinnie and Darien as they leave. I have no idea who they are but from what I've heard tonight, there's definitely some past tension with Elliot, and did I hear right? Business partner?

As they reach the door, my eyes are drawn to a large ring sat on Darien's pinkie. It looks like solid gold, and big enough to see the five emeralds encrusted in it, but it's the centre of the ring that catches my eye. A hollow, oval setting sits empty right between the emeralds.

"That's an usual ring," I say, my voice louder than I expected, as Alaric, Elliot and Axel turn to look, as does Darien. He stops in his tracks, turning with a smirk on his face.

"A family heirloom, one I hold close to my heart." This man has no heart, and if he does it's black as tar.

"It appears to be missing a stone," I point out.

Darien looks to the ring, inspecting it before turning back to me.

"Indeed it does, such a beautiful *ruby* it was too."

Chills erupt all over my body as I stare at the empty setting on the ring. *Ruby, like the one we found in Trinity's bedroom?* I still had the small stone sitting on my bedside table.

The size of it, the shape of it, everything seems to match the one missing from Darien's ring. Words failed me as I stood frozen to the spot.

Darien smiles at me before turning and walking back towards the exit.

The music starts up again as everyone takes in the events. *Dorothy's 'Raise Hell'* covers the muttering of the crowd as I look to my palm. The small, velvet box, still sitting neatly.

"What the fuck is it?" Alaric's beautiful face is twisted in anger as he stares at the box. He looks like the devil himself, but still so devastatingly gorgeous it hurts.

"I...I dunno." I lift the lid to find a gold chain, on the end of it sits a pretty heart shaped locket with intricate lattice detailing.

"A fucking necklace?"

We look at each other in confusion. Did Vinnie like my act that much? I'd noticed the way he looked at Cass when he walked in, maybe he thought I'd be up for the things she was encouraging me to do earlier. I wonder how Alaric would react to that, if he knew what she had said?

I snapped the box shut.

"Is there twenty four hour security at the Hive?" I ask, suddenly changing the conversation. Alaric looks at me like I've gone insane.

"What?...erm, usually yes but they can rotate. It's not a prison, it's a home for our staff."

I nod, "I think Darien had something to do with Trinity's disappearance."

I can't piece together all the segments in my brain but I know after seeing that ring, it had to have something to do with him.

Alaric glares at me. "Why do you think that?"

"Because of the missing stone in his ring. I have it, I found it dropped into a pile of sweaters in Trinity's apartment when I went with Morgan to get the sweater that Trinity promised her."

"It could be any ruby missing from that ring, doesn't necessarily mean it's that one."

"I know it's that one, don't ask me how but I just know it is. He's done something to her, I know it."

Al rubs his hand over his face in frustration.

"Fuck, then we need to get into that club sooner than we planned. We're not going to be able to do anything tonight, but first thing tomorrow I'm going to see what Colt can do to get us in."

I nod. Knowing that Darien probably had something to do with the missing girls had me wanting to storm out there and confront him right now but Al was right, we needed to come up with a plan on how we were going to get into Scarlet.

"Come on, I'll get you a drink."

Alaric takes me by the hand. His warm, calloused palm encases my small hand and leads me to the champagne table. I take a flute and begin to drink.

"There you are," Morgan screeches as she and Leon appear in front of me. I swear she's pissed. "Wasn't that crazy? Talk about tension."

I widen my eyes to signal for her to shut up.

"Oh," she says, looking at Alaric and then back at me. Her eyes making their way to the floor.

"Morgan, I hope you're not drinking?" says Alaric. Seriously, he sounds like her dad. I know she's young but she's not that much younger than me.

She giggles, "of course not boss. Come on, let's dance."

She grabs my hand and turns to grab Leon with her other hand, leading us towards the dance floor. I turn to give Alaric an apologetic look but he just smiles and waves me off.

Cassie's 'Me and You' begins to play as we reach the dance floor. Morgan rolls her hips as she leads us through the crowd already there.

The night kicks into full swing, and it seems the drama of earlier events are swept to the back of everyone's mind as the champagne continues to flow.

Axel opens up other doors to reveal more seating areas for people to relax. I decided to split off from Morgan and Leon to have a walk around, it's then that I spot Sully having a three way kiss in the corner with Ashleigh and Leela. Both his hands caressing a breast on each of the girls and their hands travelling up his suited thighs.

Axel is on the velvet sofa across the room, nibbling on the ear of a girl I recognise but I'm not sure of her name. I think she may have been the hostess on the night I visited La Tanière with Sim.

I try to avoid staring but suddenly the clammy feeling of nausea has me breathing through my nose as I spot Alaric on another large sofa with Sapphire on his lap, straddling him.

She moans shamelessly as she gyrates her hips on top of his groin, although his piercing stare is set firmly on me. He then licks her throat slowly, still keeping his eyes on me. My stomach lurches.

Was he trying to make me jealous? And was he even for real saying that I wasn't allowed to touch anyone but yet here he was with his hands all over that skank.

With a scowl on my face, I fled the room before crashing head on into Leon.

"Woah! You ok baby girl?"

I inhale deeply, trying to compose myself.

"I'm fine, I just need to go home."

"Ok well Jax will drive you."

He calls over to Jax asking him to drive me back to the apartment, which luckily he agrees to.

"I'll let Morgz know you're gone."

"Please," I reply, kissing Leon on the cheek before heading out to the limo with Jax.

CHAPTER TWENTY SIX

Lexi

I don't think I've ever felt so happy to be back at the apartment.

I showered quickly, slipping on a cream silk, cami nightdress that fell to my thighs and brushed my teeth ready for bed.

I couldn't stay there and watch that display a second more or I would have ended up scratching Sapphire's eyes out, and I wasn't about to do that over a guy, no matter how hot he was. Suddenly the front door was torn open.

"Alexandra."

His bellowing voice seemed to vibrate off the walls and straight through me.

I jumped from the bed as he entered my room.

"Don't you knock?" I asked in frustration, trying to keep my demeanour calm.

His hair was ruffled and his suit shirt opened slightly at the top, tie relaxed. He looked devastatingly gorgeous, the embodiment of strength and power, his eyes looking wild and *starved.*

"Why the fuck did you disappear from the house?"

I laughed in disbelief. "Are you kidding me? You think I'd really stay when the party was beginning to turn into some…"

I screwed my face up and frantically waved my hand at the wrist, "...big orgy and you had Sapphire draped all over you? No thanks."

A smirk lifted at the corners of his mouth. "Jealous?"

I narrowed my eyes as he looked at me with a smug grin.

"You can fuck her all the way into next year if you want to, just stay away from me," I snapped.

"She means fuck all to me."

I scoff again. "It didn't look that way."

God I really was sounding jealous.

"I don't give a shit about Sapphire or any other, and stay away from you? You know I can't do that little siren."

His eyes never leave mine as he speaks.

I feel the burn in my cheeks. "And why's that?"

Without even answering and in a flash he's standing before me, his lips crashing onto mine. I don't even resist as my lips part in an instant to allow his tongue access and a shiver races down my spine.

He backs me up until my calves hit the bed and rips my nightie clean off my body in one devastating tear, leaving me completely naked besides my knickers. He pulls his lips from mine, both of us panting heavily as his gaze rakes up and down my body.

"You are divine," he purrs, pushing me back onto the bed and dropping to his knees. His large hands slide up the inside of my thighs, pulling down my knickers until they're completely removed and spreading my legs wide. A low groan escapes my throat as I lie back and accept the wave of blissful anticipation.

Suddenly his tongue was on me, licking and caressing up the inside of my thigh until he reached just before the apex and sank his teeth into my flesh, breaking through and drawing blood. I gasped from the shock and then instinctively bucked my hips as he soothed the sting with his tongue. I could feel my pussy pulse as he continued his assault higher, until his head was directly between my legs. He slid his tongue all the way up my slit, forcing a sharp inhale and began circling the tip of it around my clit.

At this point I was struggling to stop myself from screaming out and as he slid two fingers into my core and the pleasure began to build, I couldn't stop from calling out his name.

He chuckled against my sex, the vibrations making me squirm even more.

"That's it baby, you let the world know who does this to you."

I buck my hips again to get more of him as he adds another finger inside of me, my pussy stretching deliciously around his three digits.

He continues to flick my sensitive nub, reaching up with his spare hand to squeeze my tit, gently pulling on my nipple ring.

"Fuck Lex, these are sexy as hell," he remarks about the tiny silver bars sitting in my nipples.

I can't help the giggle that leaves my throat.

He curls his fingers upward massaging my inner walls and I can't help but tangle my hands into his hair, gripping hard. He growls against my clit, thrusting his fingers in and out of me more vigorously until I'm coming undone

"Ahh!"

"Good Girl, come on my tongue. I want to taste all of you before I bury myself deep inside that tight pussy."

His filthy words push me over the edge as my body convulses. The beautiful torture washing over me as my back arches off the bed and I splay out my hands to my sides, gripping the silky bedsheets below me.

Al moans low as he continues to feast between my legs and then crawls up my body, his swollen lips back on mine as I open my mouth and taste myself on his tongue.

"You taste like my undoing," he gasps as I fight to regain my regular breathing. My heart hammering against my chest.

The thick, hard ridge of his cock pressed against me as he lay over me on the bed and then stood up between my legs, undoing the buckle on his belt and dropping his trousers.

God he's huge. How the fuck is that going to fit?

He opens all the buttons of his shirt and I sit upright on the bed before him, running the flat of my palms over the perfectly carved sculpture of his six pack and pecs.

I've never seen a more beautiful man in my life.

He throws his shirt to the floor and takes my wrists in his hands, pushing me back down onto the bed, pinning my hands above my head.

He leans over, skating his tongue over my aching nipple, before taking it into his mouth and sucking hard.

"Oh god yes," I cry out as he releases my nipple with a pop and flicks his tongue over my piercing.

Licking and gently biting across my collar bone and throat, he comes face to face with me again. I can feel the tip of his rock hard cock nudging at my soaked entrance.

"I take it Natalia sorted your birth control?"

"She did," I reply, bowing my back from the bed, my body begging to take him inside me.

He giggles. "So impatient little siren."

The tip of his cock begins to move back and forth in shallow thrusts.

"Please," I beg, the need for him overwhelming my entire body.

"I want to fuck you raw, I want to feel that sweet pussy clenching around my cock as you shatter beneath me and I empty myself inside you."

"Yes," I cry, squirming in his grasp.

"Tell me. Tell me what you want me to do to you."

"I want you to fuck me raw, I want you to come inside me... please."

"Such a dirty girl, keep your eyes on mine Siren."

I look straight into those deep, grey pools and with that, he thrusts hard inside me to the hilt.

The shock of his size makes me cry out, as a loud groan is forced from his mouth.

He stills to let me adjust, my pussy clenching around him like a vice.

"Fuck, you're tighter than I thought," he pants as he begins to thrust in and out of me in a slow rhythm.

He releases my hands as they travel to his back, digging my nails into him with every pound of his hips.

Pleasure begins to build deep inside my core, as his hip bone rubs against my clit with every thrust and I lift my hips to meet his rhythm.

"I've dreamt of this moment since I first saw you that night in my club," he pants. "I've imagined how you taste. How you feel. You're intoxicating."

"I've wanted this since I saw you watching me that night," I replied. His rhythm begins to significantly pick up pace.

"Harder," I beg, as he slams into me again and again, until our collective moans have taken over the whole apartment.

His mouth comes to mine, and with a final deep thrust that hits the edge of my cervix, I scream my release into his mouth.

"This pussy belongs to me," he whispers into my ear and with two more thrusts, he grunts loudly as he empties himself deep inside me, my own orgasm making my pussy pulse around him, milking him for every drop.

He drops his head into the crook of my neck panting heavily, sweat coating every inch of us.

I brush a strand of my hair that's stuck to my head to one side, as we continue to lay where we fell for a few seconds.

Al then rolls off of me, his release sliding out of my pussy and down my ass as he pulls me into his chest. I rest my head on him, still revelling in the exhilarating feel of his skin against mine.

Without another word, he kisses me on the forehead and we fall asleep, wrapped up together in bliss.

CHAPTER TWENTY SEVEN

Lexi

Opening my eyes, I gaze around the room trying to organise the millions of chaotic thoughts racing around in my head.

Did last night really happen? I had sex with Alaric Mackenzie. What the fuck was I thinking?

The dull ache between my thighs let's me know that I didn't imagine the mind blowing fuck that occurred just hours earlier, and looking down I see the bite marks staining my skin as further proof of my actions.

I touch one and flinch at the sharp burn that radiates from it.

Turning to my side, I'm greeted with an empty space. The bed, cold beside me.

Great, he probably regrets it as much as I do... wait do I regret it? Because I don't really feel like I regret it, even though I'm pretty sure I should.

Rising to my feet, I grab my black silk robe and slide it on as I hear sounds coming from the kitchen outside my door.

"You're finally awake."

Alaric stands at the stove wearing nothing but some low hanging jeans, the deep V below his stomach making my mouth water more than the smell of whatever it is that he's cooking.

"I thought you might want pancakes."

"Pancakes?" I looked at him in surprise. "The great Alaric Mackenzie making pancakes?"

He laughs as he scoops his mixture in the pan and flips it with the spatula.

"Well I kinda thought after last night you'd be hungry. We did work up quite an appetite."

I smile shyly and sit at the breakfast bar in front of where he's cooking. "Pancakes sound great."

I begin to wonder when I'm going to wake up from this strange dream. My relationship with Al has always been an odd one. We've never even been friends and now we're… what even are we? This is the most surreal morning I think I've ever had.

"What are your plans today?" He asks, popping the pancakes on my plate and adding some berries and a drizzle of honey.

"I should go and see Sim, it's been so long and she deserves an explanation."

He nods. "Fair enough, I'll send Demitri to go with you."

I laugh, almost spitting out the small bite of pancake I've just consumed. "That's really not necessary, I'm fine on my own."

He looks at me with unease. "Five of our girls have gone missing Lexi, I won't have anything happen to you, either he goes with you or you don't go at all."

I sigh in frustration. He hasn't changed that much since last night then?!

"Fine." I hold up my hands in mock defeat. "What are you going to do about Darien, about the ring?"

"I'm going to speak with Colt today, see how we can get into Scarlett undetected. If we're gonna find something, we'll find it there."

"Okay." I raise from my chair. "Al…"

"Yeah."

"Do you really believe the girls are still alive?"

He looks at me for a second, his mouth opens as if to say something but then thinks better of it.

"In all honesty, I don't know. I just have to hope they are."

I nod. "Well I better hit the road."

I stand from my chair, ready to go and get a shower.

Al nods, standing from his seat and walking towards me until we're face to face, his lips barely brushing mine. He leans down, planting the softest kiss on my lips. A low groan unexpectedly escapes me. *Embarrassing.*

He chuckles against my mouth.

"I'll see you very soon, little siren."

His eyes heated with desire, making my core clench knowing that I did that to him. *Me, not Sapphire. Fuck you Sapphire! Jesus Lexi, get a life.*

He grabs a white t-shirt from the sofa, pulling it on and grabbing his hiking boots before leaving the apartment.

I groan, throwing my head back as I waddle towards the bedroom.

As I enter the doorway, I spot the small, velvet box on the bedside table. Opening it up, I inspected the pretty necklace one more time. This time opening the locket to take a look inside. It's empty and I'm about to close it up again, until faint lettering inside catches my attention.

Bringing the tiny heart closer to my eye, I make out the faint words engraved onto the gold.

Is this some kind of sick joke?

My breath catches as I read them aloud. *'Daddy's Little Girl.'*

CHAPTER TWENTY EIGHT

Lexi

"Daddy's little girl? Huh?"

Sim sits facing me on the rickety little table in Mals coffee shop, inspecting the locket between her slender fingers, a confused expression on her face.

Demitri sits a few tables away, flicking through an old newspaper, looking bored out of his skull.

"I know right, I don't understand either."

"Hmmm, well he must have given it to you for a reason, I mean it's kinda specific don't you think?"

I sigh, leaning forward to rest on my arm, propping my chin up with my hand.

"Yeah it is, and I can't help thinking that maybe… just maybe this guy is my father."

The words feel surreal as they slip from my lips.

Sims' eyes widened, "seriously?"

"Yeah, I mean he did say that he had a kid, and that it was the mother that was the problem. I mean it kinda described what had happened with my mom and everything."

"What has your mum told you about your dad?"

"Nothing really, except he was married and tried to get her to get rid of me, but what if that was a lie? What if he wanted to know me but she wouldn't let him. I mean it kinda makes sense, and why else would he give me this necklace and show so much interest in me? It's the only viable answer."

Sim nodded as she took it all in, sipping on her cappuccino.

"Well, I mean I guess... So what are you planning on doing about it?"

I sigh. "Things are complicated at the minute, I can't go into too much detail."

Hurt flashes across Sims face.

"Oh come on, you know I'd tell you everything if I could but yeah, basically things are complicated and I want to find out more about Vinnie, but if he is my dad then I want to know where we go from here."

Sim looks at me with a sympathetic gaze.

"Look Lex, I get it, I really do but just be careful. You've spent your whole life being there for your mother and look how that's turned out. Just please don't lose yourself trying to make someone into a better person. Some people are beyond saving, and it grinds our hearts to dust to admit that, but sometimes we've just got to let that dust blow away."

I completely get what she's saying. Rushing into this is certain to end badly and I've definitely had too much faith in my mum getting better. Although now she's in an actual private rehab, she's going to get the best care I could hope for.

"Yeah I know you're right. Anyways, changing the subject to something a little lighter, how's things with Landon?"

She smiles and I assume this means good news.

"Well we've had a date. I can't believe you haven't been around, I've been desperate for someone to get all this pent up word vomit out on."

I laugh. I do feel guilty that I haven't been around lately for Sim, as we've never spent more than a few days apart since we were kids.

"Well I'm around now, and I should be getting my own place soon at the Hive, so you can come and stay with me."

"The Hive? Jeez Lex, these people are intense. You've got a new job, a new home..." She lowers her voice to almost a whisper, hitching her thumb towards Demitri, "a bodyguard...it's crazy how things have turned around for you."

"Yeah I know." I pause and I already know Sim caught my hesitation.

"What? You are happy there aren't you?"

"I am, I just... I dunno, my head is all over the place I just..."

"There's a guy?" Her eyes widened again.

"Well I mean.."

"Who is he?... not the guy we saw here?"

I roll my eyes. "No, it's his brother."

"Haaa," Sim cackles at the top of her lungs. "I knew something was up."

"Nothing is up, I just... I don't know, it's strange, I hated him... I thought he hated me."

"Girl, those are the best relationships. I bet the sex was hot as hell."

I laugh, "I mean, it was only the first time it's happened but yeah, it was kinda hot."

"Only the first time? That means you wanna do it again." She giggles like a schoolgirl.

I laugh at how crazy she sounds right now.

"Ok yeah, I suppose it wouldn't be too much of a pity if it happened again but hey I'm not expecting anything, this guy is ridiculously hard to read."

She smiles, the mischievous grin tugging at the corners of her mouth.

"Is he hot?"

I can't help but laugh as I explain in detail about my situation with Alaric, primarily leaving out the part about him being a top assassin who murdered my stepfather and blackmailed me into working *and* living with him, but hey at least I'm *aware* this is probably a bad idea, right?

Fuck! I'm the one beyond help!

Arriving back at the club, Elliot, Alaric, Axel and Colt were sitting around one of the booths. Rio and Sully stood beside them. They all looked deep in conversation, not one looking up until I released the door I'd just walked through, pulling them from their discussion.

"Anything on Vinnie and Darien?" I ask.

"Yep, We're on the guest list." says Colt, tapping into a laptop in front of him.

"We?"

Alaric stands from where he's sitting by Axel.

"Rio and Sully will go, they're the ones Darien and Vinnie haven't seen yet, they won't be recognised. They'll wear a camera linked to my laptop so we can see everything. Not a single other person besides the ones who are here right now know about this Lex, the last thing we need is someone finding out about the infiltration."

"I wanna go with them," I replied.

Alaric laughed. "That's out of the question."

"No it isn't, it's my decision, you're not dictating this for me as well. Look…" I showed him the locket I had tucked away in my pocket. "It says *Daddy's Little Girl* inside, I think Vinnie might be my father."

I see Elliot flinch in the corner of my eye as Alaric raises his eyebrows in surprise.

"What the fuck?" Alaric looks to the ceiling in disbelief and runs a hand through his hair, before taking the locket and inspecting it closely.

"I don't know what game Vincenzo De La Hoy is playing with you," says Elliot from where he's sitting, a thick cigar in his hand. "But this is too dangerous for you."

"Fuck yeah it is," adds Axel from beside him. "That club is no place for you little siren."

"Plus he's seen you," says Alaric. "There's no way you're going, he knows what you look like."

"Then I wear some kind of disguise, I dunno but I can do this,

I know I can," I plead. The room is silent. "Anyway, how did Colt get us on the guest list? I thought it was strictly members only?"

"It is," replied Al. "We took the identities of two members who would have been attending tomorrow night."

I stare at him in confusion. "So where *are* the two members who were supposed to be going?"

A darkness takes over his features as his mouth curls into a snarl.

"Dead."

CHAPTER TWENTY NINE

Alaric

She wants to go with them? Is she fucking crazy?
It's going to take more than some fake eyelashes and a bit of glitter to hide who she really is.

My heart pounds in my chest, such a fucking little brat. I'll deal with that later.

For now however, I've got to deal with the screeching in front of me from Lexi, who wants to know *what the fuck I mean by two people are dead.* Jeez she's sexy as fuck when she's mad.

"We'll leave you to it," says my uncle, stepping out from the booth.

Axel lights a cigarette, blowing out a plume of smoke before laughing and heading off with the others. Fucking prick.

I stand before the little siren, watching her intensely.
Her tiny fists placed on her hips, she's fucking adorable. I try to hide my smile.

"So, you gonna tell me what the hell you've done?"

"Some things have come to light today, since we had Colt take a look at the kind of people on Scarlet's guest list."

"What kind of people *are* on the guest list?" She frowns.

"Bad ones." I lower my voice as I lean against the table where the guys were just sitting. "The two we killed were Jameson Dunning and Neil Winters, they were both known child abusers. Rich. Powerful. Think they're above the law kinda guys. They were new members of Scarlet."

"What, and you think that's the kind of guys that go there?"

"They *are* the kind of guys that go there. I had Colt check out many of the people on that list, and every single one of them was filthy rich, and had some kind of criminal record. Most of it covered up."

She nods, inhaling deeply.

"It's a dangerous place, little siren, one I don't want you around."

"I'm a big girl, I can take care of myself."

She walks up to me, her hips swaying and stops so close to me, I can smell the sweet mint on her breath. *Fuck I'm rock hard already.*

I still for a second, before grabbing her wrists and twisting her around so she's facing away from me, before leaning forward to whisper into her ear. I hear a low gasp escape her lips.

"You know, I don't take too kindly to being spoken to that way in front of my brothers, you need to be punished for your attitude, pretty siren."

Her breath hitches and I see the goosebumps prickle across the pale flesh of her neck.

"I didn't speak to you in any…ahh!"

Before she can finish her sentence, I push her head down so she's bending over the table of the booth. The very place I conducted my meeting minutes earlier.

One hand on her back, I use the other to loosen my leather belt before pulling it from my jeans, threading the end of the belt back through the buckle. I feel her shiver below my palm.

She tries to turn her head to look up at me.

"So what? You're going to beat me now?" She snarls in defiance.

I chuckle at the remark. "Oh Alexandra, if only it was that simple."

She gasps as I loop the belt around her neck, pulling the slack tight. Her body bowed from the table.

I stare down at her slender shoulders, and perfect breasts as she breathes heavily making them rise and fall. The urge to take them in my mouth overwhelming and almost painful.

"You need to learn, little siren that I don't always play nice."

I tug on the belt, causing it to tighten as she lets out a low groan. I lean down to bite gently on her bare shoulder, exposed in the little cami she wears, and *fuck* her ass presses into my groin as she begins to gyrate against me.

"Well, well, well my filthy little slut, tell me you want me to fuck you over this table where anyone could see at any minute."

"Yes," she begs. Her reply almost hissed.

"Tell me you want them to see, tell me you want them to watch me as I ram my cock into that tight little hole."

She pants quickly as I hold the belt in one hand and reach around between her legs with the other, rubbing her clit over the top of her jeans.

"I want you to fuck me hard while they watch."

I grin into her neck as I nibble all the way up and along her ear.

I bring my hand from her pussy, flicking open the button of her jeans and yanking them down, so they're around her ankles. I pull her knickers down to join them and kick open her knees to spread her legs wider, the jeans and knickers restricting them opening any further. With her soft, perfectly round ass right in front of me, I raise my hand, bringing it down in a sharp slap across her butt cheeks. A high pitched yelp is forced from her throat.

"Naughty, disobedient little siren."

I open my fly as my hard cock springs free and glide my hand down the thick shaft, pumping once. A bead of pre cum already dripping from the slit at the end.

"Al... I..."

Before she can speak, I slam inside her cunt in one brutal thrust until I'm fully seated, my hips slapping against her ass cheeks. I feel her ridiculously tight pussy constrict around me and I can't help the feral grunt that escapes me.

I continue to pound into her in deep, hard thrusts, gripping her hip firmly in one hand and the belt in the other. After a minute, she backs up, meeting my thrusts halfway as we sink into a rhythm, our desperate moans colliding.

I tilt her hips to raise her ass further in the air, looking down at her ankles still bound by her jeans and knickers. The filthiness of the quick, hard fuck right under the occupied office windows above, making me almost finish at just the thought. Her nails dig into the table as she drags them down, leaving claw-like marks in the wood.

"I want you to touch yourself," I whisper into her ear. She lowers her hand between her legs and begins to rub her clit quickly as I continue to drive into her.

Her moans get louder and I feel her body convulse as she comes, while I slam harder and pull the belt as taut as it will go. The stuttered sounds of her gasps letting me know her breathing is now severely restricted.

Four more pumps and I'm following, my body exploding with pleasure as I empty myself deep inside her, filling her with my seed. I release the belt and she slams forward onto the table, gasping for air.

Breathing hard, I lean down and run my palm over her back again. The light blue cami, sticking to the sweat coating her silky skin.

Her body still trembling, I pull out of her, feeling the slip of my warm release as it slides from her pussy and down her thigh.

"This," I say, stroking my fingers through the cum on her thigh and collecting it on my fingers, "is what you do to me." I reach around pressing my fingers between her lips onto her tongue as she sucks them clean, turning back to look at me and smiling. The glint of mischief in her eyes.

"If that's how I get punished, remind me to make you mad more often."

CHAPTER THIRTY

Alaric

"Remind me again why we're here?"

"That smart mouth of yours never seems to let up, does it?!"

Standing in the gym I face Lexi. Our clothes changed from what we were currently wearing, into workout attire. I try to avert my gaze as she stands looking at me, one hand on her hip, rolling her eyes.

I don't think I've ever met another woman who could infuriate me as much as she does. Her stubbornness is like a force field that's impossible to penetrate, but I'll be fucking damned if I'm sending her into the snake pit without any fucking training whatsoever.

"You need self defence training. We won't have time to go into everything but I'll show you the basics, just enough to get you more prepared."

After what happened with the mothers pimp boyfriend, I wasn't taking any risks.

"Right then Mister Miyagi, let's get to it."

She waves her arms around in some ridiculous mock karate pose before attempting the fucking crane kick from *Karate Kid*.

"Concentrate!" I bark. She salutes. *She fucking salutes.*

"We'll start with the palm-heel strike."

I go through positioning and demonstrate ways to move to catch your attacker off guard.

"And what happens if I can't use my hands?"

"Front kick to the groin area." I push out my leg, demonstrating how to move before getting her to imitate what I'd just shown. "Good, that's good."

She smiles over at me with pride, running her hand through the loose strands of hair that have escaped her hair tie. Her lips part and I imagine that sweet, sweet mouth over my cock for just a second.

"We need to go through what to do if someone attacks you from behind, grabs you before you realise."

"Okay," she nods. "Want me to turn around?"

She smiles and I don't miss the glint in her eye as she giggles.

"Yes Siren, I want you to turn around."

As her back is towards me, I wrap my arm around her shoulders, slamming her back into my chest. A gasp escapes her lips.

I lean into her until my lips are grazing her ear.

"If anyone is fucking insane enough to risk touching you like this..." I lower my mouth to her bare shoulder, my lips barely skimming over the warm flesh. She trembles slightly in my hold. "Then you drop your whole body weight, it'll catch them off guard for a second and make it more difficult if they have to carry you."

She drops slightly, mimicking what I have just explained.

"Then grab the index and middle finger before pushing back, this will incite pain, and finally twist and throat punch."

I hold her arm bringing her fist out to show her the points at which to attack.

"You're good at this," she smiles.

Fuck she's pretty.

"Well in my line of work, you're either good at it or you're dead."

"And what about fire breathing? Is that a life skill?"

I laugh. "Call it more of a hobby."

We stand, staring at each other, our breathing in sync, almost like each of us is waiting for the other to say something but nothing comes.

"Hey fuckers."

We both turn at the distraction.

Axel strides into the gym, looking completely out of place in a black leather jacket and torn black jeans. He inhales deeply on the cigarette in his mouth.

"Axel." Lexi dances over to where my brother has entered. She dives at him and he catches her, her legs wrapping around his waist.

The smile on Lexis' face makes my insides sour, but my brother is the only one I would never have issues with when it comes to her. The loyalty we have to each other is solid and always has been since before I can even remember.

"Come to help out little brother?" I ask with a smirk.

"Count me in, what's going on here anyway?"

"Self defence class," says Lexi jumping in.

"Sweet, wanna wrestle little siren?" He winks at Lexi, who giggles before jumping into a ready stance.

"Right, let's go again."

This time the three of us get into a routine and soon Lexi is throwing punches and blocking like a pro.

"This is fun, I wanna learn more," she says through panting breaths.

"You will, for now we only have time to go through the basics but in time I'll have you trained up fully."

"So no one can ever hurt me again."

She stares at me with those beautiful big doe eyes. I walk towards her, taking her chin between my thumb and forefinger.

"Oh little siren make no mistake, if anyone even *attempts* to harm you again, they will feel pain like no other."

She smiles, and just for a second I think I see a flash of darkness in her eyes similar to my own.

I shake the feeling. Its fucking crazy, I've had the best upbringing with my uncle but becoming swept up into his business as a contract killer, over the years had made me a fucking monster, and I wasn't under any illusion that I was anything different.

"You got this baby." Axel throws his arm around her shoulder, kissing her forehead. She smiles.

"Well I better take a shower." Lexi grabs her sweat towel, throwing it around her neck. "Any last words of wisdom before we end our class?"

She stands waiting patiently for my reply.

I pick up my sweat towel, wrapping it around my own dripping neck and look straight at her.

"If all else fails, you bite that fuckers face until your tooth hits the bone."

CHAPTER THIRTY ONE

Lexi

"Your name is Andromeda Rose. You're the recent love interest of Jameson Dunning, who is none other than our very own... Oliver Sullivan."

Colt points to where Sully has entered his office, as he fiddles with the thick, diamond choker around my neck that houses a tiny camera, invisible to the naked eye.

"Oliver huh?" I tease. Sully grimaces at the name, making me giggle.

"Don't ever call me that, my mom calls me that. I'm Sully through and through."

"Yes you are," laughs Colt, throwing me a teasing look.

Sully grabs the wire from his small camera, threading it through a button hole before adjusting it into his tie.

It's taken hours for La Tanières makeup artist to conceal my identity. Lip fillers that dissolve within a few hours have been added to enhance my pout. Green contact lenses added to hide my heterochromia and a long, flowing wig of chestnut brown curls covers my usual flaming red hair. My wrists are adorned with diamonds, matching the choker I'm wearing.

Luckily Colt made no comment regarding the light marks on my throat. Something I was extremely grateful for as I felt my face heat when he had fastened the choker around my neck.

I smoothed out the beautiful yet revealing crimson plunge dress before taking in my appearance in the small mirror.

"Wow, that's incredible." I stare at my reflection, wondering if it's really me under all of that camouflage.

"Amazing what a bit of makeup can do, ey Siren?!" Axel stands behind me as I continue to glare at myself.

"Hey, how's everything going?"

"Good, Als got the laptop set up now, we'll be listening and watching your every move."

I nod.

"You know Lex I wish I could be there with you. It should be me and Al."

"It's too risky, he knows the two of you too well and come on, could you pull off this sexy wig?"

He laughs as I twirl around.

"Where's Al?" the words feel knotted in my throat.

"Right here Siren."

I turn to face those beautiful grey eyes I've come to know so well as Alaric stands before me.

"You know I'm only allowing this because you have Rio and Sully, I trust my brothers with my life and more importantly I trust them with yours. If it was anyone else, there wouldn't be a chance in hell you'd be going."

I smile. "I know, but I need to do this. If Vinnie is my father and they have anything to do with the missing girls then I'm the best one to end whatever this is. He knows I'm his daughter, the locket proves that so he's less likely to harm me if we do get discovered."

"That's not an option. You stay with Rio or Sully and you keep your head down Lexi. I mean it."

I lean forward, raising on my tiptoes to lay a tender kiss on his lips. His hands snake around my back and into my hair as I part my lips to give access to his tongue as he deepens the kiss. As we part, he hands me a tiny earpiece.

"Push this into your ear, these ones go deep into the ear discreetly so they can't be seen by anyone, plus your hair will cover it. The guys have one too."

I nod, staring at the minuscule piece of equipment.

"Remember the training. I'll be watching."

With that, Alaric heads back to his office where laptops are set up to keep watch on everything we see tonight.

"Right, let's get this show on the road," Rio calls from outside the door.

We head out and down the staircase leading to the front of the club. Rio and Sully ahead of me.

"Lexi."

A rough voice calls from behind me. I turn to see Elliot standing there, his face looking pained.

"Elliot, are you okay? Should I call Al?"

"No…no I just wanted to speak to you is all."

"Okay."

I can see the hesitation in his expression, almost like he's fighting some internal war with himself.

"Don't go tonight. Let Rio and Sully go and stay with Alaric, he can protect you."

I smile. "Elliot I can't, I…"

"You have no idea what Vincenzo De La Hoy is capable of and let me tell you, if they have anything to do with those missing girls, I guarantee it's because of me."

I frown, "Elliot, what happened between you and Vinnie?"

His face pales. "I can't go into ancient history now but I know that that club is not safe for you. Please stay."

I kiss him on the cheek.

"You know for an assassin you have a pretty big heart."

"All I wanted was to rid the world of evil, I've never killed an innocent, not once."

I smile. "Thank you for your concern but I have to do this," I pause. "I want to do this."

He lets out a long exhale before nodding silently, knowing there's no changing my mind.

"Then take this."

He hands me a holster that straps to my thigh and a small

handgun.

"It's a G36. Trust your gut Lexi, if anything doesn't feel right, you pull that trigger."

I look down at the G36 in my hand in surprise before nodding and strapping it to my thigh, pulling my dress down to conceal the weapon.

Heading out of the door, I see Rio and Sully jumping into our chauffeur driven limos ready for a night at Scarlet.

Stepping into the car, I slouch down onto the firm, leather seat. The material, cool against the sliver of my thigh exposed from my dress. Switching on the tiny earpiece, I press it into my ear before adjusting my hair.

Rio takes my hand in his and squeezes firmly for reassurance, but for the first time since I made up my mind to attend the night at Vinnies club, a strange feeling begins to settle in my chest, a feeling I hadn't known until now.

Fear.

CHAPTER THIRTY TWO

Lexi

Compared to La Tanière, the club is discrete from the outside. All black brick and simple neon lettering, not at all what I was expecting from an elite, gentleman's club.

Two, burly security guards stood on the entrance in classy, black suits. Their expressions never changed as we left the limo, my hand in Sullys, and approached them at the end of a small red carpet. You could tell a mile off what kind of moody fuckers these two were.

Sully coughed, clearing his throat.

"Jameson Dunning, Andromeda Rose and Neil Winters, here for an audience with Mister De La Hoy and Mister Steele."

The security guard peers hard at Sully, before turning his attention to me. My heart begins to pound at a rapid rate, the force so strong that I worry at any minute it might burst through my rib cage.

"Breathe baby." Als words feel like a safety blanket wrapped firmly around me.

"Identification?"

His voice is sharp and commanding as he waits for us to hand over the fake IDs that Colt forged for us.

The tightening in my throat was almost painful as the small identification cards were thoroughly checked. *Oh my god, he's going to recognise us! Fuck, why did I think I could get away with this?*

"Go on through."

My eyes widened and I looked to the guard as he jerked his head towards the inside of the club.

I let out a silent, slow exhale as Sully took my hand, holding it tightly in his grip and we entered the building.

Walking down a long, dark hallway, lit only by small candles in brackets on the wall, it felt more like entering some medieval torture chamber than a gentleman's club, but the walls vibrated with the bass of the muffled music, which became clearer the closer we got to the main doors inside. *K Flay 'High Enough'* broke through the speakers as we entered the main room of the club.

The room was large, with seating areas positioned around four podiums where exotic dancers were gyrating in sparkly g-strings and nipple tassels.

A large bar covered the whole back wall of the club, selling a range of whiskeys and vodka amongst ridiculously expensive bottles of champagne.

At first sight it reminded me of a casino from a *James Bond* movie as all the men were in fancy suits. There were probably only two other women besides me, minus the strippers. I suppose the name gentleman's club was a giveaway as to why. *My poor attempt at a joke.*

"Everything seemingly above board so far," whispered Sully as I scanned the room.

"Any sign of Darian or Vinnie?" asked Rio.

"Not yet, let's get a drink."

My nerves were starting to get the better of me now we were here and I needed a touch of liquid courage, so as soon as we got to the bar, I ordered a double shot of whiskey.

Throwing back the glass, I winced as the amber liquid burned my throat, warming a trail right down to my stomach.

"Nervous Baby?" grinned Sully, sipping his vodka and coke. I rolled my eyes, gently tapping my thigh to feel my gun.

Rio turned to face Sully and I.

"Four o clock."

We both turned to look in the direction Rio had indicated, seeing Vinnie chatting to one of his guests.

An icy shiver coated my skin at just the sight of him. It was the angry scar and white glass eye that gave him a creepy, almost evil look. If his club was the *Bond* casino, then he was the *Bond* villain for sure.

Darian was nowhere to be seen. My eyes fixed to the floor, trying to avoid contact but as I lifted my head to quickly check that he was still chatting to the guest, he was staring straight at me.

His face looked more sinister than it had the night of the Feast of Fire.

My breath hitched and I quickly averted my gaze to Sully, who placed an arm around my shoulders.

"You guys stay here, I'm gonna take a look around," said Rio, downing his drink and patting Sully on the back.

A small poker table was set out in the corner just by the bar.

"Fancy a game?" laughed Sully.

I smirked, "no but by all means," I gestured to the table. The whole room was littered with men, I couldn't believe how busy it was.

"Let's grab a seat." Sully picked up our drinks and led us over to one of the free tables.

"Wow a lot of men sure do like strippers."

"Yeah a little too many," Sully eyed the table next to us with suspicion.

"Maybe they do extras like La Tanière."

Sully caught the sarcasm in my tone.

"Nah, it's something more than that. A private members club doesn't get this busy for four strippers who are average at best." Sullys eyes continued to scan the room.

"Maybe it's Vinnies charming personality," I laugh. "Or the vodka."

Sully smirks while rolling his eyes. "Well you were the one wanting to know all about daddy dearest' business."

"Very amusing, I just want answers, that's all. Like why he left my mother alone at sixteen and if he ever thought about me, even once."

I shake my head, I didn't expect Sully to have any clue what I meant.

"You know my dad was a piece of shit too, used to beat on my mom and me, even had me arrested when I was fifteen for hitting him back to stop him hurting her. Nearly all of us at La Tanière have been there. That's why it's there, to help people like us."

"And the other business?"

"That's one question I can't say I know the answer to."

I was surprised by Sully's honesty. He's usually the joker of the pack.

I felt a clammy hand land on my shoulder. In shock I looked up to see a man in roughly his late forties standing above me. His beard, perfectly trimmed, matching his salt and pepper hair. His suit looked designer and I could tell by his smile that those things were bought, not the natural teeth god gave him that's for fucking sure.

"Hi there, I'm Michael and you are?"

I looked to Sully, who was staring at the man with contempt.

"Andromeda," I smiled. "Andromeda Rose." I held out my bejewelled arm and he planted a soft kiss on my hand.

"Tell him to back the fuck off."

Jeeeez having someone in my ear was distracting.

"Andromeda Rose, what a beautiful name… and for a strikingly beautiful girl."

His stare roamed the length of my body and something in his eyes changed for just an instant. The friendly smile seemed to be eclipsed by an almost depraved image as he licked his lips. Within a second the friendly look was back.

"Jameson Dunning." Sully stepped forward, thrusting his hand out to Michael, "Andromeda's partner."

Michael slowly shakes his hand.

"Partner? Interesting, and you have an open relationship?"

My eyes widened.

"Absolutely not," I protested, causing a smirk to appear on Michael's face. *Smug bastard.*

"Please forgive me I meant no disrespect, I just simply find it strange is all, you know, the girlfriend being aware of her man being here. Mister Dunning here is a very lucky man."

"Well plenty of men with girlfriends and wives visit strippers don't they. It's not always a big deal."

Michael narrows his eyes, watching me for a second.

"Strippers… yes… strippers. Of course." He nods and turns to leave. "Excuse me please, have a great night both of you and the… strippers."

He turned in the direction of the bar and walked away.

"That guy was a creep," I shuddered. Sully nodded, still looking in Michael's direction.

"Yeah and something was really strange about the way he was talking," said Al into my earpiece.

Sully takes hold of my hand again.

"Keep touching what's mine Sullivan and you'll be lucky to make it to next Christmas."

Sully laughs at Als threat. "Just keeping it realistic boss."

"There's Rio." I pointed to where Rio is heading back towards us. "See anything?"

"Not yet, but keep your eyes open, it seems odd there's no sign of Darian yet."

The lights lower all of a sudden and the strippers leave the podiums. A bright spotlight shines from the back of the room onto the podium furthest from where we are standing and I notice Vinnie standing there, looking like he's ready to address the crowd.

"Gentleman, and of course our few ladies we have in attendance, I hope you are all having a wonderful time this evening. Now if you would like to make sure you have your wallets to hand. We will take you down to the auction."

I stare at Sully.

"Auction?"

He shrugs his shoulders.

"If you form an orderly queue, we can get you down there swiftly."

We begin to follow the crowd, including our mate Michael who begins to exit through a large door that resembles a fire escape. It leads to a dark, stone staircase and my whole body breaks out in chills as we start to descend.

I begin to feel like I've been walking down hard steps for hours but the journey must have only been a couple of minutes before we reach the bottom, facing another large door.

The security guard leading us down, types in a code and the door swings open, revealing a large, brightly lit stage. Around it are lots of small, cell-like booths each with buttons inside. The booths were shrouded in darkness and concealed from the stage by two way mirrors, meaning whoever is inside the booth can see the person on the stage, but the person on the stage cannot see inside the booth.

My breathing begins to grow more erratic as I see Vinnie on the stage.

"Now as before, at our previous locations that some of you may have visited, those wishing to purchase may enter the booths and spectators may reside around the stage. Thank you, gentleman."

An eerie sensation feels like cold hands running across the back of my neck and I hold my breath in anticipation as strange classical music begins to play.

Suddenly Darian Steele enters the stage pulling a long thick chain, attached to the end is a metal dog collar around the neck of a naked young girl.

I gasp in horror, holding my mouth to conceal the sound, as well as the bile rising in my throat, as she is dragged roughly across the floor. Her body, covered in dirt, bruises and lash marks. I try hard to muffle an escaping sob.

"Son of a bitch." I hear Als voice but even that isn't enough to distract me at this moment.

The girl can't be any older than about fifteen. My hand instinctively goes to the gun at my thigh. Rio sees, grabbing my hand.

"Not now Lex, it's too dangerous," he whispers under his breath. I've never felt so helpless in my entire life. My whole body burns with adrenaline and anger.

Vinnies voice booms over the tannoy.

"Our first girl, Lara, celebrated her sixteenth birthday with us last week. She was previously a virgin, only broken in the once by Darian, so she will be a slightly higher price than the others we have on sale tonight."

The girl's sobs ring in my ears as lights begin to flash above the booths, indicating a bid has been placed.

When the highest bid is in, the sale closes announcing who gets the girl. Once she has been bought she's dragged brutally from the stage, falling back onto her knees. Darian doesn't even give her time to get back to her feet as he continues to pull the chain, forcing choking grunts from her throat.

I'm going to be sick any minute.

"Now our second girl has impressive skills, she's a former dancer of the infamous La Tanière nightclub."

My heart sinks to my stomach, my chest tightening.

"And rumour has it, this little birdie would offer extras at the end of the night, so she has plenty to bring to the table in terms of experience. Please welcome Trinity."

I gasp as a beautiful, petite blonde is dragged, again by a dog collar onto the stage.

I feel Rio still beside me and hear a low growl from Sully.

This girl is different from the last. Unlike how timid and terrified Lara looked, Trinity stands straight and defiant.

She growls at Darien as he forcefully pulls on her leash. Also unlike Lara, Trinity's hands are bound in front of her. Something tells me she didn't go down without a fight.

I looked around the room. I have no idea where the security guards came from but there must be at least seven of them, plus with the amount of people in the room, I know we're completely outnumbered and will have to remain unseen for now.

Trinity's long blonde hair is matted and her skin dirty like she hasn't been bathed in months. A sharp contrast to the impeccably dressed men and women here tonight.

A man whispers into my ear. "See anything you like?"

I shudder, shaking my head. I don't even bother to turn to see his face but the rustling noise I hear from behind me is enough to indicate that he's playing with himself.

The lights begin to flash to indicate buyers for Trinity as we look on in horror. Finally the highest bidder is selected and I see Darien ready to drag her away.

With all her strength, Trinity digs her heels into the ground, preventing him from moving her.

The crowd start to jeer, shouting obscenities towards Trinity as she tugs against her bonds.

"Move you bitch, your masters waiting," shouts Darien, but she growls at him more, like a dog turned feral.

"Teach the whore a lesson," shouts someone from the crowd, and it takes every muscle in my body to stop from reaching for my gun and putting a bullet right between the sick fucks eyes.

Darien strides forward to grab the metal collar around Trinity's neck, but as soon as he stands in front of her face, she spits straight into his eye.

Darien wipes the saliva dripping from his face with his free hand, looking straight into Trinity's eyes. Then without warning, he punches her as hard as he can in the nose. A sickening pop echoes in the air as blood bursts from her nose. She screams, grabbing her bloodied face as Darien grabs a clump of her hair and tilts her head backwards.

"You're damaging the product." A shriek comes from the booth containing the highest bidder, as an overweight, balding man rushes out and onto the stage.

"You've broken her nose," he screams at Darien. "I'm not paying for a faulty one."

Darians face twists in anger. "This bitch is trouble, she needs putting in her place." He sneered.

"Myself and my cousins wanted to be the ones to beat her, now she's damaged goods."

As Darien is about to reply, Vinnie enters the stage.

"Now gentleman, I'm sure we can resolve this. We will keep Trinity here a few days, patch her up and then she's all yours."

The man stares at Vinnie. "Fine but she better look good as new."

Vinnie nods, snapping his fingers as two security guards enter the stage, taking an arm each and dragging Trinity, who appears to be semi conscious at this point off the stage.

As the next girl is prepared to be brought out, I keep my eyes on the guards dragging Trinity, before shuffling through the crowd after them.

"No, wait!" I hear Rio but it's too late, I can't lose sight of them.

"Lexi, what the fuck are you doing? Get back to the guys now," Al bellows through the ear piece but I can't stop my feet from moving.

"I have to know where they're taking her."

"Lexi, FUCK!"

His voice becomes a roar as I keep walking, weaving in and out of the baying crowd.

"Lexi, you're getting the fucking spanking of your life when you get back here."

Through the back exit and down more cold, concrete steps, I sneak out and quietly follow them as they carry Trinity even further into the basement.

"Stupid Bitch, just didn't know when to quit," one of the guards laugh.

They enter the basement and I peer through the small window of the door they just entered. Horror strikes me, my mouth running dry.

I see Trinity thrown into a dirty cage, lined up next to several other cages containing half naked young girls, most of them crying or cowering in terror. I'm willing to bet my life on the fact that these are the other girls missing from La Tanière.

CHAPTER THIRTY THREE

Lexi

"What are you doing down here?"

A rough voice echoes behind me. I freeze, squeezing my eyes shut before turning on my heel to see the owner of the voice.

Another security guard stands before me.

"Oh I'm so sorry, I think I got lost looking for the ladies room." I flutter my eyelashes, pouting my plump lips at him for distraction. Beads of sweat begin to collect on my forehead.

He looks me up and down cautiously, and I'm beginning to wonder if he's going to be so easily charmed. "Bathrooms upstairs."

I nod, "thank you." I don't hesitate any longer. He watches as I start to climb the stairs.

"Customers aren't allowed down here," he calls after me.

I turn back to face him. "Of course, my apologies."

I force out my sweetest smile before heading back to the guys.

Stepping through a door, I come face to face with a long, empty hallway. *Shit*, I don't remember there being another door on the stairwell but I must have missed it because this is definitely not the way that I came.

I slump against the door for a second to gather my composure.

"Lexi, get back to Rio and Sully now. I knew letting you go was a fucking mistake," Al continues to yell in my ear.

"We need to get them out. They're keeping them in cages. Filthy cages Al, and they're hurt, hurt really bad."

My eyes sting with the tears desperate to fall. I inhale and exhale slowly.

"Lex, we will. I promise we will, and then every fucker in that place will burn. They'll burn til their bones are nothing more than a fucking pile of ash."

I stand back up straight and brush off my dress. *Get it the fuck together Lex.*

I notice a door to the left with a small window so I decide to peer inside. It looks like a security room with several screens focused around the club *and* the area of the auction. Luckily it's empty but I'm willing to bet a security guard will be back soon.

"Security room straight ahead."

"Perfect, we'll need to know the location of that for future reference."

I turn on my heel to head back the way I just came when I smash straight into a hard, broad chest.

"Michael," I look up to see the guy from earlier standing right in front of me. "What are you doing here?"

He smirks down on me. "I could ask you the same thing, pretty girl."

"LEXI!" I can hear Als voice in my ear as Michael places his outstretched hands on either side of my head, caging me against the wall.

"I was looking for the bathroom, took a wrong turn."

"I see, well did you and your partner... Jameson was it? See anything you liked at the auction?"

The very mention of it makes my stomach churn.

"Not this evening," I smile. "Now if you'll excuse me."

I try to leave but he keeps his hands firmly in position.

"Yeah tonight's show was a little dry I'll say that much,

pretty girls that's for sure but someone else caught my eye first, unfortunately for the girls on stage tonight."

I know exactly where this conversation is going. "I better get back." I try to leave but his hand presses to my chest pushing me back against the wall.

"How about you and me have a little fun while we're alone down here? No one will ever know."

"I don't think so."

"Oh but I do."

He grabs the neckline of my dress to pull it down and with that I slam my knee into his groin as hard as I can.

Before I can run to the door, he grabs my ankles, pulling me to the floor, my body slamming down hard.

"LEXI!" I barely hear Alaric through the earpiece, as flashbacks of Anton race through my head.

"I know you want this, you slag." Michaels hands roughly paw at the hem of my dress to pull it up.

Fuck no, this is not happening again.

"PULL THE GUN NOW!" Al bellows in my ear. *Elliot told him about the gun.*

I flip over onto my back and lunge forward, sinking my teeth into the flesh of his cheek. *'Bite that fuckers face until your tooth hits the bone.'*

"AHHHH YOU BITCH," he screams, trying to push me off as I quickly reach down to my thigh, grabbing my G36. As soon as I press it to his forehead, he freezes, panting erratically.

"What the fuck?" His hands shoot up as if in surrender. "Who the fuck are you I'm sorry?"

The rage is burning through my veins like poison and I know I'm seconds from killing this creature if I don't regain control.

"You disgust me," I sneer. "Men like you think you can take what you want, when you want it, no matter the cost to the woman."

"Men like me?" he laughs nervously. "You're in a club with your boyfriend, buying little whores to be your fuck puppets. Take a closer look in the mirror sweetheart."

My hands shake, knuckles turning white as I squeeze the gun in my hands, feeling for the first time an urge to end someone's life, but if I do this now, we'll never get the girls out.

I keep the gun pointing straight at Michaels head.

"Look I'll do whatever you want okay, please, just don't kill me."

I see the snivelling coward he really is, what they all are.

"I want you to lick my shoes."

He stares bewildered for a second. "Okay." He leans down, this tongue poking between his lips.

"No."

He pauses.

"I want you to lay on the floor like the piece of shit that you are and stick out your tongue so I can rub my shoe over it."

He screws his face up in anger as he hesitates for a moment.

"DO IT!" I shout, holding the gun closer to his face.

He slowly lowers his body to the ground, laying face down but sticking out his tongue.

"Good boy, now you'll lick my heel." I lift my shoe, pressing the tip of my thin, stiletto heel to the flat of his tongue.

Before he can move to lick it, I stomp down, crushing his tongue with my heel. A blood curdling crunch fills my ears and a terrifying feeling overcomes me. Satisfaction.

He screams in agony as blood rushes from the wound, flopping like a fish out of water on the floor but I don't relent.

"Now repeat after me, I'm a dirty rapist and the only way I can get my tiny dick wet is by forcing it inside some innocent woman…oh no wait… you can't." I laugh.

He tugs for a few more seconds before passing out.

Suddenly the door bursts open.

"Lex?"

Rio and Sully hurry through the door, weapons at the ready.

"We've been looking everywhere for you," Rio looks to Michael. "Is he…"

"No he fainted."

"Let's get out of here," whispers Sully.

"He might talk," says Rio.

I shrug, "If he does he'll have to admit the truth. That he attacked a guest while her partner wasn't around."

"Fuck, Als gonna kill us."

"Yeah I fucking am," Al shouts down the line.

"Come on let's go, we can slip out if we leave before someone finds your mate." Sully grabs my hand and we hurry back to the main room.

Everyone is clearing out and we manage to mingle with the crowd until we're safely back on the streets, limo waiting.

As soon as I'm back in that car, I feel like I can breathe for the first time. My heart pounds and sweat coats my whole body.

Not only is Vinnie almost certainly my father but he's a human trafficker, stealing vulnerable girls from the street and selling them to these monsters.

I know I did the right thing by taking on the infiltration tonight, but I know I've entered this limo right now a different person than I was when I exited it a few hours ago. I lost a part of my soul in there tonight, a part that's now engulfed by shadows and I know one thing for sure, that part of me is never coming back.

CHAPTER THIRTY FOUR

Alaric

FUCK!
I stand from my hunched over position watching closely at the monitor screen and slam my fist into the office chair. It flips over violently, crashing to the ground and smashing into the small sofa.

"I knew that bastard was up to something, but I never had it down as this." Elliot paces the office, his hands covering his face.

We've all been awake the whole night, keeping watch on how everything played out at Scarlet, and saw first hand the horrors that those pieces of shit have been hiding.

They have our girls! They have our fucking girls! Rage flows through me like electricity, charging through my veins.

I hear the doors of the club fly open downstairs. I don't even wait for Axel and Elliot to catch up before I'm racing down the stairs to get to Lexi. Her dress is torn and her face red and tear streaked. I take her in my arms, pulling her close into my chest as I feel her sink into me even closer.

"You did good baby, you did so good," I whisper into her hair as I hold her head to my chest and kiss her scalp. She looks exhausted.

I turn my attention towards Rio and Sully before grabbing Sully by the throat and slamming him against the wall

"ALARIC!" Elliot's voice booms like thunder.

"What the fuck bro?" Sully looks at me like I've gone insane and to be honest I think I fucking have. I want to kill the prick, in fact I want to kill both of them for letting her out of their fucking sight.

"If anything had happened to her, I'd be making you dig your own fucking grave by now... both of you," I roar.

"We fucked up Al, it won't happen again," says Rio.   Sully still stares in shock, pinned by the throat to the wall.

"Oh I know it fucking won't."

I let go of his throat as he staggers forward.

"What are we going to do Al?" Lexi walks over, looking up at me, tears frosting her eyes. It's strange looking down at her with those contact lenses in. She looks as stunning as ever, but that's not my little siren.

"We wait until they least expect it, and then we attack. Get the girls out and deal with Vinnie and Darien."

"They're in cages Al, filthy cages, I couldn't get a proper look but I did see some of them tied with ropes around their neck, they've been beaten and by the looks of it starved and who knows what else. We have to get them out."

"We will. We need to be careful, I've seen guys like them before in my line of work. Taken hits on many, and the girls won't always be kept in the club basement. That, I'm certain of. It's too risky with the cops amongst others."

Lexi looks at me and then blinks as if an idea has just popped into her head.

"Trinity's hurt, she only has a few days and then they hand her over to the guy who bid on her. I think they'll keep her at the club, at least for those few days so we won't have long. When she's handed over, who knows what will happen to her, we need to get her out fast."

"Then we come up with a plan and get her out. I'll re-watch the footage from your body cam."

The thought of watching that bastard touch what's mine again feels like someone drilling nails into my chest but I'll deal with that later.

"I'll see if I can find any doors, entrances, anything that could get us into that building without being seen."

Lexi nods, her face pale and wiped out.

"We can't do anything without sleep, and none of us have had any since yesterday so everyone out, showered and to bed. After sleep we sort out a plan of attack." Elliot looks at me and I nod, sliding my arm around Lexis shoulders and pulling her into me as we start to leave to go back to the flat.

As we get outside, I turn to see Axel behind me.

"Take her home. I'll be with you soon," I say to him as he throws his arm over Lexis' shoulder.

"Where are you going?" He asks.

"The other girls were taken from the street, but we've found out that Trinity was taken from her room at the Hive. That's impossible as we have twenty four seven security, so someone helped the fucker get in. Plus from what we saw on the cameras from last night, Vinnie has information on the girls, stuff he wouldn't know unless someone was feeding it back to him. We have a rat and I wanna find out who it is."

"Who are you going to see then?"

"I'm going to speak to Zayn, he's head of security for the Hive. Now it's confirmed that Darien has been in that fucking building, I wanna know how, and more importantly *who* the fuck let him in."

Zayn sits at his desk in the small glass cubicle outside the entrance to the Hive.

We placed security outside as we figured it was more private for the staff who lived here. Plus the cubicle that the security guards sit in is made from bullet proof glass, so it's safer for everyone.

I've always liked Zayn, probably because I've always had so much respect for him and Natalia. They've always been two of our most loyal employees.

I turn my hand, tapping my knuckles on the glass window to get Zayn's attention. He looks up from his desk and walks towards me, outside the cubicle.

"Boss?"

"I need to know who was working on this date."

He looks at the piece of paper in my hand where I've jotted down the date that we noticed that Trinity hadn't turned up to rehearsals with the burlesque team.

"Sure thing." He goes back inside and taps into the system to find the rota for that particular day.

"Kenny Ryan, looks like it was his shift on this date boss."

I nod. Kenny Ryan was our youngest security guard, a bit of a live wire at times but Elliot had a soft spot for him. He wasn't the brightest guy you'd ever meet so hardly a mastermind you'd expect assisting a human trafficking abduction, but something had definitely happened that day and I was going to find out what.

"Bring him in. Now."

Zayn doesn't ask questions as he calls Kenny who comes down straight away to the security desk.

"You called for me boss?"

Kenny stands in a white t-shirt and black sweatpants, his mop of curls laid messily on his head.

"I need to know why you let an outsider into the Hive on this particular day, namely this man."

I hold up a print out of Darien that I managed to get from Lexis body cam. Kenny peers at the picture.

"I've never seen that guy in my whole life."

His expression looks bored and I'm starting to think this little prick isn't aware of just what he's done.

"This guy got into the Hive and took one of my girls on the day you were working. Now I want to know how that happened." My voice remains calm.

He rolls his eyes. "Like I said I don't know…"

SMASH! I plough his mother fucking face into the table in one swipe.

"My nose!" He screams. "You broke my nose."

"Someone has taken one of my girls and she's been beaten, raped and kept in a fucking cage like an animal. Now you better start thinking long and hard about what happened on that day before your nose is the least of your worries." I grab the swollen, bloody pulp of his nose and give it a twist for good measure. He screams again.

"I would never let anyone in, I swear, it wasn't my fault."

"Then who let him in that day?" I bawl.

"I... I don't know, I was feeling rough with food poisoning and I managed most of the day, but then Cassidie came and said I could take a break and..."

"Cassidie?" I snapped. My eyebrows rising. *That fucking bitch, I knew she couldn't be trusted.*

"Yeah, she let me take a break, said she'd cover the desk and to take my time so I did. I'm sorry, I came back and she said everything had been fine and she wouldn't tell you or Elliot about me going off like that and that was it."

Tears leak from his eyes as he clutches his nose. Zayn stares on from the corner.

"Maybe ask her if she saw anyone."

I run my hands through my hair, seething. I'm going to destroy that fucking snake. Her days are numbered.

"Oh don't worry I will." I turn back to Kenny who's sat staring at the floor.

"And you, you're fucking fired."

CHAPTER THIRTY FIVE

Lexi

I lay back on the cool sheets, my body fighting the urge to fall into a deep sleep. I'm feeling better after my shower and changing into my silk cami and shorts pjs, but I know if I let sleep take over now I'm going to be greeted with my nightmares. Nightmares of what I saw, what I heard. I thought after Anton it would be the end of them, but how wrong could I have been?!

"You need anything?"

Axel pops his head around my bedroom door.

"No, I'm good but thanks," I smile.

He returns the smile. "I'm proud of you for how you handled yourself last night Lex."

"I don't feel very proud of myself right now."

Axel smiles again, showing his perfect set of bright, white teeth. It amazes me how something so perfect, can do the things he does. I guess the same could be said with Alaric, but Al has always maintained that Axel was the crazier one out of the two. Maybe I just got a different side of him.

"You rammed your heel through the fuckers tongue, he ain't gonna be speaking for a while."

He laughs a dark chuckle, and I try my hardest not to join in but I can feel myself smiling.

"Where's Alaric?" I ask.

"Not sure, but he'll be back soon, of that I'm certain."

With that, he walks from my room, closing the door behind him.

I must have fallen asleep because when I wake Alaric is sitting on the end of my bed, his head in his hands, wearing nothing but his grey sweatpants.

The room is pretty dark, it seems like he closed the curtains for me.

"You been there long creeper?" I joke.

He looks up. "Long enough."

Goosebumps speckle across my skin as he pulls the duvet slowly down my body. The cool air caressing my bare skin.

"Everything okay?" I ask.

His face looks pained, like he has the weight of the world on his shoulders.

"We've uncovered our little rat." His voice is low, almost whisper like.

"Really?" I sit up straight as he twists his body onto the bed and starts slowly moving up towards where I'm sitting.

"Yes... Cassidie." His hands skim up my thighs.

"Cassidie?"

"The one and only." He watches his hands as they slide up my thighs and over my waist, and then gently digging his fingers into the meat of my hips.

He pulls me down towards him quickly until I'm on my back beneath him and he's staring down at me. His breathing slow and his eyes hooded.

"What have you done with her?"

"Nothing yet, but I will." His lips go to my collarbone where he litters light kisses all the way along and then around my throat before travelling up under my jawline.

My whole body shivers as I feel his hand slide across my breast, making my nipples pucker, and up to cup my jaw as he continues kissing my neck.

His face is then above me, his intimidating eyes staring

straight into mine.

"I don't want to talk about her now anyway. All I want…is to be inside you."

He leans down and his lips touch mine, more gentle than he's ever been with me before and my lips part instinctively to allow his tongue to enter, he entangles it with mine, caressing slowly and I know that that one kiss holds more passion than I've ever felt in my entire life.

His hand skims over my bare shoulder slipping down the strap of my cami until my breast pops out of the top. Moving down he takes my nipple in his mouth, the feel of his tongue flicking over my piercing sending shocks of adrenaline surging throughout my body. I arch my back, pressing myself into his mouth, aching for more.

He shifts slightly, positioning one of his legs between mine as he softly brushes the outside of my thigh, before inching his fingers upward and slipping them into the band of my shorts, bringing them down my legs until they're removed completely.

His fingers graze over the cotton of my white g-string, sweeping over my slit through the small, moist patch on my underwear.

"Fuck baby, you're soaking already."

He continues stoking the parting of my lips over my panties, up and down, up and down.

"You like that?"

"Mmmm," I moan gently, my back still slightly arching from his touch. He increases the pressure of his fingers.

"I'm going to ruin you little siren, I want to possess your heart, your body, your mind. I want to come inside you so deeply that no amount of time can erase my claim."

"Fuck me…Alaric please." I beg, between panting sighs.

In one swift movement, he rips my panties from my body. My stomach is knotted in rapture as I lay bare before him.

He pulls the waistband of his sweatpants down to release his ridiculously thick erection. My mouth salivating at the sight.

"Get on your knees, little siren."

I slide from the bed onto my hands and knees and crawl towards where he's standing at the foot of the bed. I rise up from my hands as I reach him, still on my knees I look up to him, his gorgeous grey eyes burning with lust.

"Open your mouth."

I do as I'm told.

"Wider."

I try, then close them slightly as hesitation sets in. He's huge, how the hell does he think he's gonna fit himself in my mouth? As if by reading my mind, he grins at me slightly before gently wrapping his fist in my hair, tilting my head further back.

"You can take it baby, now open for daddy."

It's as if some light had switched on inside me at his dirty words, as my lips part and my tongue slides over the hard tip of his cock. I glide my hand over the shaft to the base to pump him at the same time as he begins to thrust, meeting the rhythm of my warm, wet mouth. I flick my tongue over the slit at the end of his cock and then slide it down the underside, along the throbbing vein that runs along his shaft. My saliva lubricates his length and after a few more thrusts, he pushes down past my gag reflex into my throat. I jolt with the force, as his grip tightens on my hair, keeping me in place.

"Good girl."

I breathe rapidly through my nose as he fucks my throat harder.

"Fuck!" His growing moans fill the silent room. I continue to keep a rhythm with my mouth, until it feels as if he's almost over the edge and he rips his cock from my throat, leaving a burn in its absence.

Saliva drips from my mouth, down my chin.

"Fuck, you drive me insane," he breathes, lifting my cami top over my head and staring down at me, completely naked, trails of saliva over my face.

He takes my hands and gently lifts me from the floor before pushing me back on the bed, spreading my legs wide and kneeling between them.

"I kneel for no one, but for you I would fall to my knees and fucking bow to the queen that you are."

"I want you, every inch of you." The words come out strangled as he slowly kisses up the inside of my thigh. The anticipation is pure agony, and all at once I want him to just give in and crawl inside me. No matter how much I get of this man, it will never be enough. I can never get close enough to him.

His tongue glided over my opening before massaging my clit in lax circles. I resist the urge to call out as my desire stirs like a hurricane in my stomach. My hands tangling in his hair.

With one hand on my hip, he brings the other to my pussy, plunging two fingers deep inside me without warning and thrusts twice in long, torturous strokes before entering a third. I clench around him, the sensation of being stretched and filled making my eyes roll to the back of my head.

"Oh God."

It doesn't take many more aching thrusts, and just as he curls his fingers up, hitting that sweet, sweet spot, I'm coming undone. His name on my lips and rolling my hips, chasing every last drop of my orgasm.

"That's it, little siren, ride my fingers."

As the feeling subsides, a bead of sweat trickles down from my forehead. He stands between my legs, looking down at my naked form.

"I've never seen anything so perfect in my entire life."

Despite my body only just going through its release, I want more. I *need* more.

"I need you." I'm trembling, my voice barely a whisper as our eyes continue to stay locked on each other.

Heat pools in my lower belly again and all I can think about is how much I want him inside me, fucking me hard.

Alaric lowers his body onto mine, pressing me into the mattress and gently grazing his lips over mine until I wrap my hand around the back of his head and pull him down, his lips crashing on mine. Raw, animalistic hunger takes over me as I moan into his mouth, but he's determined to take it slow this time, dragging out my torture.

"Al… please."

His lips meet mine in another penetrative kiss as he lowers his hands, gripping my butt cheeks and then flipping us over until I'm on top of him.

I look down at this gorgeous, ripped god below me, the tattoos decorating his tanned skin.

I slide back, feeling his rock hard cock teasing my entrance.

"Take what you need Siren," he whispers as he digs his fingers into the meat of my hips, lifting me until the tip of his cock has already started to enter me.

He lowers me, agonisingly slow onto his cock until he is fully sheathed. Our groans filled the air as my pussy stretched around his width.

"Fuck, so good," he moaned.

I began to grind my hips, sliding my pussy up and down along the length of his cock.

He lifted his hips, meeting the rhythm of mine until neither of us could maintain control and he sat up still inside me, taking my breast into his mouth and sucking hard. His hands on my ass in a vice-like grip, he pulls me in, continuing to let me ride him until I'm teetering on the edge yet again.

He fucks me harder, our cries bouncing off the walls and as I'm about to come, he kisses me, consuming my cries of pleasure into his mouth. I shatter around him, squeezing my eyes shut tightly, and seconds later he's following, bucking his hips and driving his cock as deep as he can, before spilling inside me.

We remain in position, panting heavily, our sweat licked bodies fused as our arms stay tightly entangled around each other, his head nestled in the crook of my neck.

He sits back, looking straight at me, a sated smile on his face.

"Who would have thought we'd be here now, after you hated me?!" I laugh.

He narrows his eyes, a serious expression on his face.

"I never hated you Lexi. I've never feared anything in my life, but when I'm around you I fear the things you make me feel, that's why I couldn't stand to be around you."

I nod, staring at him in surprise, not sure how to react to what he's just said. So instead of saying anything, I slowly lift myself from him, his seed spilling out of me and running down the inside of my thigh as I head to the shower.

I switch on the fawcett. The hot blast of steam overtaking me, clearing my head.

Before I can step in, I feel warm hands slide around my waist once again. He's not the only one who's afraid of these feelings. I've been hurt, abused, broken by so many, my trust in men has been non existent for so long. So many emotions race through my body but as we step into the shower, body's tangling and tongues exploring, the racing thoughts are silenced, and all I see is him.

CHAPTER THIRTY SIX

Alaric

She sits there with the arrogance she's always possessed, and it takes everything in me not to string the bitch up right now and make an example of her. But if we're going to get the girls out, then Cassidie Sloan is our only way in.

The gym has emptied out for the day, so it was the perfect place to set up a meeting between Elliot, Colt, my brothers and I to get to the bottom of what this fucking poisonous snake has been up to.

"So, what is this about Al?" She shrugs her shoulders, crossing her legs with a bored expression on her smug face.

"We know, Cass," says Axel. "We know everything. About the missing girls, about Vinnie and Darien, about how you helped them get into the Hive and take Trinity so she could be sold off to some sick pervert like a dog on a leash."

I say nothing as she looks at my brother in surprise.

"I don't have a clue what you're talking about," she scoffs. She looks down at her manicured hand, rubbing her thumb and forefinger together as if waiting for us to tell her the meetings over and to get out, but fury rages through my blood and I'm a ticking time bomb ready to fucking explode.

"Why Cass?" Elliot steps up from the old wooden chair where he was perched. "Why betray us like this? Why betray me?"

She looks at him for a moment, I see the tick in her jaw as she clenches her teeth before swallowing slowly. I half expect another lie to come out of that disgusting mouth of hers when she finally speaks.

"Because I could."

Her voice is like venom, no remorse, no regret, just pure hatred.

"Oh come on Elliot, me and you were nothing more than a pass time. I couldn't get him," she points at me, "so I went for you. Vinnie was my future."

Elliot nods, his tongue skimming his bottom lip. He will never show his emotions but I know he's hurting. Hurting over some low life whore. She doesn't deserve to lick the shit off his boots.

"You were the one who suggested we allow the girls here to offer business after hours, we were against it but you were the one who pushed for it." My teeth bared as I spoke. "You were grooming them, scoping out which ones that bastard could take. Letting him swipe them off the streets." My fists clench by my side. "Letting them into the Hive." My breathing grows erratic. "The Hive. You let them take her from HER FUCKING HOME!" I roar.

Cassidie shoots back in the chair but I lunge for her, grabbing her by her skinny throat and launching her in the air.

She chokes as she struggles, wiggling her legs to get back on to her tiptoes.

"HER HOME, WHERE SHE WAS SUPPOSED TO BE SAFE!"

I throw her like a rag doll with all my might and she flies through the air, landing onto the hard, parquet floor with a thud.

I stalk towards her as she shuffles backwards on her hands and her arse.

"Please Al," she begs.

"Give me one good reason why I shouldn't tear your throat out now? You lying, manipulating, filthy BITCH!"

Grabbing her by the throat again, my saliva sprays from the corner of my mouth in pure rage and litters on her terrified face.

This is the reaction I wanted, not the arrogant, self assured, little cunt from before, but the terrified animal ready to be shredded to pieces by a pack of wolves.

"I...I..." she struggles to speak.

"You're going to help us get into that club unseen. You're going to help us get those girls out and then I'm going to fucking kill you."

Her eyes widened in fear. "I... I can't help you, Darien will kill... kill me...I..."

"If you don't, then I will finish you off right now. I want to know everything, when they're not around, who is at the club and how we can get in undetected."

I can feel her lanky body shivering under my grasp.

"Vinnie and Darien have meetings with potential buyers every night between seven and nine. It's the only time they're away from where the girls are. Security are watching everything though. The only other way in is the back door but it's usually watched by at least one guard."

She scratches her nails against my hand that still latches onto her throat. "Please I don't know any more I swear."

I don't know if I believe her but I intend to keep her around just in case.

"You'll stay in the basement, Demitri and Jax will keep an eye on you while we find out if you're lying or not. You're gonna be useful to us Cassidie."

"I'm not lying, but I can't help you even more, I'm dead anyway for what I've said already."

I nod to Rio and Sully who stride over grabbing an arm each and lifting her up.

"Let me walk. I can't run anywhere, not in these heels anyway."

The boys release her so she can walk alongside them.

As they begin to exit the gym, I turn to Axel and Elliot who are watching me with concentration in their faces.

"She's pretty useless to us now," says Elliot. "She's told us all she knows and now we know how to get into the club."

"True," I agree, "but if we let her go, she goes straight to Vinnie and Darien and so far they have no idea we're even on to them. We keep her here for now."

A horrifying bang thunders just outside the gym as the three of us instinctively duck our heads in sync.

"Gun shot!" says Axel, fury in his eyes.

We run out of the gym, dread knotting in my gut that Cassidie has somehow got a hold of Rio or Sully's gun and aimed straight for them.

As we dash through the exit, there lies Cassidie in a pool of her own blood leaking from the back of her skull. A gun in hand. Her cold eyes open and staring straight at the heavens.

"Boss, she grabbed my gun, she shot herself." Sully looks down at the mess of a human being on the floor before him.

I sigh. "Clean this mess up."

"Yes boss," says Rio.

Relieved, Elliot and Axel make their way back to their offices.

Sully and Rio get to work, cleaning up the evidence of Cassidies suicide.

"Sull."

He turns to me.

"Boss?"

"I've worked with you for almost eleven years, ten of those years as a hitman and never once has anyone been able to pull a gun from your holster, not a single one."

"Yes boss," his eyes went to the floor before coming back to mine. "Those girls have been brutalised, worse than you can imagine."

I nod. Sully may be a professional killer by occupation but he's always been a good man.

He smiles at me, sadness clouding his expression.

"Trinity was my friend."

CHAPTER THIRTY SEVEN

Alaric

Trusting Cassidie when it came to the lives of innocents wasn't something I really wanted to go with, but I knew it was our only angle right now.

She was dead, and to be honest she wasn't going to spill anything else anyway, that was for certain. She'd been too afraid of the consequences.

Rio and Sully were out getting rid of the body, and I'd spent the day with Elliot, planning tonight's attack on Scarlet.

I sat at my desk wishing this whole fucking day wasn't happening. Tonight was going to be risky, that much I fucking knew, and we had to be careful, even more so for the girls trapped at the club. One wrong move and I didn't know what Vinnie or Darien would do to any of them.

"Right so we have this sorted then!" says Elliot, picking up my mock up map of Scarlet. I'd used the footage from the body cams and also information from Lexi, Rio and Sully to draw up the inside of the club and where everybody needed to be. It helped that Rio and Sully had been inside before, so this gave us an advantage when looking for the girls as hopefully my brothers could lead us straight to them.

Colt was assisting us tonight, as was Axel, so we had six bodies to cover all bases.

"Sorted," I confirmed, taking the paper in my hand. "I'll make sure the weapons are ready."

He nods. "How's Lexi doing?"

I continue staring at the makeshift map in front of me.

"She's training in the gym with Leon and Morgan I believe." Keeping my tone casual, the last thing I wanted was more questions from my uncle.

"She's a nice girl."

"She is."

"And you're a good man."

I snort. "Come now uncle, this is not the time to be getting soft."

He laughs, "I care about you Alaric, I always have. No matter what, I want you to know that."

Despite Elliot's choice of career, he has always protected me and my brother and brought us up well.

"I know."

He looks at me without saying a word as I walk from the office.

Heading back to the flat, my chest begins to tighten. When it came to Hit contracts we've had before, we only had to worry about ourselves and witnesses but now we had to worry about the safety of god knows how many girls. Their lives are literally in our hands.

The door to the flat was already unlocked. Knowing Lexi, I doubted she would have finished training so early. Even if she had, she loved to hang around and gossip with Morgan and Leon, so the only person I could think of that would be in the flat was my brother.

As I walked through the front door, Axel was sitting on the sofa, beer in hand in just his black sweatpants.

"Didn't know you'd be here," I said. He looked over and smiled.

"I did have a better offer in the form of a Miss Ashleigh Court but to be honest, that resource has pretty much been exhausted on my part."

I laugh. "So she doesn't interest you anymore?"

He rolls his eyes. "She interests everyone, that's the problem. I'm her side piece rather than the other way around."

"A new experience for you brother," I joke.

"The only person who really has Ashleigh's heart is Leela Dawson. Men are just toys to her."

Ashleigh's heart? I laugh. I've never heard my brother speak like this. Axel has never cared about what women thought of him, just as long as one of them was on the end of his dick.

I slouched next to him on the sofa.

"Are you going to tell me what this is really about? Because let's face it, you've been fucking every girl we've had at La Tanière for years and you've never once mentioned about their *hearts.* Pussy perhaps but never heart."

A long sigh leaves his mouth as he stares at the floor and I can tell he's avoiding eye contact with me.

"What have you done?" I ask. He closes his eyes for a few seconds before finally opening them.

"I'm in love with Lexi."

He stands, waiting for my reaction. Is he fucking kidding me right now?! A bitter churn twists in my stomach at his words.

"I'm sorry bro, I see the way you look at her and she looks at you and I can't help but want that. There's been a few times I've seen her look at me and…"

Crack! My fist lands on his cheekbone.

Axel jumps to his feet, staring straight at me, one hand to his cheek.

"See this is why I didn't tell you before."

A red mist clouds my vision and all I can think about is making him stop talking. This is my brother for fuck sake and he's telling me he's in love with Lexi, with my fucking girl. He's my flesh and blood, our bond is thicker than anything but lines are being crossed when he thinks he can touch what's mine.

I lunge for him, grabbing him by the throat. His hands latch on to my wrist but he doesn't try to stop me. Axel may be a few years younger than me but he's built well, just as I am, so he could put up a fight if he really wanted to. He was a killer to the core, as was I, so the fact he wasn't retaliating told me that he had no intention of doing so.

"This isn't even up for discussion Axel, you're not in love with Lexi."

A sea of rage is coursing through my bones and the last person I want on the end of that rage right now is my own brother.

"I don't want this to come between us, but she's just not like other girls."

"I know she's not fucking like other girls," I roar.
My head split between letting him go and letting him feel the charge of my fist once more.

"I've seen the way she looks at you too and the way you look back at her, and you both think I don't see the chemistry there. I can fucking feel it, but you tip
toe around it and you should feel fucking lucky because that feeling, I would do anything for that feeling, I..."

"Wait a minute," I disrupt his confession, letting go of my grip. "You would do anything for that feeling? I should feel lucky? Have you heard what you're saying? You're talking about the feeling, not Lexi. Is it the girl you want or what we *have*?" I say that with hesitation as to be honest I don't even know myself what the fuck we have.

"I'm done with fucking around Al. A different girl, maybe two or three together each night, I mean yeah it's been fun but I want that connection now. Maybe I'll never have it."

I turn to face away from where Axel is standing. He's always been a player, completely the opposite to me but I get the sense that now, at twenty nine he's trying to tell me he wants love, not just a quick, convenient fuck. I don't think it's Lexi he's in love with at all, I think it's the idea of her. *It better fucking be the idea of her.*

"You'll find that feeling with someone Ax," I say quietly.

"There's someone out there for you, someone who makes you feel like you wanna be a better person, someone who makes you feel like less of a fuck up, but even if you are still that fuck up, then they still care about you anyway. It's what you deserve, and it's what you'll get."

He walks over to the round mirror hanging on the wall.

"Jesus, no chicks gonna come within a mile of me now you've fucked up my face. Other than my dick, this is my best feature."

I laugh as I look over at his face, a dark bruise beginning to stain his skin, at least I didn't aim for the nose. His pretty face can handle a light tap.

"I'm surprised that mug hasn't had a few slaps from someone's husband already to be fair."

Axel chuckles. "I guess there's time," he replies.

I think about the danger we'll be facing tonight and it makes me look back on all the other times we've taken jobs, not knowing if we'll be coming back again that time but thinking fuck it and doing it anyway.

"Yeah," I say finally. "I guess there is."

I turn to walk towards my room.

"When are you going to tell her?"

I look back over my shoulder. "Who?"

"Lexi… when are you going to tell her that *you're* in love with her?"

CHAPTER THIRTY EIGHT

Lexi

"Where do you think she left to go?" Morgan tightened the microphone into its holder on the little makeshift stage she was using to practice on.

"I don't know Morgz, I didn't really know her."

Lies.

I knew exactly where Cassidie was, *okay maybe not exactly where she physically was,* but I knew she was never coming back after she put a bullet through her own head. Alaric didn't even bother pretending with me when I ask what had happened following their confrontation.

I didn't think it was right to let Morgan know that Cass had anything to do with Trinity's disappearance, but I couldn't hide it from her that we'd found her and were literally on borrowed time before she got shipped away to a life of god knows what horrors.

"I never liked her anyway, I always felt like she put pressure on the girls to... you know... give extras to the customers, plus she was a total bitch when I first came here. I think Sapphire was probably the only one who liked her."

I nod. I had to admit she wasn't the most friendly person to me either and she certainly wasn't going to be missed.

"Anyway on other matters, I'm still thinking Leon is keeping something from me."

"You're not still hooked on that are you?"

I smile over at Morgan, this overactive imagination of hers refuses to rest.

"Mark my words, I will figure that shit out."

I laugh at Morgan's determined expression as she looks at me with arms crossed, tapping her little ballet pump shoe.

"I've no doubt about that. Anyways I'm going to go see Al, find out what's going on, do you need any more help setting up your stuff?"

She looks around the floor at all her music equipment that she's arranged to help her practice her performance.

"No I'm good, you go see your man." She smirks and wiggles her eyebrows at me.

Giving her an obvious eye roll, I turn to leave the gym.

"He's not my man," I called back over my shoulder.

"Sure thing." Morgan answers, the sarcasm blatantly present in her reply.

I continue walking without another word. Alaric was not my man, I mean yeah we had good sex, ok fucking *mind blowing* sex but it wasn't like it was anything exclusive and I didn't want it to be anything exclusive. *Did I?* He was danger personified. The whole relationship is fucked up, beyond fucked up.

Pushing the thought from my mind, I headed back to the apartment to find out what the plan was for Scarlet. My insides fluttered like a million moths had been trapped inside me. Was Vincenzo De La Hoy my father? The thought still lingered.

Part of me had hoped that he was, just so that I could have some closure, maybe get closure for my mum, *if she was even clean enough to care*. Now that I knew he was using his club as some base for human trafficking, the thought of being his bloodline repulsed me. I began to itch in my own skin like I wanted to scratch the DNA right out of my body. I knew the day would come when I had to confront him, but I think deep down, the idea of Al ending him was a welcome relief.

That seemed highly unlikely tonight however, due to the fact Al had told me they were planning on getting into the club while Vinnie and Darien were away. I doubted Alaric or the guys cared whether he was there or not, but I knew that Al thought it was safer for Trinity and the girls if they got out before Vinnie and Darien were back at the club.

Walking into the apartment, the tension was abundant.

Axel leaned on the breakfast bar, scooping cereal from a bowl into his mouth and Alaric was lining up a row of guns on the dining table.

The first thing I noticed even before anyone spoke a word, was the shiner emerging on Axel's face.

I ventured further in, warily observing the room.

"Everything okay?"

"Everything's great, little siren," Axel replied through each spoonful. Alaric kept his focus on the guns.

"What happened to your face?"

Axel throws me a cheeky smile. "Walked into a door princess."

I narrowed my eyebrows. "A door?"

"Yep." He smiled and continued chewing.

Right because trained killers often walk into doors, yep happens all the time.

I dropped my tote bag on the chair right by where Alaric was organising his weapons.

I looked at the table. "Have you used all these before?"

He started loading the guns, making no eye contact with me. "Yes"

"Which one has killed the most?"

He hesitates before picking up a black matte gun that looked like something I'd seen in a *Die Hard* movie.

"The Beretta Brigadier."

He turned it in his palm, inspecting all the angles of its shape. "I'd like to see... maybe... one day."

Alaric looked at me for the first time since I walked through the door.

"See what exactly?" His eyes narrowed, focused solely on mine.

"See you kill someone, I want to know what it feels like, to end someone. Does it feel powerful?"

The words came out gravelly as heat flowed through my veins.

I don't know why I was asking these things but something happened that night at Scarlet. Something I couldn't explain. One minute I was fighting for my life against Michael and the next I was hesitating when I should have been leaving with Rio and Sully. Hesitating because it felt good punishing a man who had wronged so many women. Causing him pain had felt like a release to me, and I had to admit it had fucking turned me on like crazy.

"Something like this is too dangerous for you, little siren," Alaric said the words, but I could tell in his eyes he was intrigued by what I was saying. He dampens his lips with his tongue.

I lifted a revolver from the table, circling the end with my forefinger.

I heard the chair creek behind me as Axel headed to his bedroom, leaving Alaric and I alone.

I could hear Als breathing growing more ragged.

"I want to know, I want you to show me."

I placed the gun to my lips, parting them slightly and circling my tongue around the end before sliding the barrel into my mouth.

Alaric's eyebrows lifted slightly and a flash of lust grazed his eyes.

Within seconds his hand was at my throat, massaging my windpipe. His erection evident through his grey sweatpants.

He pushed me back against the table, pulling the gun from my grip. He slid the barrel down my loose tank top between my breasts and over my toned stomach, traveling lower.

"I can show you many things with this gun, little siren, and killing is not one of them."

With that he slid his fingers into the band of my leggings, tugging them down slightly over my ass until my pussy was bared to him. Heat rolled through me, causing my thighs to quiver.

He tutted. "No underwear? Naughty, filthy little siren."

"Mmm," I groaned, closing my eyes as the tip of the revolver skirted over my pubic bone and grazed my clit. I shuddered under the touch.

"On the table." It was a command not a question and without hesitating, I perched up on the edge of the table.

Alaric grabbed my calves, pushing my heels up and spreading my legs further, my pink pussy open and glistening before him and the band of my leggings stretching with force.

He stroked the end of the revolver over my opening and I could feel myself getting slicker by the second.

He leaned into my ear, his hot breath sending shivers along my spine.

"You're so wet Siren, your sweet slickness is covering my gun, your tight little cunt is begging me for it. Is that what you want?" His voice now practically hissed. "Do you want me to fuck you with my gun?"

My eyes roll to the back of my head at the thought.

"Yes," I pleaded. "I want you to fuck me with it… please."

His grin turns devilish as he presses the tip into my pussy. The cool metal easing between my lips.

"Look down Siren, watch while I take you with my weapon."

I look down to see the revolver sliding all the way inside me. The sight alone makes me feel like I'm going to come any minute.

Alaric takes his free hand and begins to circle my clit, hard and fast. I lean into his shoulder to muffle my cries so that Axel doesn't hear what's going on right outside his door.

"You were asking for this."

His thrusts speed up as I try to look down again and see the slick gun, sliding in and out of me.

With the pressure on my clit and the revolver hitting that sweet spot inside me, I'm coming undone within seconds. I lean back on the table, biting my lip, tasting the copper tang as I draw blood while trying to silence myself and roll my hips against Als fingers and the gun. Wanting him to force the object inside me as deep as he can, as I ride out my release. My pussy pulsing hard with the wave of ecstasy rushing over my body .

As I come down from my high, Alaric withdraws the gun from inside me. The barrel coated in my climax.

I inhale deeply, trying to control my panting as I stand and pull up my leggings.

Alaric looks at me, a satisfied smirk on his face.

"I'll be thinking of this moment tonight siren," he says. He turns the gun in his hand, before gliding his tongue over the base of it.

"I will be thinking of your desperate cries when I'm using this very weapon to end someone's life."

CHAPTER THIRTY NINE

Alaric

Scarlet stood in a shroud of shadows as we approached the club just after seven.

The old building looked as sinister on the outside tonight as we knew it was on the inside, but the eerie silence surrounding us wasn't going to lead us into a false sense of security that was for sure.

Colt had been staking out the place since around six. As much as I hoped Cassidie's final words were true, I knew what a lying snake she had been now and I struggled to believe anything that had come out of that vile mouth.

However, by six forty five, Colt had signaled through the earpiece to alert us to Vinnie and Darien leaving the premises in a blacked out suv.

Axel and I had taken the back route straight away and were stationed in an old, abandoned building opposite Scarlet. It gave us direct vision to the back doors, where I could see two armed security guards standing. Both looked like they were pumped to fuck full of roids

Rio and Sully were down on the ground towards the side of the building. I'd already seen one of the guards go through the back door so I knew it wasn't locked right now. Good. *Now's our perfect chance.*

Rio and Sully attached the suppressors to their guns before stealthily rounding the corner.

Rio grabbed the first guard in a chokehold around the neck, and by the time the second guard went to retrieve his gun from his hip, it was too late. Sully raised his gun, putting two bullets into the back of his head with a low pop.

Rio mirrored the action by taking out the guard in his arms, both bodies dumped to the floor at their feet. "Keep watch at the front, we're going in," I ordered Colt through the earpiece.

"Yes boss," he confirmed.

Elliot joined us from where he'd been stationed with Colt.

"I'll keep watch on the back, go."

He tapped me on the shoulder as I nodded and ran down the old stairwell with Axel, across the yard to the back entrance of Scarlet where Rio and Sully were waiting.

Sully pulled on the door and the four of us slid inside.

The back entrance was nothing like what I'd seen through Lexis' body cam. It was dark and cold and not a single trace of any of the glamour from the club.

"We need to get to the security room, turn off the camera," whispered Rio. Luckily the stairwells were camera free as customers didn't ever use them, except when escorted by Vinnie or Darien to the bidding room.

Sully and Rio already knew how to get there. We followed them to the floor where the room was located, and stepped through the door. I recognised the place straight away as the area where Lexi had been attacked.

Fury began to simmer within me as I squeezed my fingers tightly around the grip of my gun.

An overweight fucker, eating a stack of doughnuts was sat lazily watching the monitors in front of him in the security room.

He lounges back with his feet crossed and perched on the table. It didn't take long for him to become aware of our presence when Axel burst through the door. The guard tried to squirm as Axel gripped him by the scruff of his neck. He had a good seventy pounds on Axel, but still he wasn't going anywhere as Rio disconnected the cameras and I quietly put a bullet through the guy's head, before dragging him to a cupboard and shoving his body inside.

"We need to get to the girls," said Rio. "From what I remember it's not too far from here."

We followed his lead, keeping watch around us as we stalked through the corridor back into the stairwell.

Screams radiated from the room below, echoing through the cold stone of the building.

Fuck we were close.

As the guys retreated down the stairs, I remained at the back, ensuring we weren't being followed until we reached the bottom.

The door to the basement was locked with a security code. I could hear three or four guards inside.

Peering through the small window in the door, I spotted the guards. Three of them. This definitely worked in our favour as we would be able to outnumber them.

One of the guards was holding a young blonde girl by her hair, her head forced back as her terrified eyes stared up at her tormentor. Her small hands tied in front of her with thick rope. The other two guards were laughing as he groped her breast while she kicked and screamed.

Fuck waiting anymore, the guys turned their heads as I slammed the butt of my gun into the small glass panel, shattering it into thousands of tiny shards. Screams rang from the cages, the sobbing intensifying.

The guards spun around in shock as one of them walked towards the door, opening it from the inside. The other guard dropped the girl to the floor and drew his gun along with guard number three.

As soon as the door opened slightly we pounded through, the force of my fist smashing straight into the first guard's nose, breaking it open like a smashed papaya.

Gunshots were fired as we jumped behind stray beer barrels laying around the room. Screams filled the air from the terrified women and my only thought was making sure they were not harmed by any stray bullets.

Guard three fired a shot grazing Rio's arm.

"FUCK!" he shouted before standing, rage in his expression and opening fire. Five bullets penetrated the chest of guard three, before Axel took the fatal shot that ended the life of the second gaurd.

The women cowered in their filthy cages, crying and some clinging to each other. There were more than I had anticipated, probably around fifteen now.

"ALARIC."

I heard the voice and knew it was her before seeing her.

"Trinity."

I turned to see the pretty, little blonde, her face beaten and bloodied. She shivered in the little bikini she was wearing. Welts covering her back and legs, most likely from where she had been punished following the last auction.

Sully ran to her cage as we grabbed the keys from guard two, who was laying in a pool of his own blood.

"Alaric, Axel." I heard the cries of the other women. The women who had gone missing from La Tanière. They were all here. I breathed a large sigh of relief. The guys pulled open all the cage doors, as the women crawled out.

Sully ran his hand through Trinity's matted hair.

"Come on," I called. "Let's get out of here."

A rumbling laugh came from the direction of the door, as we all shot around to see Darien standing in the way of the exit.

What the fuck? Why didn't Colt tell us he'd come back to the club?

"Well, well, well, what do we have here?" He stood tall, a thick cigar in his mouth. "What's wrong Alaric?" His beady eyes stared in my direction. Piercing.

"Didn't expect to see you this evening Darien," I replied in a cool, calm tone.

He laughed, exhaling a long cloud of smoke.

"I can see, I should have put more guards on tonight, good thing I forgot some things from my office. Is that the reason why you thought it was okay to come into my club? Kill my security?" He looked to the girls who were beginning to cower again. "Try to take my stock?."

I glared into his eyes. There was nothing there. The man had no soul, he was a monster. A monster like me, only one of the worst kind.

"I think you'll find these women belong to me, Darien," I gesture towards Trinity and the La Tanière girls. "And if you ask anyone they will tell you, I don't like to share what's truly mine."

Darien stood, his eyes still glued to me. His hand began to creep slowly to the hem of his suit jacket.

A murderous laugh leaves his throat.

"Oh Alaric Makenzie," he lifts the gun and it's like time is drifting by in slow motion. "I can't wait to see the look on your face when you find out that…"

BANG! Darians eyes bulge as his blood paints the exit where he stands. A bullet hole right through his forehead. Screaming and crying fills the room. He was dead.

I blew out a breath I didn't even realise I'd been holding.

Turning my head I see Axel, his face void of any emotion as he stands with his beretta in hand.

I knew in that second that his action had potentially saved my life. I didn't know what Darien was going to say to me and to be honest I didn't fucking care, all I cared about was getting out of this place with the girls and beating the shit out of Colt for not letting me know about Dariens return.

"Quick, through here."

Rio and Sully began helping the girls out of the building. Relief filled my bones.

"Alaric."

Elliot's voice echoed through the ear piece.

"Elliot," I replied.

"Alaric, I'm around the front of the building now, it's Colt. He's been shot!"

CHAPTER FORTY

Lexi

La Tanière still seemed like a whole different place to me when the room wasn't roaring to life with the flamboyant laughter and cheer from the drunken crowd.

The place was dimly lit with small, golden orbs mounted on the walls, and so quiet you could hear the echo of my tumbler as I placed it down on the empty bar top with a clink.

Picking up the half empty bottle of vodka, I poured myself another glass.

I'd tried to stay in the apartment tonight, until I'd gotten word that everything was alright over at Scarlet but I was restless beyond belief and needed something strong to calm the nervous waves that were lapping in my stomach.

So in my pjs, I headed across the courtyard from the apartment to the club, where I could sit with my intrusive thoughts and bottles of alcohol.

All I could think about was would Alaric, Elliot and Axel make it out of the building alive?! Would the girls make it out of the building alive?!

"Room for two more?"

I was pulled from my daydream by Morgan and Leon approaching with caution.

"Penny for your thoughts," said Leon, grabbing a tumbler and the vodka bottle and pouring himself a glass half full.

"You're gonna need to rob a bank for all the thoughts going through my head right now."

I sighed, leaning my shoulders down onto the bar.

"Well, friends don't let other friends get drunk alone," said Morgan, placing a warm hand on my shoulder and reaching out to take a glass from Leon.

"Any word yet?" she asked.

I shook my head, swallowing another mouthful of vodka. The neat, clear liquid burned my throat as I swallowed. "Nothing!"

Morgan poured the vodka into her glass. "Well all we can do now is hope."

It sounded trivial. I felt like sitting here and waiting was destroying me from the inside out. I worried about the girls but deep down I was petrified something was going to happen to Alaric. I hated myself for letting a casual fuck take over so many of my emotions, but I was severely in deeper than I wanted to admit when it came to him, and the feelings he evoked in me where completely alien. I'd felt lust and desire but not this weird thing I was feeling in my gut right now.

"I hope to god I'll see Trinity again," said Morgan. Her face filled with sadness.

I threw my arm lazily over her shoulders. "You will, she's coming home Morgz."

Leon backed two shots of vodka, wincing at the sting as he swallowed.

"You okay?" I asked, narrowing my eyes. "You seem really off lately. Is there anything you wanna talk about?"

"Yeah," said Morgan, jumping in. "I've been saying something weird is going on with you, I know you're hiding something. Disappearing all the time, ignoring my calls."

Leon's face pales.

"It's nothing."

"And you always say that too when I ask you anything, we're supposed to be besties Leon."

I can feel the frustration in Morgan's tone. Her and Leon are my closest friends here, but they've been friends with each other even longer.

Leon stares at his glass. "I can't tell you... at ...at least not right now, it's... complicated."

"But complicated? how?"

Suddenly, the doors of La Tanière burst open as the guys race into the building. Rio, Axel and Zayn, the Hives security guard in front, then Sully and a bunch of half naked women, clutching the blankets Elliot had thrown into his car earlier in the day, and finally Alaric and Elliot carrying a slack body between them which I instantly recognise as Colt. His arms draped over Alaric and Elliot's shoulders and his eyes barely open. Natalia, the staff doctor and Zayn's wife, is following close by and it's then that I notice the large stain of pooled blood under Colts jacket, just above the right side of his rib cage. *Fuck, he's been shot!*

Cold sweat prickled my forehead and the back of my neck as I watched Alaric and Axel lay him on the floor, Rio throwing his jacket down onto the cold stone as cushioning.

Natalia grabbed her stethoscope and knelt down to tend to him, as Alaric tore open Colts shirt and applied a rag to the gushing wound. His hands, adorned with bright red blood.

A deafening cry filled the atmosphere, a sound of pure, animalistic pain and I realised it was coming from Leon.

He ran to Colts side, throwing himself to the ground, tears streaming from his sorrow laced eyes.

"What happened?" He sobbed.

"Darien came back to the club," said Alaric, continuing to apply pressure to Colts bleeding chest.

"He came back?" My voice shrill with the horror of what I was hearing. "Where is he now?"

"Dead."

Alaric's words sent a shiver down the length of my spine.

"What about Vinnie?" I asked, my voice significantly lower.

"Oh don't worry, daddy's still alive." His words were laced with venom and I could feel the bite.

Was he angry at me? Did he blame me for what had happened to

Colt?.

I knew now wasn't the time to be discussing this.

"The bullet is in too deep, I'm calling an ambulance or he's going to die," said Natalia.

Elliot nodded to give her the go ahead and she grabbed her phone from her jeans pocket.

The ambulance was here within minutes. Elliot had Natalia check over the girls and they all huddled together in his office.

The initial reunion between Morgan and Trinity had been emotional, with plenty of hugging and sobbing but soon they were happy and smiling despite what was going on around them, and Trinity was helping Morgan get coffees and hot chocolate to the girls to warm them up.

The paramedics managed to get Colt stable and onto a stretcher.

Leon sat on the floor clutching Colts bloodied black denim jacket, staring straight ahead. I knelt down beside him as his grip on the garment tightened.

"So, anything you wanna tell me?" I said gently, stroking my palm over his hair.

Leon looked up at me from where he was cuddling the jacket. His eyes glittered with tears.

"We were together," he sighed quietly. "Me... and Colt, we've been seeing each other in secret for a while now."

My eyebrows raised slightly at Leon's confession.

"Oh I see."

Leon dropped his chin back down onto the jacket.

"And was this the great secret you've been keeping from Morgan?"

Leon nodded. It finally made sense to me why he was always sneaking off, refusing to answer calls.

A secret romance was definitely something I'd suspected, but certainly not with Colt.

Leon wiped a hand over his reddened face.

"Colt wasn't ready to come out, not yet. I guess I can't blame him after everything *I've* been through. But he made me feel like the most attractive man in the world, like my scars were perfect because they were a part of me. I knew how he felt about everyone knowing about us but he was just... we were just so..."

His pained expression told me everything I needed to know and my heart ached for him. I'd never seen someone as strong as Leon look so broken and wounded at that moment.

"Leon, do you love him?"

Leon's face snapped straight to mine as if I was crazy for a second, but then all of sudden his features softened.

"More than anything."

I took his hands in mine and gave him a gentle smile.

"Then go to him, go to the hospital, be with the man you love."

Leon's eyes widened. "You really think...?"

"Yes," I giggled. "Go."

Leon nodded, offering me a nervous smile and quickly kissed me on the cheek before standing and making his way towards the doors, to catch up with the ambulance.

Things had taken an unexpected turn tonight, and with Darien dead, it wasn't going to take a miracle for Vinnie to now know that the Mackenzies were on to him.

The question was, what demons had tonight's events awakened now?!

CHAPTER FORTY ONE

Alaric

When you kill for a living, you come across some pretty fucked up shit.

I'd faced humans who'd committed every sort of crime but none turned my stomach in the same way as the trafficking of women and children.

It was easy enough contacting the families of the women we'd rescued from Scarlet.

The tears and cries of happiness when they were reunited had filled the atmosphere like oxygen, and of course our girls were safely back in their homes at the Hive which was a huge relief. But it didn't mean the terrors of what they had faced would just disappear now they were back.

This was one of the reasons I had hardly laid eyes on Lexi this whole last week since we infiltrated Scarlet and brought Vinnie and Dariens little business venture crashing down.

Trinity had struggled since the first night she got back to her apartment in the Hive. At first it was just the feeling of unease, and the fact someone had taken her from her own home meant she didn't even trust having the security guards on the door anymore.

After reassuring her that Zayn would be taking full control of the security on the building, she seemed to relax a little, until it became clear that the trauma was a lot more deep rooted when she began having night terrors the second night she was back.

Due to this, Lexi and Morgan had set up camp in her apartment and stayed with her twenty four seven to offer her the support she needed.

I had no doubt Lexi was probably relieved to be out of my apartment anyway, seeing as the last time we spoke, my anger and frustration had gotten the better of me.

I hated what Vinnie and Darien had done, to the women, to Colt and I knew that wasn't Lexis fault but she was his flesh and blood, obviously I was gonna be slightly pissed off at that. But I kept reminding myself that she was nothing like him and my reaction was just fucking stupid.

Maybe I should be trying to make it up to the little siren. *As usual, that's going to have to wait for now though.*

There had been no word from Vinnie, and with Colt still in the hospital, following surgery he ended up needing to remove the lodged bullet, we were an informant down.

We hadn't even heard if Vinnie had come back to the club after Darien was killed, but we knew it would only be a matter of time before we needed to hunt for him. He was too dangerous to simply let go, but one thing I believed was that he was definitely at a disadvantage now Darien was gone.

This last week, the nights at La Tanière had been busier than ever. And as Lexi was with the girls on the nights I wasn't needed at the club, Axel would run the show with Elliot, and I headed back to stay at my house.

The apartment seemed like it was missing its soul without Lexi, and I never realised how her presence really affected the place.

The small bar we'd chosen to hang out this evening was completely dead except for a couple of customers lounging by the jukebox and a bar worker lazily polishing glasses with an old rag.

Everyone was doing their own thing tonight so Elliot, Axel and I decided to shoot a bit of pool and just chill, something it seemed like we hadn't done in fucking forever. Chaos seemed to reign my fucking life at the minute.

I took my turn to break before handing the cue to Elliot.

"There's been no sign of life at Scarlet at all this week, we need to be on our guard, something doesn't feel right."

I nodded, things had been extremely quiet on Vinnie De La Hoy's side since we got the girls out of the club. Too quiet. Part of me considered if it would have been better after all to attack when we knew Vinnie would be there and take him down with Darien. But with the amount of security he has, and would have had with him, I knew we would have been outnumbered and the chance of getting all the girls out alive would have been significantly slimmer. At least by attacking while he was away, we had the best chance of executing our plan while security was at its minimum.

"We'll keep watching, without Darien things are going to be a lot harder for Vinnie. He has nothing left at the club."

"He'll move on," said Elliot. "Find another psychopath to do business with, take more girls."

"Then we kill him." Axel interrupts between swigs of his beer bottle. "Now we have the girls out safely there's nothing stopping us from putting a bullet straight between his eyes... or having a bit of fun with him first." He winks, using his knife to pick his teeth. *Animal.*

"He's a dead man walking," I reassure Elliot. "He'll be dealt with in due time."

My phone buzzed in the back pocket of my jeans.
I checked the text which was from the interior designers sorting out the apartment at the Hive for Lexi. The place was all finished and ready for her to move in.

I swallowed hard, my mouth dry despite the beer I'd been drinking.

I should have been ecstatic, hell a few weeks ago I would have been. The thought of getting the apartment back to how it was before. No more finding bras around the living room or searching for one of my work shirts, only to find a hot, little redhead wearing it as a dress that barely covers her perfectly shaped ass, making my dick hard while she makes breakfast, listening to some god awful nineties boy band music blasting from the radio. Yep definitely how I wanted it to go back to. *Fuck! Was I miserable that the time had come for her to move out? What a fucking chump!*

"How about we take a trip over to Scarlet this evening, see what's going down?" said Axel.

"We could drive that way back I guess."

Axel and Elliot nodded. I suppose it wouldn't hurt just to take a quick look.

After a couple more rounds of pool we jumped into Axel's *Audi* and headed a few blocks up from the bar to where Scarlet was situated.

As we rounded the corner, I wasn't prepared for the sight before us. I wound down the tinted glass window.

The place had been completely boarded up and left derelict.

"He's gone." said Axel, staring at the empty building. "Guess now Darien's gone, he didn't want to hang around."

"Hhmm." I squinted at the club, suspicion flowing through my bones. This all seemed a bit too straight forward. "What about Lexi? He didn't even try and make contact with her again after the Feast of Fire."

Axel shrugged. "Maybe he realised he didn't want to be in her life after all, he never wanted to be in her life before did he?"

"So why give her that fucking locket?"

"You don't know Vinnie De La Hoy, and things are never that straightforward with him. He took our girls to send a message, that much was clear," said Elliot. "By the looks of things he has left town, so for now we just need to keep our wits about us and hope he's realised messing with the Mackenzie's was the wrong move."

Winding up the window, I sat back in my seat as Axel drove us back to La Tanière. At least for the time being I could focus on the little siren, and that was definitely what I intended to do this evening... and put to bed a little problem that was still playing on my mind.

CHAPTER FORTY TWO

Lexi

Receiving the text message to say that I now had my very own apartment at the Hive was both surreal and bittersweet.

I had to admit, as much as I had hated the thought of living with Alaric before, I'd actually grown used to having the grumpy asshole around. Who would I have to piss off in the mornings now?

This last week had pretty much been a blur and I'd only seen Alaric or Axel in passing in their offices or hauled up in a booth with Elliot, heads down, deep in concentration regarding god knows what.

I knew things were still pretty tense between us.
So many people had faced hell because of Vinnie, but I was pissed off that Al had taken his frustrations out on me.

The message I'd received about my new home had stated that I could move in as early as tomorrow so there was no point beating around the bush. I decided to get back to Als apartment and pack up my stuff, ready to get settled into my brand new place at the Hive tomorrow.

Walking into the apartment, the tension in the air was thick and potent. I could hear Axel in his room and Al was sitting on the sofa, his legs parted, elbows resting on his knees. His dress shirt was untucked and the top three buttons undone. His hair, a little ruffled. He looked like he'd had a rough day but my god he was the picture of perfection.

He ran his calloused fingers over the sharp curves of his jaw and I swallowed hard as the memories of those fingers over every inch of my body sent shock waves through my veins.

"I take it you heard about my leaving."

He turned his head to look at me with those gorgeous grey eyes.

"I heard."

His face remained stoic as always, as I walked towards my room, *god it drove me mad that I couldn't read him.* I was growing fed up with this constant mask.

"Well I guess I should go and pack. The maintenance guy said I should be good to move in from tomorrow."

He remained silent as I turned to walk, but was suddenly halted by a warm hand grasping mine.

I turned to see Alaric standing before me, his eyes seductively hooded and the intensity of his gaze burning through my skin.

I kept telling myself that my body was immune to him, but the way the heat began rushing between my legs with only a stare confirmed that that was complete and utter bullshit.

"So I became aware of a little problem recently that I thought we should probably clear up." His voice was like gravel and he ground his teeth as he spoke.

My breathing accelerated as I tried to form words clearly that were lodged in my dry throat.

"And what would this problem be then?"

He smiled wickedly, a telling smirk that revealed I was in for a world of pleasure... or possibly pain.

A muscle flexed in his jaw as he stalked forward just an inch.

"My brother seems to believe he's in love with you."

I glanced quickly between Axel's bedroom door and back to Alaric's gorgeous smoky eyes in surprise.

Suddenly Axel exited his bedroom and stared straight at us. I could tell from the look on his face that he knew exactly what we were discussing.

"Personally I think it's just the thought of being with someone that appeals to him now, I suppose there's only so long you can fuck around, hey bro?!"

Axel grins mischievously over at his brother. I wasn't sure if what Alaric was saying was true, if that's really what Axel believed, but I could tell they were getting some fucked up kick out of this game and seeing my reaction.

I wasn't about to give them the satisfaction of seeing me squirm. No, I intended to take full control of this situation.

Releasing Alaric's hand, I turned to where Axel was standing, tugging the hair tie from my ponytail letting my thick waves of auburn hair tumble down my back.

I swayed my hips gently as I prowled towards Axel and placed a finger on his bare chest, gently stroking it down the painfully hot indentations of his shirtless torso.

"Well if you're not sure if what you're feeling is real, maybe we need to do a little…experiment."

Axel's eyebrows rose as lust glittered in his beautiful eyes. The same eyes that matched the ones of his brother who was standing merely feet away, his laboured breaths audible. Was he jealous? He was definitely reacting in *some* way that was for sure.

I looked over my shoulder to see Alaric frozen to the spot. His expression, stony and cruel. A muscle feathered in his hard jaw.

My head was screaming at me to stop, to turn back to Al and abandon this crazy idea but my heart told me to continue, to take what my body was craving in this moment.

Axel's hands instinctively slipped onto my hips, squeezing gently and I expected Alaric at this point to put a stop to it, to switch to the possessive, dominating alphahole that I knew he was inside, but he didn't. He did nothing, just watched with ice in his gaze until I glanced at him again and noticed that the chill had been replaced with something else, something animalistic and feral. A pure look of starvation.

He stalked towards where I was standing as Axel pulled me into his firm body. I slammed against his solid chest, my hands crashing against the smooth, flawless skin of his pecs.

Alaric came up behind me, caging me between himself and Axel. His large hands sliding over the curves of my ass cheeks over my leggings, squeezing roughly.

He leaned into my ear from behind, so close I could feel the warmth of his breath grazing my skin and sending goosebumps down the back of my neck.

"Be careful how you tread little Siren, I've told you before I don't like to share my things." He looked up to Axel who was standing with a smirk on his handsome face. "But he is my brother and I'll allow him this moment to help him realise what it is he really feels for my possessions."

He continued to caress my ass while Axel unhooked the buttons on my shirt, sliding it over my shoulders to expose my braless tits, heavy and aching with need.

"Fuck!" Axel sighed, staring at my bare chest and flat stomach. "You are perfection, I could actually come just staring at you."

Adrenaline kicked into my body and I felt like my skin was charged with electricity as Alaric reached around cupping my tits in his large, masculine palms and kneading them. The rough skin of his fingers slid over the most sensitive parts of my nipple as a whimper escaped my throat.

Axel slid his fingers into the waistband of my leggings and tugged them down to my ankles where I shrugged them off, standing in nothing but my little red thong.

Then, without warning, they were both on me like starved lions fighting over a single carcass.

I stood between them, throwing my head back as they both began to kiss, lick and bite my shoulders, collarbone, and neck. Axel in front of me and Alaric behind. The feel of both their hands touching, feeling, exploring my body made liquid heat surge between my thighs until I could feel the dampness pooling inside my thong.

Axel took one of my nipples into his mouth, sucking hard as Alaric's fingers snaked around my hips sliding straight into my thong. He began rubbing slow, tortuous circles over my clit until

I was struggling to keep myself standing as my legs turned to jelly.

Axel released my nipple with a wet pop.

"Tell me how wet she is for us brother," said Axel. A breathy laugh came from Alaric's mouth, the light sound vibrating against my skin as he continued kissing my shoulder from behind.

"My little siren is soaking for us. She's going to be a good girl and let us use her however we see fit."

Alaric's words released what felt like a thousand butterflies swarming around my stomach as my skin pebbled beneath his touch.

I moaned softly as Al pushed me further into Axel, his erection pressing into the naked flesh of my groin through his jeans. *Jesus, he was just as huge as Alaric.*

Axel began walking backwards towards his bed, guiding me with him by my hips as Alaric followed.

He dropped onto his back on the bed, propping himself up on his elbows.

"See how sweet this little pussy is," said Alaric from behind, and without warning he ripped the red thong clean off my body, leaving me fully exposed.

The feeling of both of their eyes on me, gave me a confidence I never thought I had. The need in their gaze made me feel desired and powerful and at that moment I knew I had two kings on their knees, completely at my mercy.

Axel unbuttoned his jeans, freeing his long, hard erection. My pupils dilated at the sight and my mouth salivated as I went to lean towards him.

"No!" Alaric's voice was sharp and commanding. "Your mouth is mine, he only gets you here." His fingers slid down my abdomen and between my slick folds, hovering at my entrance before impaling me with his long, thick finger. I shuddered a breathy moan at the delicious intrusion.

Alaric began to fuck me with his finger, bringing it in and out of my wet heat as my hips bucked with his rhythm, then he entered a second and the intoxicating feeling of fullness made me cry out.

"Jesus, she sounds so good when she sings for us," Axel panted as he took his cock in his palm and began rubbing up and down the thick shaft.

Alaric retreated his fingers and placed a hand flat between my shoulder blades before pressing me down towards where Axel remained on the bed. I followed his direction, crawling onto all fours on the bed until my face hovered above Axels' as I straddled him, our lips barely sweeping against each other.

His hand brushed the side of my cheek, disappearing behind my neck as he pulled me in for a kiss. It began gently, his tongue teasing mine, in smooth, caressing strokes before the hunger inside me began to take over and I pressed into his mouth taking all that I could. He shrugged off the rest of his jeans until he was completely naked and I took his hard cock into my hand, pumping firmly as he groaned in pleasure.

I looked over my shoulder to see Alaric watching us with hooded eyes as he began to remove his shirt and jeans. The sight of him ignited more fire inside me and I stared in awe at this man's devastatingly beautiful form before me, while I continued to tease his brother's cock.

Just the sight of Alaric alone did more to me than any man could ever do with his touch and I wanted him inside me, claiming me, more than anything.

As I released Axel's cock, he began grinding his hips against my sweet spot as I continued looking over my shoulder at Al.

"Alaric, touch me... please," I begged desperately as Axel's thrusts created devastating friction between my thighs.

Alaric grinned as he rubbed his finger down the crack of my ass while I straddled Axel, and again pushed me forward until my ass and pussy were on show before him. He rubbed my clit from behind.

"Such a needy little cunt, my siren has."

I groaned again at his filthy words.

"Please, I need to come." I squirmed against Alaric's teasing fingers.

"You hear that brother, she wants to come," said Axel, licking my breast that was dangling straight over his mouth.

"She'll come when I allow it," barked Alaric. His voice was cold as steel.

Axel gripped the back of my hair, dragging my lips to his in a rough, punishing kiss as I felt Alaric bend towards me, his tongue spearing straight into my pussy. I cried out against Axel's lips as he swallowed every one of my moans.

Axel worked his fingers back onto my clit in hard circles, the pressure making the pleasure border on the side of pain. I squeezed my eyes shut as Axel then reached around, squeezing my ass cheeks, holding me in place while Alaric feasted on my pussy.

Just before I felt like I was going to come, Al pulled away and Axel's rough hands gripped the meat at my hips, lining my entrance up above his cock.

I felt Alaric's palm glide down my back as Axel lowered me down onto his solid, throbbing erection, impaling me in one thrust until he was fully seated to the hilt.

I cried out in surprise as his cock filled me to the brim and my body squirmed to adjust around his sheer size. *Fuck he was almost as big as his brother.*

He started to move inside me as Al grabbed my hips from the back and started to move me in time with Axel's thrusts. The pleasure began to build between my legs and in my stomach as we got into a harmonious rhythm. Our moans filling the air.

"Such a fucking tight little siren," grunted Axel. His head rolling back.

Suddenly Al lifted me from his brother, slamming his fingers back inside me. I cried out from the pain of being sore from just taking Axel's cock and then the sudden invasion of Alaric's fingers. He pulled back his hand, glistening in my arousal and placed me back onto Axel's throbbing cock. Confused, I began to grind my hips again until I felt Alarics fingers spreading the slickness he's just retrieved from my pussy along the crack of my ass.

Pressing me down until my chest was flush with Axels', I heard him spit and felt the trail of warm saliva run between my ass cheeks and land perfectly onto my arsehole. I knew exactly what was going to happen as Al rubbed the lubrication around my tight forbidden hole.

I'd only ever been touched there once and it was during the horror of what I'd experienced at the hands of Anton, I flinched at Alaric's touch.

As if sensing exactly how I was feeling, he ran his fingers through the back of my long, flowing hair and leaned over to whisper into my ear again.

"I'm going to take you here." He glided his finger over my arsehole again. "Show me, little siren. Take back what he stole from you, what they all did."

My hesitation eased as I nodded and with that he began to slide the tip slowly into my ass.

I inhaled sharply as he continued to push himself into me.

"Breathe Siren," he whispered as he continued on, pushing past the ring of tight muscle and finally burying himself in my ass right to the hilt.

Once he'd given my body time to adjust, he began to move in sync with Axels thrusts. The fullness of the double penetration sent shock waves through my body as the three of us moved in tandem.

I panted as their grunts became louder and more feral and soon, what started out as a slow rhythm became desperate and selfish as they both slammed into me with force, taking what they needed from my body, and it was the most intense and liberating feeling I'd ever experienced.

I desperately wanted to feel them both pulsing and coming inside me at the same time.

A few more thrusts and I came, screaming into Axel's chest. My orgasm crashing through me like tidal waves against the rocks, shaking me to my core.

I slammed my eyes shut as stars danced behind my eyelids

with the force of my release.

A second later, Axel drove up into me with force that jolted my whole body as he roared his release while Alaric continued the assault on my backside, gripping a handful of hair in his palm and tilting my head around towards him so his lips could meet mine in a passionately hot, messy kiss, with tongues tangling and moaning exchanged. With one final thrust he came deep inside my ass, his roar radiating through my lips as I kept my head turned towards him.

Exhausted and completely sated I dropped onto Axel's strong, sweat licked body as Alaric pulled out of me from behind. I winced at the withdrawal as he flopped down onto the bed beside me.

Lifting myself from where I was connected to Axel, I lay down next to Alaric, my thighs sticky with his and his brother's seed.

The three of us laid there silently in peace, but part of me worried about the consequences of the actions we'd just taken.

Axel was the first to move, standing from the bed and grabbing a towel from the chair in the corner of his room.

He wrapped it around his waist before turning to me, leaning down to lower his forehead to mine.

"Thank you," he whispered before kissing my cheek and retreating to the bathroom.

I laid still next to Alaric, our breathing slowly regulating until I felt his fingers entwine with mine, sending my breathing ragged once more.

He raised himself onto his side as I turned to face him.

"That was the one and only time I share, Siren." His fingers lightly stroked my cheek.

I nodded, looking innocently into those pools of smoky grey. Then his full, supple lips brushed against mine in a gentle, feather light kiss.

In that moment there was no greed, no urgency, no battle for domination, just the two of us, sinking into each other, wrapped in a perfect bubble of bliss... and love.

CHAPTER FORTY THREE

Lexi

"What if she's not ready to see me yet?" Nerves coiled in my stomach and I felt like at any second my breakfast was about to make a reappearance.

"Havencroft has assured me your mother is making steady but positive progress. I think it's about time you made that visit."

Alaric straightened his black silk tie against the crisp white of his shirt as I fastened up the last of the buttons on my cream midi dress.

Today was the day that I was supposed to be leaving the Mackenzie brothers' apartment and moving into my new home at the Hive. But that plan had been pushed back one more day, as Alaric had surprised me this morning with a visiting pass for my mother, who was still recovering in Havencroft rehab.

I was both thrilled and nervous when I'd been presented with the pass as I desperately missed and wanted to see her, but I was also worried about whether or not she actually wanted to see me. I was terrified that there would be any hindrance to her progress. However, I trusted Alaric and if he felt now was a good time to visit my mum, then that was exactly what I was going to do.

I clutched the heart shaped locket that I'd received the night of the Feast of Fire from Vinnie, tightly in my palm. Today would be the perfect time to confront my mum about my father, but something inside told me that I couldn't risk anything that might send her spiralling back into addiction.

I set the locket back on my bedside table, leaving the room and closing the door. Vinnie and his identity would remain locked in that room for now, today was about me and mum and no one else.

As soon as we were ready, Alaric escorted me outside. I assumed he was taking me to meet Demitri or Jax, who would be travelling with me to the rehab facility, but as soon as we got to the front doors I saw Alaric's Porsche parked up on the curb.

"You're coming with me?" I looked at him in surprise.

"Of course I am, I wouldn't let you go alone, even with Demitri or Jax."

I couldn't help the smile forming on my face. "Thank you... for helping her."

When he looked at me, I couldn't determine whether that mask he hid behind was back in place or he was going to show me the real him again, then he spoke.

"I didn't do this for the lowlife junkie who bore you, I'm not my uncle."

His words stung, I couldn't pretend they didn't.

My gaze dropped to the floor until I felt his fingers brush underneath my chin, lifting my head.

"I did this for you. Only for you."

He leaned down and planted a soft kiss on my lips before opening the car door and letting me in.

The drive to Havencroft seemed longer than I imagined it would be. We travelled down country lanes and by fields littered with wildflowers until we arrived at the grand, old building.

I'd pictured the place to be very modern with almost a clinical feel, but this was more like someone's home. Pretty gardens surrounded the large premises and as soon as Alaric and I entered the doors, I could sense the welcoming, homely feel to the place. It was definitely somewhere I would have wanted my mum to be.

We approached the reception desk where a small, dark haired woman was typing on her computer.

She lifted her head to greet us, looking twice as her small, jade green eyes met Alarics'. Her cheeks flushed a brighter shade of pink. *Of course they did, not a fucking woman alive could control the way their body reacted to* that *face.*

"Mr Mackenzie," she stuttered, straightening her blouse and playing with the curls in her hair. "What a surprise."

I rolled my eyes at the blatant flirting.

"Hello Pearl, we're here to see Miss Power if she's ready?"

Pearl stood from her chair and walked around the desk towards us. She headed straight to Alaric without even giving me a single glance.

"This way."

We followed down a long corridor, I noticed how everything appeared so immaculately clean and tidy.

Eventually we arrived in a large room, almost like a Georgian sitting room, with a large, pink velour chair in the corner.

My mum was sitting in the chair, staring out through the floor to ceiling window in front of her into the large garden which contained a pretty, stone fountain in the centre.

She was wearing jeans and a large blue knitted cardigan, wrapped tightly around her body despite the sweltering temperatures of the room.

Alaric held back with Pearl while I approached my mother with caution until I was standing right next to her chair. She didn't move so much as an inch.

"Mama?"

Tears stung the backs of my eyes as I looked at her, still glaring out of the window.

She looked the best she'd looked in as long as I could

remember. She'd gained weight on her petite frame and there was a slight colour to her usually pale white complexion.

Carefully I sat on the chair next to where she was sitting and finally she turned her head towards me.

"Hi mama," I said quietly. I couldn't stop the tears from falling at that moment as they rolled down my cheeks and onto my lips. I could taste the salt of my sorrow.

"Lexi?"

It was as if she'd only just recognised me. Her lips curled up at the sides in an attempt at a smile but then the tears began to fall until she was sobbing, her palms pushed into the hollows of her eyes.

I inhaled sharply to regain my composure as I slipped an arm around her slender shoulder. She reached for me and for a few seconds, I had no idea how long, we held each other. Neither one of us saying a word.

When her tears began to subside, I sat back in the chair holding her fragile hand.

"How have you been?"

She glared at me with confusion on her face.

"I didn't know where you were. Some men...they came and took me from my house. There was shouting and banging and then I ended up here."

She looked around the room as if she was still trying to decipher where she was.

"You're in rehab mama, it's the best place for you. Have they been good to you here?"

My heart was breaking with every word I was saying. I struggled to control the quiver in my voice.

"They've been amazing," she answered.

Relief flooded my body as I smiled.

She glanced over to where Alaric was now standing. I hadn't noticed that Pearl had already left.

"I haven't seen you but he..." she pointed to Al, "He told me you were safe and he visited me often. Even brought me some of those butterscotch sweets that I like."

I turned to Alaric who glanced away, clearing his throat. He'd been visiting my mother, caring for the *lowlife junkie* as he called her. All this time I'd disliked him and he'd done his best to make sure I saw no emotion from him, and he was coming here and caring for someone who he had no obligation to. Maybe he was more like Elliot than he'd care to admit.

It was at that point that I realised, that even though I was forced to stay at La Tanière, it was all for the best cause possible and seeing how much my mum was benefiting from the care here, made me realise that I would never do anything to jeopardise that.

I turned back to my mum. "I'm so glad you've been okay. I've missed you so much."

She looked at me for a second. Her eyes sparkling with more tears before she started to sob again.

"I'm so sorry Lexi. I'm so sorry I wasn't the mother you needed, the mother you deserved. I couldn't manage, I was so lost. I wish I could start again. Show you how much I wanted to be that mother for you."

My face reddened with more hot tears as we sat together, our hands tightly entangled.

"It's okay mum, it's okay, because when you get out of here, you're going to be better and we're going to start again. Me and you. We can have that perfect life."

She nodded and lowered her head, keeping a firm grip on my hands and I realised just how much I had the Mackenzies to thank for. How different my life would have been if I hadn't met Alaric, and that thought, all of a sudden terrified me.

Saying goodbye to my mum after our visit was bittersweet. We hugged, we kissed, there were more tears but I promised I'd come for another visit soon.

I left with my heart heavier but my shoulders lighter after seeing the difference this place was making to her health and well-being. She was right where she needed to be at this moment in time.

Alaric strode around the Porsche, opening the passenger side door for me.

I hesitated. "Thank you."

The words flew from my mouth before I even knew what I was saying. All I felt after today was gratitude. No one had done anything even remotely as nice for me as what this man standing before me had.

"I never knew you were visiting my mum."

He looked at me, his lips parting slightly, dampening them with his tongue and that simple movement alone was enough to coax a shiver through my body.

He looked like he was about to say something but then changed direction at the last minute.

"You're welcome." The words came out softly as we stared at each other for the briefest of moments, which felt like an eternity in my mind, before I broke our eye contact and jumped into the car.

CHAPTER FORTY FOUR

Alaric

Rolling over, my eyes were met by the breathtaking beauty splayed out before me.

Last night after getting back from Havencroft to see her mother, Lexi and I had spent the evening packing her belongings, then deep in conversation on my bed before I wrapped her slender body in my arms and she'd fallen asleep.

It was something I'd never done with another woman before. The only time a woman was in my bed was to fuck and even then there was no emotion, no attachment.

Last night was different. If someone had said that I would be laying on my bed *talking* to a woman and then falling asleep without so much as a kiss, I would have said they'd lost their fucking brain, but that's exactly what happened and neither us wanted or pushed for more.

I lay watching the gentle rise and fall of her breasts, her adorable soft snores coming from those sweet, full lips, and the way that mass of silky red hair fanned out across my pillow. I wouldn't even call her a queen, she was too perfect for that, a goddess was the only way I could describe that beauty.

She twitched and gently opened those beautiful eyes, one

brown and one blue, a content smile on her flawless face.

"Good morning." I gently leaned over and kissed her forehead.

"Good morning Mr Mackenzie. It seems you're getting into quite the habit of watching me sleep."

I chuckled. "Watching you sleep is one of my favourite pastimes."

She smiled sweetly, hooking her arm over my waist.

"I need to get everything together for the move."

I nodded. I knew she needed her own space but it was secretly killing me to let her move out. I knew in the end however, it would be the best for both of us.

"I have a few things to take care of today but I'll help as much as I can. Axel will be around some of the time today so I'm sure he'll pitch in too."

She smiled. "Thank you…for everything."

Things seemed to be a lot more chilled at the club since Scarlet permanently closed its doors.

The only one who seemed still on edge was Elliot but I sensed that was because he knew Vinnie better than anyone and was anticipating his return.

I kept myself on guard for it but I wasn't worried. He'd lost Darien and a pack of his heavies, so he was significantly weaker than he was before.

Lexi seemed happy to have her own space when Axel and I helped her take her stuff up to her new apartment at the Hive. The place was bright and spacious and I made sure the bathroom was filled with those little shitty moisturiser things she likes. *Fucking women!*

"This is amazing Al."

Lexi skipped over wrapping her arms around me, squeezing like a little kid. I hated to admit it but it was fucking adorable. My arms wrapped around her tiny waist, hugging her back.

Axel emptied out some of the boxes we'd brought up to the apartment.

Since the time we'd all participated in our little *'experiment'* things had improved between myself and Axel and even between Axel and Lexi. I fucking loved my brother and I had no idea he wanted to stop fucking around and settle down. I was glad he realised his infatuation with Lexi was purely him wanting the connection I had with her, but it left me wondering what it was that was going on between us.

Axel and Lexi laughed as they organised the boxes in Lexi's room. If any guy so much as smiled at her I'd have torn his throat out, but I didn't feel that way with Axel. He was my brother above all else and loyalty ran in our blood.

"I'm gonna split, got some bits to take care of but can probably help out later," said Axel, grabbing his leather jacket from the sofa.

"Sure thing, thanks bro."

He headed out of the door leaving me and Lexi alone.

I walked over to where she was standing, her back to me as she emptied out some bits from one of the boxes onto the table. I slid my hands around her waist,
leaning round to speak into her ear.

"I have some things to take care of too, you gonna be alright for a while?"

She stilled, I felt her body tense before she turned to face me.

"Al…" The words seem lodged in her throat. She swallowed and looked up at me under that fan of pitch black eyelashes. "I want to come with you."

I squinted my eyes in confusion.

"I want to come with you, on a kill."

My eyes lifted, almost reaching my forehead.

She continued staring at me innocently, her white teeth gently gnawing on her plump bottom lip.

I wanted to take that lip between my own teeth.

"Why would you want to do that?"

Her tempting mouth curved up in a half smile.

"I want to see what you do, I want to know how it feels, to have the power to end someone, to know the world is free of one more piece of shit."

A shocked chuckle left my throat.

So my little siren wasn't as pure and innocent as I had her down as. I looked into those painfully exotic eyes and a flash of savage hunger caught my gaze. All along I'd thought I was the one who would be doing the corrupting but something confirmed to me, in that moment, that there was definitely a darkness in this little princess that she kept buried well. A wolf lurking under the ruse of a lamb.

"If that's what my little siren wants, then that's what my little siren will get."

Her smirk lifted to a full smile, brightening her face and showing all her beautifully straight, white teeth.

I had intended to take care of a particular task today, and this one would be the perfect job for my little siren to accompany me on.

CHAPTER FORTY FIVE

Lexi

Something squeezed in my gut as Alaric unlocked the large bolts and chains leading to the basement of La Tanière.

I'd heard the rumours of a sound proof basement from Leon and Morgan, but I was yet to see if this story was true.

I ached to go with Al and see what his work entailed. But after letting him convince me that it was simply too dangerous to just *tag along* on a hit, I agreed to join him on a job that he had told me was *personal* to him.

Opening the large iron door, I was surprised but not horrified at what lay before me.

A man stretched out vertically in the middle of the room. He was chained by his wrists in rusty shackles hanging from the ceiling. His feet barely touched the floor putting all the pressure on his arms. I winced at the thought of how uncomfortable he must be. He was gagged and blindfolded and completely naked.

Rio and Sully entered the room behind us and closed the heavy door.

I felt Alaric drift up behind me, his breath fell on the back of my neck and I froze.

"This one's for you Siren," he whispered, nodding towards where the man was standing.

I walked towards him, sliding the blindfold from his eyes. He glared at me with instant recognition, but instead of seeing fear, I saw nothing but anger and hate.

He looked nothing like the polished aristocrat I'd set eyes on that night in Scarlet, with his designer suit and slicked back hair. This man looked almost feral.

I removed the gag from his mouth, a trail of saliva dripping from the rag.

"Hello Michael, how's the tongue?"

He glared at me, snarling, his teeth bared like a wild animal.

"Well if it isn't my little bitch Andromeda."

He spat the words at me, struggling to pronounce them and letting me know that my punishment at Scarlet had left its mark.

Alaric walked beside me, staring at Michael.

"Now, you don't know me," he began, "but I know you very well Michael, or should I say Jean - Miklaus Denova. Known for your help and contributions towards various sexual and domestic violence charities. Quiet ironic really considering you attempted to rape my girl here."

Alaric gestures towards me as Michael continues to snarl in my direction.

"Now before we begin I was hoping you could tell me where the fuck Vincenzo De La Hoy has disappeared to? His absence has become a little concerning to me."

Michael scoffed at Alaric's words.

"No? Ok well just to enlighten you on your current predicament, I had Rio and Sully here take you from your cozy little meeting last night. I'd been doing a little research of my own as I saw first hand what kind of man you are, and imagine my surprise when I uncovered even more of your little secrets."

Michael glared at Sully as if realising for the first time he wasn't the predator he'd pretended to be that night at Scarlet.

My breath hitched and I stood frozen to the spot as I watched Alaric begin to circle Michael like a beautiful, powerful vulture.

"So it came to my attention that your little shopping trip to Scarlet, the night you met my beautiful siren here, wasn't the first time you'd attended such a thing. In fact I'm now aware that you've purchased four women over the course of a year, isn't that right?"

Michael remained silent as Alaric unbuckled his belt, sliding it through the rings of his trousers and folding it in half.

Blood raced through my ears as I braced myself for what was about to happen.

"What's wrong Michael? Don't want to answer?"

Faced with yet more silence, Alaric's eyes turn wild, his fists clenched, body shaking in rage as he lifts the belt and brings it down, buckle first, on Michaels cock with a sickening crack. The sound startles me so much my body jolts.

The blood curdling scream pierces the air and my body breaks out in chills as I continue to watch in silence.

"Was that a yes, Michael?"

Michael whimpers, his body trembling. Alaric lifts the belt again.

"Yes…yes," Michael cries, he thrashes against his restraints.

"Well done. So four women purchased in one year and where exactly are they now Michael? See I've been made aware that you have friends on the right side of the law. Friends who were able to quash any suspicion when human remains were found on your land."

Alaric laughs, throwing his head back but it's completely void of any humour. Instead the laugh is laced with sinister intent.

"How strange, isn't it Michael?! That despite the fact human remains were found on your premises, female nonetheless, you are still out here, walking around, looking for your next victim."

This time he didn't give Michael a chance to answer anything before he brought the belt down in another chilling crack.

More screams filled the air as Alaric shoves the old rag back into Michael's mouth to muffle the cries. He then turned towards Rio and Sully.

"Leave us." He ordered. They both exited the room now, leaving me alone with only Alaric and Michael.

"Look at her." Alaric walks over to me, his eyes filled with danger and lust as he grips me at the back of my neck and pulls me to him. "So beautiful, no wonder you wanted to fuck her that night at Scarlet."

He moves his hand from my neck to my jaw, pressing his thumb against my bottom lip to open me up and sliding it inside.

I caressed his digit with my tongue, tasting salt and sin as I stared into those intoxicating pools of grey.

"Maybe I should show you what you missed."

With that he pulls his thumb from my mouth and replaces it with the force of his lips. Kissing me brutally and owning every part of me as our tongues tangle in a fierce, passionate dance.

It felt like he was drowning and I was the air he so desperately craved. He was like a mad man. I swallow a gravelly moan that escapes his mouth as he slides his hands under my ass, gripping tightly and lifting me from the ground.

My legs automatically wrap around his strong waist as he carries me to the edge of the room, right within Michael's direct eyeline.

"Put your hands against the wall." He commands, dropping me to my feet and spinning me round until I'm facing away from him, my back flush against his broad, solid chest, kicking my legs open wide with his foot. He begins to claw at the hem of my dress.

I'd worn a slinky, orange mini dress today that hugged every one of my slender curves and showed them off to their full potential.

It didn't take long for that dress to be hoisted up around my waist, my bare ass and pussy on show as I'd chosen to go without underwear today.

"Such a dirty little slut," he grunts, sliding his calloused palm over my arse cheek, before raising his hand and bringing it down in a merciless slap.

I cried out in shock at the burn, hearing a dark chuckle behind me.

Alaric grabs my hips. His fingers digging in so roughly, I know he's going to leave marks as he lines himself up at my warm, wet entrance before thrusting up through my arousal and impaling me on his huge, rock solid length.

He hisses through clenched teeth as my eyes squeeze shut, trying frantically to adjust to the size that I'll never seem to be prepared for.

"Oh Michael, if only you knew how amazing this hot, tight cunt feels right now."

He taunts his prisoner as he thrusts inside me, hard and deep, over and over again. The sound of skin on skin as his hips slap against my arse cheeks.

Our collated moans bounce off the walls and it's all I can hear besides the tortured groans of Michael, who can do nothing but watch helplessly as Alaric slams into me with hard, pounding thrusts.

He bites down on my shoulder as I cry out at the sensation, my orgasm building deep inside my core. Then he reaches around and all of a sudden his fingers are on me, massaging my clit as I gasp for air.

"Al, I'm going to come," I pant, as he continues to rut and claim.

"You hear that Michael, she's going to come and it's going to be all over my cock. God she feels so fucking good."

He lifts the hand still fingering me and brings it down, slapping my clit so hard and then again until it pushes me over the edge. Bright specks of light flash behind my eyelids and I come with a scream as he thrusts harder while I ride out my release, panting heavily and dripping down his cock.

"FUCK!" With a final roar he follows. I feel him pulse deep inside me, his hot cum flooding my cunt as I clench, milking every last drop.

He collapses against me, pushing me flush against the wall. My sweat slicked cheek sticking to the cool concrete before he slips out of me, zipping up his trousers.

I turned, thoroughly sated, to see Michael staring. His eyes threatened a fate worse than death. Shame he'll never get to carry it out.

I tug down my dress and smooth my fingers through my sex tousled hair before going to stand beside Al, who's now looking straight at Michael.

"Well now we've got that out of our system…" Alaric's hand goes to where his gun is strapped to his hip and I knew he planned to finish this here and now.

"Wait!" My hand instinctively shot out, halting Al before he reached the gun. "This one belongs to me."

A dark smirk curled on those luscious lips as he retreated his hand, allowing me to take over.

I turned to look Michael straight in the eye.

"I've known men like you my whole life." The words came out clear and assertive and I even surprised myself by how calm and confident I felt. I began to stalk forwards and backwards as I spoke.

"They take, they hurt, they destroy and nothing ever happens to them." I spot a broken bottle lying in pieces on one of the tattered shelves. "Whether it be pimps praying on defenceless women drowning in addiction,"

I reached the shelf, picking up a large shard of broken glass, gripping so tightly that the jagged edges severed into my palm. "Or billionaires who allow innocent women to be taken from their homes, so they can be sold like cattle." I walk back to where Michael is chained, standing before him. "You're all the same, and you all deserve to die."

He scoffed behind his gag as violence sears through my veins. I rip the rag from his mouth.

"Anything you'd like to say?"

He throws back his head, spitting in my face, the vile liquid hitting my cheek.

I see Alaric tense from the corner of my eye. Turning my head, I hold up my hand to signal to him to be still. He stops in his tracks as I turn back to Micheal.

"Go to hell," he grunts, eyes flashing with pure evil.

I lean in, the smell of stale sweat invading my nostrils as I whisper into his ear.

"Oh don't worry I will… and I'll see you there."

Potent adrenaline and rage flow within me and I steer my arm around, driving the shard of broken glass straight into the side of his neck before dragging it across and slitting his throat wide open.

His eyes bulge as choking and gurgling sounds vibrate from his mouth and blood pours from the gaping wound, pooling at my feet.

Alaric comes to stand beside me as we watch Micheal bleed out in front of us. His body twitches for a few seconds before he goes completely limp.

I drop the glass to the floor like it's scalding me.   Shaking, I bring my blood-covered hands to my face, blood from the man whose life I've just ended.

Alaric grips me by the wrists, pulling me into the warmth and safety of his arms. There he holds me until it feels like all my broken shards are sticking back together.

"You did good babe." He sighed as he kissed the top of my head.

I hesitated, breathing in and out, waiting for the guilt to arrive or the horror of the realisation of what I'd done
to kick in, but neither came. I didn't care that Michael was dead. There was one less murdering rapist in the world, and I was glad.

CHAPTER FORTY SIX

Lexi

Music roared through the building, almost raising the roof right off of its foundations. The bass pounded through my body like a second heartbeat as I stared around the club from the balcony, seeing La Tanière come alive in all its splendour.

After leaving the basement yesterday, I felt like a different person. I'd been given the control back, and the power and the feeling was incredible. The way my body responded to what had happened scared me and made me wonder if there had been a darkness in me that had been lying dormant.

However it was performance night at the club, and rather than being my usual nervous self, I was excited and dripping with confidence.

Donning my usual gold attire, I skipped down the staircase to go backstage and hang out with Morgan, Leon and Trinity.

Colt was finally on the mend and limping around like *Kevin Costner* in *The Bodyguard* and his relationship with Leon had become stronger than ever. I guess a live or die situation really makes people realise what it is that truly matters in life. Seeing Leon happy was the most amazing feeling.

Trinity was getting the help she needed and although she wasn't ready to just step back into her role at La Tanière, she came along to offer support to us all.

She'd opened up about a lot of the abuse her and the other girls had suffered at the hands of Vinnie and Darien, and I could only be thankful that at least one of them was dead. We hadn't got any more information out of Michael on Vinnies whereabouts, so that one was still a loose end for now. I knew the boys were working tirelessly to locate him.

Trinity had also been spending an unusual amount of time with Sully, and it didn't take a genius to notice the way he looked at her. He was like a little lovesick puppy and I swear it was obvious to everyone but Trinity.

Backstage, Morgan stood in a stunning floor length silver gown with spaghetti straps. Her hair in long, dark waves secured on one side with a sparkly clip shaped like a nightingale. She looked like a glamorous fifties movie star.

"You look incredible." I smiled.

"Thanks Lex, I'm performing my version of *Kodaline's 'Brother'* tonight. I'm so nervous."

I combed my fingers through the loose side of her silky hair.

"You're going to be amazing. When are you ever anything but amazing?"

Morgan's already pink cheeks flushed with heat.

"And you are the friend every girl needs." She grinned.

Leon approached with Trinity in tow, carrying what I assumed was alcohol for us.

"Hey lovely ladies," he handed me a small glass filled with clear liquid. "Sip of dutch courage?"

I sniffed the tumbler, the fumes of neat vodka stinging my nostrils.

"Paint stripper?" I laughed as he rolled his eyes, giving my shoulder a playful push.

I downed the glassful, winching as usual at the burn in my throat.

Trinity came forward, wrapping me in her slender arms.

Spending time with her at her apartment in the Hive had helped us form a close bond and I was sure that, like Morgan and

Leon, I now had another friend for life.

"Nice to see you girl," she chuckled. "I can't believe I'm back here seeing the show from the other side. God I've missed this."

I smiled, Leon handing her another one of his glasses filled with neat vodka.

As we carried on laughing and joking, the music switched to *Carry your throne* by *John Bellion* and the whole room stared in awe at the stage. Bright white strobe lights focusing on the centre.

Alaric headed onto the platform in just *those* tight leathers and no shirt. Two orbs of fire hanging from chains in each hand.

I would never get used to the sight of that powerful chest, muscles straining under taut skin and those abs!   The sight of the deep V trailing below the waistband of the leathers made the skin on my chest flush and my legs feel like they were made of marshmallow.

The way that man owns the crowd is the most mesmerising thing I've ever seen. The men whistle and roar along with the music and the women just stop and gawk as he makes an actual element bend and bow to his will. *Fuck it makes me horny!*

I spot Sapphire in her usual place at the other side of the stage, her cornflower eyes hungry and wide as she takes in the sight.

I know Sapph is in love with Al. That much is crystal clear and I don't want to be the one to cause anyone heartache, but these growing feelings I was experiencing for him were getting harder and harder to ignore, and I knew our relationship was taking a much deeper turn than just sex.

Sapphire continued to stare at Alaric as he moved like liquid across the stage, but his penetrating, wolf-like eyes were fixated on mine. Never breaking the intense stare even while performing with the scorching fire.

I grabbed another glass from where Leon was standing, not caring what was in it and threw it back. I hated the jealous pangs that seemed to infiltrate my body when I saw the way Sapphire looked at Al.

I guess their history together was tougher to just brush off than I imagined.

Maybe if the guy was more straightforward it would be a little easier. But all this possessive bullshit left me wondering what the fuck was actually happening and yesterday, with Michael, he'd called me *his girl.* Talk about a mindfuck.

The music faded and the crowd went wild as Alaric finished up his performance, leaving the stage to the same side Sapphire was standing.

My act was up next, so rolling my shoulders and taking a deep breath I expelled all thoughts of Alaric Mackenzie from my brain to concentrate on the music. The crowd silenced as *Madness* by *Ruelle* started to play and I walked light footed onto the stage, my hands feeling the stream of silk between my fingers and slowly starting to climb.

The night as always ended on a high. The crowd were cheering, the stage alight with fountains of fire and the staff finishing off their performances with popping champagne.

Alaric had changed back into his usual business suit and had the stern but gorgeous frown to go with it as he oversaw the end of night exit routine.

Exhausted, most of the staff collected their belongings and headed back to the Hive. I had to admit I was nervous to spend my first night there. It felt extremely odd knowing I was going back to an empty apartment and neither Alaric nor Axel would be there. Still, having my own space where I could veg out and have girly nights with Morgan and Trinity did seem like heaven.

Tossing on my old ripped *Nirvana* T-shirt with some Jean shorts and converse, I grabbed my old tote bag and prepared myself to leave.

Morgan, Leon and most of the others had already split.

"Siren."

The words sounded like silk and honey and my whole body quivered, turning slowly to see Alaric waiting behind me.

I smiled, "Mr Mackenzie, you looked amazing tonight."

He smiled. Although for the first time that smile didn't seem to reach his eyes. "As did you."

The words came out softer, quieter and a strange feeling of anxiety clawed inside my chest as he dropped his gaze to the floor.

"Are you okay?"

Panic was starting to evolve now and I had no idea why I was feeling this way. *Jesus Lexi, stop being such a pussy.*

Alaric smiled, looking back towards me. Suddenly he sighed loudly. "Fuck Lexi, this is killing me."

I narrowed my eyes in confusion, waiting for him to continue.

He stared at me, emotion burning in his gaze but I couldn't work out what emotion it was.

"Since you've been here everything's changed." He ran his palm over his face. "I try to work, I try to sleep, I try to fucking hang out with the guys, and the only thing I can fucking think about is you and how I just wanna curl up on the sofa with you or drag you to my bed and fuck you until you can't even remember your own name."

My cheeks heated at his words. A tingling sensation stirring in my stomach.

"Al what are you saying?"

All I wanted was to grab hold of him and kiss that tortured look from his face, but I stood paralysed to the spot waiting for him to answer me.

"I'm saying you're changing me little siren, you're making me give a shit and it's fucking brutal."

Words deserted me and all I could do was stare down at the floor.

"I'm saying you're free."

My head jolted up to meet his gaze, startled at what he had just said to me.

"What do you mean?" I asked.

Confusion whirled around in my brain. What did he mean I was free? Free from what? Him? Did he not want me here anymore?

"I mean I'm no longer keeping you at La Tanière against your will. You're no longer obligated to stay here if it's not what you wish. Your mother will still receive her treatment from Havencroft. That will be ongoing for as long as needed, but I can't do this to you anymore."

I felt like I'd been hit by a double decker bus. Did he not realise how happy I'd become here? It wasn't just about staying for my mum anymore, I was staying for me. Did he not realise how I'd started to see these people as my family? Where did he think I was going to want to be instead? With Vinnie, father of the year? I don't think so. I only had Sim on the outside of La Tanière and even then it didn't mean I wanted to just up and leave. I'd only just got my own apartment at the Hive for god's sake and what about Elliot? Had he even consulted things with him?

So many questions thrashed inside my mind, desperate to come out of my mouth but there was only one thing I could manage to say,

"Why?"

He swallowed and a muscle ticked in his neck.

"Because I love you."

CHAPTER FORTY SEVEN

Alaric

I swear the next ten seconds felt like the longest time of my life as I stood, my fucking soul bare for this girl who right now was standing as still as a god damn statue. I'd never felt so fucking vulnerable in my entire life and I hated it.

I'd never told a woman I loved her before, I'm pretty sure my brother had told many women he loved them in the hope he'd get into their knickers, but I was different. There was no way I was going to say it until I fucking meant it, and up until this moment I hadn't found anyone who I even wanted to say it to but I knew now this was it.

I felt it now with my little siren. This wasn't just sex or a good time. I fucking loved the bitch and I wanted her in my life, her and only her but I couldn't keep her at La Tanière confined in the chains of blackmail.

I wanted her to want to be here, for herself, for me, not because she needed the money to fix her fucking mother.

Those gorgeous doe eyes stared at me as her little tongue darted out and ran along her plump bottom lip.

I hadn't asked her how she felt about me, but I was pretty sure with the sounds she was making when we were alone together that there was definitely some kind of chemistry there.

Finally she opened her mouth.

"I should get back to the apartment. I'm really tired."

Fuck! What was I supposed to say to that? Had I expected her to say it back? Yes? Maybe? Fuck knows but I swear my stomach felt like it was digesting rocks.

She turned towards the door to leave the club, tossing her bag over her shoulder.

"Goodnight Alaric."

I let go of the breath I was holding, my shoulders slumping forward and the weight of the world crashing back down on top of me.

"Goodnight Alexandra."

Those were the only words I managed to choke out, as she pushed through the swinging door and out of my sight.

Growing up, three things had always brought me comfort in life. My brother, my uncle and a bottle of Jack. Well two out of three ain't bad as I slouched back in the cushioned booth of the club, with Elliot and a large bottle of my favourite whiskey. We'd already managed to polish off half of the bottle.

Axel had already confirmed he wouldn't be coming home tonight as he was seen groping Ashleigh backstage before her performance, so there was no need to wait up for him.

Elliot puffed away on his fat cigar as I drowned my sorrows.

"I let her go." I could feel my eyes sting with a mixture of exhaustion and the alcohol kicking in.

"Did you tell her how you feel?

I scoffed, "yep! Fuck lot of good it did me though."

Elliot nodded. His face was emotionless.

"The girl loves you."

I threw my head back, barking with laughter.

"She turned and left." I replied.

"Love is a tricky thing to navigate," said Elliot, "if it was easy then the world would be a much simpler place. Hell, I should know I've been there myself."

I looked at my uncle. His face aged with the stress of life.

"Chloe?"

Elliot nodded.

"Chloe was a good woman, the love of my life. She would have done anything for me, gave me a beautiful daughter if only for a short time."

I swallowed more of my whiskey, watching as my uncle poured out his heart.

"Chloe always taught me to be a better person. It was her who almost managed to convince me to go straight. Give up the life on the wrong side of the law. If my head hadn't been so fucked over Kayla then hell I might have even done it." He hesitates, taking another drag of his cigar and looking back at me. "Before Chloe there was someone else, another woman."

My eyes widened at the revelation.

"Someone else? You dirty dog, I never knew this." I chuckled. My uncle was always a private man. Most would even call him secretive, so the fact he had another love is weird as fuck for me to hear.

"Her name was Sienna, she was the most beautiful woman I'd ever laid eyes on. I thought she'd be the one I'd marry but it wasn't to be. She didn't feel the same."

The pain in his voice was almost tangible as he squeezed his hands into fists on the table, his knuckles turning white.

"Alaric, there's something I need to tell you..."

The door burst open with a mighty thrash, as Rio darted in, a look of wild terror on his face.

"BOSS, THE HIVE. IT'S ON FIRE!"

CHAPTER FORTY EIGHT

Lexi

Why the fuck didn't I say it back?!

What is wrong with me? *Goodnight? I'm tired?*

The guy I'm literally head over heels for has told me that he loves me and what do I do? Absolutely fucking nothing!

I pace up and down my new apartment trying to wrap my head around what the hell just happened tonight.

I didn't understand what had prevented me from telling Alaric the truth, that I was in love with him too and I didn't want to go anywhere. I wanted to stay here with him, with my La Tanière family. I was a coward in the worst possible way.

Fuck it! I grabbed my bag and headed to my front door. I was going to go straight over to Als apartment now and tell him exactly how I feel, *and then probably beg him to fuck me.* I was ready to take control for once in my fucking life.

Grabbing the door handle, I yanked my hand back in shock as the burn from the knob penetrated the skin of my palm in an instant.

What the fuck?

I ripped open the door to be greeted by an overpowering

shield of thick black smoke. It battered against my face and body, invading my mouth and nostrils and forcing itself into my lungs.

I threw my hand protectively to my mouth in instinct as I squinted ahead through the mist to try and see the exit to the stairwell.

Wading my way through the thick blanket of smoke, the piercing screams of my colleagues, my friends, rang out all around me.

I ran down the corridor, throwing my head over the balcony of the stairwell, only to see the horrifying lick of white hot flames growing and crawling its way up the building.

Deciding to make a run for it, I began descending the stairs.

As I got closer to the ravishing heat, the ground shuddered beneath me and all of a sudden a huge beam crashed down with devastating impact, blocking my exit and trapping me where I was.

Fuck!

"HELP! PLEASE SOMEONE!"

I screamed as loud as I could, my airways tightening with the smoke, forcing me to cough uncontrollably as I fought for more oxygen.

I began to move back up the stairs to my apartment. If I wasn't going to make it through the door then my only other option was the window.

Adrenaline surged through my body as I forced the feeling of nausea down and used every bit of my energy to fight my way through the smog, down the corridor, back to my home.

"HELP ME! PLEASE!"

I heard the cries coming from an apartment not too far from mine as I changed direction to seek out the owner of the voice.

Sapphire sat curled into a ball in her doorway. She was grasping her knees, which were drawn up to her chest as she rocked back and forth.

"SAPPHIRE." I called to her as her head darted up to see me standing in front of her.

She burst into tears.

"Lexi, help me please!"

I ran to her, gripping her upper arm and dragging her to her feet.

"Come on, we have to get out of here."

She followed me back to my apartment where I pushed open the sliding window.

Deafening sirens wailed outside as I saw the firefighters arriving down below.

Fuck! This was such a bad time to be living on the top floor.

Sapphire continued to panic behind me as I scrambled to think of some way out of here.

I glanced down to see Elliot and Leon. So far below, they almost looked like tiny ants.

"LEXI!"

I heard Alaric's bellowing call, before I saw him dive into the burning building.

"NOOO!" I screamed but it was too late. He'd entered the Hive with Axel on his tail.

Turning from the window as quickly as I could, I grabbed Sapphire's wrist.

"They're headed for the stairs, come on."

Suddenly I felt resistance.

"Wait!" She called. "I just want you to know, I'm sorry, for everything with Alaric. I was jealous and I wanted him for myself. I loved him but he never loved me back and it killed me. It's you he wants, he's never looked at me the way he does with you."

I smiled gently, wrapping my arms around her in a quick embrace and then taking her face in my hands.

"All of that doesn't matter anymore. We need to get out of here. Right now. Because if we don't, we're going to die!"

Sapphire nodded and circled her shoulders like she was trying her best to pull herself together.

"Now let's get out of this place."

We darted through the door, the smoke becoming even more

challenging to get through as we made it back to the stairs.

"LEXI!" Al was yelling at the top of his lungs up the stairs.

"WE'RE HERE," I called back, waving my arms, hoping desperately that he'd see me.

"Axel, she's here," I heard him shout to his brother.

Both of them fought through the devastating flames as much as they could but it wasn't enough, it was simply too dangerous to reach us.

Fear gripped my chest like a vice, choking the air from me more than the smoke itself. Then an idea suddenly hit me.

"Al, quickly I'm going to lower Sapphire down and I want you to catch her."

I looked to Sapph, her eyes red and bulging as she contemplated what I was saying before shaking her head frenziedly.

"I'm not leaving you," shouted Alaric. "No fucking way."

Tears began to stream down my cheeks as I fought back the sob lodged inside my throat.

"We have to do this."

I pulled Sapphire to the banister.

"Quick, climb over the rail and hold my hands. I'll lower you as much as I can and Alaric and Axel will catch you."

Sapphire's beautiful face was painted with horror.

"I can't do it Lexi, please I'm so scared, I can't…."

I took her hands in mine, squeezing tightly.

"Yes you can, and you will. You owe me this Sapph for being an absolute fucking bitch to me all this time."

She laughed nervously through her tears as I wiped her ash covered cheek with my palm.

"Now go."

With that she quickly climbed over the railing as I gripped her hands for dear life, my knuckles turning white as snow from the strain.

I lowered her as far as my arms would stretch. The ache searing through my shoulder muscles. Al and Axel braced to catch her below.

"On three," I called. "One, two…"

Without warning I let her go. A blood curdling scream rang from Sapphire's lips as I watched her delicate frame drop down and down, almost in slow motion, as she plunged into the brothers' combined grip.

A wave of relief powered over me. She made it.

"Lexi, come on, now you."

Alaric stared at me in pure horror and anticipation as I steadied my grip on the banister, throwing one foot and then the other over the edge.

My hands trembled as I fought with all my strength to hold on to the rail. *I can do this, I've climbed higher on the silks, granted not over a burning floor but still.*

I glanced below, ready to jump until a harrowing crash shook the rail, as another beam dropped right where Alaric, Axel and Sapphire were standing. They all dove rapidly to the side but the tremors from the impact shook the rail I was balancing on so violently I was tossed from it.

I fell, throwing out my arms in panic and managing to grab the next rail down.

"LEXI!" A horrified cry from Alaric felt like it was shattering my heart into pieces.

Holding tightly with all my strength, my legs dangling, I looked down to see the raging flames that had now consumed the whole building below me. The force of the flames pushed Alaric, Axel and Sapphire back out of the building.

I could hear Alaric's muffled cries as he fought to reach me but I was now completely alone. Everyone out of sight, just me and my fate laid out. This was it. This was how I was going to die.

Suddenly a powerful arm, clad all in black with black leather gloves reached over the rail, gripping me by the hair. I screamed in pain as the arm lifted me back over the edge of the banister and onto the floor. Coughing and spluttering on my hands and knees, I forced my head up to see who my rescuer was, only to be met with nothing but complete and utter darkness.

CHAPTER FORTY NINE

Alaric

The heat was unbearable.

Excruciating pain lanced my hands as I fought against the flames to get to my little siren.

Someone frantically gripped my shoulders and I turned back to see Axel, his skin tarred with ash and his eyes red with irritation.

"We need to get the hell away from here," he choked. His tattered T-shirt covering his mouth.

"NO!" I barked. There was no chance in Hades that I was leaving without Lexi.

As soon as I saw a slight break in the flames, I charged back into the burning building.

"AL!"

Sapphires screams were the last thing I heard, ringing in my ears as I fought through the torturing heat.

My lungs rebelled against every inhale as they were filled and suffocated, and a collection of thick, rancid dust attacked my eyes, my vision becoming more and more impaired.

Coughing and spluttering, I managed to fight my way back to the area at the bottom of the stairs where I last saw Lexi as she fell from the rail.

The flames were now overwhelming and it was pretty much

certified death if I took another step, but fuck it I wasn't going to live without Lexi, that much was certain.

I took one last deep breath and charged at the crumbling staircase, fighting against gravity as the floor gave way under my feet. Managing to get myself to the next floor up, I looked around, frantically searching for any signs of my girl, but there was nothing.

A large, padded set of hands came behind me and I turned to see a firefighter signaling me to follow.

"I need to go up," I shouted. "The woman I love is in there."

The firefighter looked at me in confusion behind his mask.

"There's no one here."

I stared at him in disbelief for a few seconds. *She was out? Lexi was safe, away from the burning building?*

I followed the firefighter as we made our way back outside. Ambulances were situated in the courtyard tending to the staff.

I ran from the building, doubling over to cough up all the shit my lungs had been subjected to. Axel and Elliot came to my side.

Standing together, the three of us looked on as the Hive burnt to the ground. Several of the La Tanière crew had been taken to hospital for burns and smoke inhalation, but all in all the main thing was that everyone got out alive.

All the homes we'd built for our club family were destroyed and I had no idea how the fuck this had even happened.

"Where's Lexi?"

I turned to hear Elliot's question as my eyes scanned the crowd searching for the little siren.

"I thought she was out here?"

"I haven't seen her."

I ran to the fire engine, grabbing the arm of a firefighter who was about to step back into the vehicle. "There's someone still in the building," I yelled.

He stepped down onto the path in front of me.

"No sir, we're finally on top of the situation and the building is now completely vacant I can assure you."

My head was spinning and I wasn't sure if it was the effects of the smoke or the fact I couldn't find Lexi.

"Look sir, we have reason to believe that this fire wasn't an accident. Fuel cans were found at the bottom of the stairwell, blatantly left there to be seen. I'm afraid we're looking at an arson attack."

A fucking arson attack? What the fuck?

Elliot was at my side in an instant.

"This is Vinnie, I know it's him," he whispered.

"What? What are you talking about? You think this was caused because we took back our girls? Or killed Darien?"

Elliot's eyes stared into mine. Sorrow pooled inside them.

"No, this was caused because of me."

I shook my head in disbelief. I knew my uncle had his secrets but I sure as hell wasn't letting him feel guilt over the fact we killed a known sex trafficker and freed a bunch of fucking women, caged liked animals. My blood raged.

Vinnie would be ended, and quickly. I was done with holding back. It was time to find him and put a bullet in his skull, but the only thing I cared about right now was seeing Lexi and holding her in my fucking arms.

Rio and Sully jogged towards us from where the ambulance was parked.

"Have you seen Lexi?" I grabbed Rio by the collar, his eyebrows narrowed.

"No, no one has a clue where she is. She's vanished."

Suddenly Leon raced towards me, panting heavily.

"Alaric, Lexis gone… and so has Morgan."

CHAPTER FIFTY

Lexi

It felt like hours. Long torturous hours that I was kept in complete darkness.

I heard voices. They were male but I didn't recognise a single one, all of them muffled by the thick, black bag I had secured over my head.

My hands were tied behind my back and even though I had no idea where they were taking me, I knew it wasn't anywhere close by, as I was hauled into the trunk of a car and the feeling of movement below me seemed to last forever.

Finally we came to a stand still and I felt the chill of the night air on my body as the trunk door was opened and large, rough hands grabbed me by the waist, dragging me out.

I considered screaming but I'd done so much of that back at the Hive when the bag was forced over my head, that my throat was now raw and painful.

The sound of large, metal shutters being wrenched open filled my ears and I was marched forward inside a building.

Suddenly I felt a presence behind me as a hand shoved me forward so violently I fell to the ground, my knees smashing on the cold, stone floor. I whimpered at the pain, trying hard to steady myself.

Suddenly the bag was ripped from my head, the bright lights

burning my eyes as I squinted to adjust. It looked like some kind of abandoned warehouse.

"Good evening Miss Power."

Lifting my head, I was met with the terrifying gaze of the scarred man with one eye. Vincenzo De La Hoy.

Fear rose from my stomach but I fought to control the trembling of my body. The last thing I wanted was for this bastard to see me scared.

"What do you want?" I snarled, trying drastically to keep my composure.

Vinnie smiled. His face was a vision I'd only seen in my nightmares.

"Well it's nice to see you too Alexandra."

I scoffed, tugging at my binds. They didn't so much as budge an inch.

"There's nothing nice about you Vinnie, we all know who and what you are. You can't hide anymore."

His eyes widened as he tilted his head slightly to the side.

"You know who I am? Oh I sincerely doubt that. It's nothing personal Alexandra, you're simply a means to an end for me."

Every word that left his vile mouth enhanced my rage.

"I know you're my father."

My eyes stung with tears as I said the words out loud for the first time.

Vinnie froze to the spot, his eyebrows pinching inwards until it looked like realisation had hit him.

"Your father?..."

A muffled scream stops him in his tracks and I snap my head around to see Morgan being dragged into the warehouse. Her small body thrashing against the two burly men carrying her in. They throw her to the ground before standing back.

"Morgan!"

I rush to her side, trying to comfort her the best that I can with my hands still tied. The rope biting into my wrists.

"Lexi, what's happening? Where are we?"

"Miss Nightingale, so good of you to join us."

Vinnies voice was sinister and taunting, causing my blood to feel like it was turning to ice.

"What do you want with us, Vinnie? Alaric will find me," I screamed.

He threw his head back in a thunderous laugh before stalking towards me, gripping me by the hair and yanking my head backwards to an unnatural angle. I steadied my body in fear that my spine was going to snap at any second.

"He won't need to try very hard, as a message to let him know exactly where you are is on it's way to La Tanière as we speak. You, my little beauty, are going to bring Elliot, Axel and Alaric Mackenzie here to me and I'm going to finish what was started twenty nine years ago."

I shook my head in confusion. *What the fuck?* I had no idea what the hell was even going on anymore.

Vinnie released my hair, forcing me back onto the floor as he walked towards Morgan.

"And you..."

His finger landed on her cheek as he slid it down her jawline onto her throat and then trailed down towards her breast. She squirmed against his touch.

"You're going to make back all the money I lost when you're little friends raided my club and took my girls."

His smile was like venom as Morgan whimpered.

"You're a sick fuck," I screamed, "and you're never going to get away with any of this."

One minute Vinnie was looking at me, and then the next I felt the back of his hand smash against my cheek knocking me to the ground. Blood pooled in my mouth as I spat it to the floor. I could hear Morgan sobbing as I tried to shake off the dizziness. A strangled laugh escaped my throat.

"Is that all you've got?"

Vinnie snarled at me, baring his razor sharp teeth.

"I've had enough of your voice," He shouted. "Put them in a cage."

With that, four large men gripped both of us and dragged us

to another part of the warehouse. A room containing the filthy cages that we'd seen the night at Scarlet.

I fought with all my strength, kicking and biting but the men were too strong, forcing me into the small cage like a rabid animal and pushing Morgan in after me.

We huddled together on the floor. I laid my head against Morgans as she cried, doing my best to reassure her and remain strong for the both of us.

"Lexi, what are we going to do? I don't even know how I got here. One minute I was trying to get out of the Hive when I saw the smoke and the next I was here." Her voice trembled fiercely.

"Well at least we know who started the fire now," I replied. Fear drained Morgan's face.

"Morgz I promise you it's going to be okay, Alaric and the guys will get us out of here. Then we're going to go home and you're going to tell Oake exactly how you feel about him."

She smiled through her tears, leaning into me as we cuddled together in the cold, dirty cage.

We must have fallen asleep because the next thing I knew, two guards entered the room where we were being kept, staring through the bars of the cage.
I thought after the infiltration at Scarlet that most of Vinnies security guards had been taken out, but here he was with a whole lot more that we had no idea about.

The men glared at us with savage, hungry eyes and for the first time I felt like I was right back living with my mum in our old crack den, with the pimps and druggies looking at me like I was a prime steak ready to be devoured.

I shuffled back, pressing towards Morgan as best as I could with my bound hands, as the cage door was opened and a hand reached in to grab one of us.

"Don't you dare touch her," I snarled, venom laced my voice. I was a cornered animal and I was going to defend myself at any cost.

The guard laughed, and I could smell his rancid breath from

where he was standing.

"I don't give a fuck which one of you bitches sucks my dick, but you better decide now before we fuck both of you until you fucking bleed."

I pushed Morgan further towards the back of the cage.

"Bring that disgusting, disease ridden little pisser anywhere near me and I swear I'll bite the fucking thing off."

The guards hand shot out, grabbing me by the throat as Morgan screamed. Suddenly the door slammed open.

"What did I tell you about fucking touching?" Vinnie stormed over to where the guard was standing, still gripping my throat and punched him hard in the face. He fell to the ground with a smack. I shuffled back to where Morgan was sitting.

Vinnie turned to the other guard.

"Bring them. It's almost time."

My heart pounded as we were ripped from the cage and taken back to the main part of the warehouse.

I was both relieved and terrified at the thought of seeing Alaric again, as part of me wondered if this reunion was going to be our last.

CHAPTER FIFTY ONE

Alaric

Forcing my foot down onto the accelerator of my Porsche, we flew through the town, heading in the direction of the warehouse where Lexi and Morgan were being held.

Only thirty minutes before, I'd received an urn, delivered to the club with my little sirens name on it, containing a note telling us exactly where Vinnie De La Hoy was waiting, and that he only wanted myself, Elliot and Axel at the warehouse or he'd kill both the girls.

"He's dead, he's fucking dead."

Rage coiled within me, shaking me to the core and I'd never felt murderous intent as intensely as I did right now.

"This ends today," said Elliot loading up his glock on the passenger side. Axel attaches his weapons inside his leather jacket on the back seat.

Elliot turned to face me. "Whatever happens today, I want you both to know how much I love you, how much I've always loved you and I've only ever wanted what was best for you both."

My eyes narrowed in confusion. "Nothing is happening to any of us today. We go in, we end this and we go home together. All of us."

Elliot nodded. I'd been on so many jobs with my uncle, seen him take on men twice as big and twice as deadly as he was and he never flinched, but this felt different. This time I sensed fear in his tone, fear mixed with something else but what that was, I had no clue.

I knew Vinnie wouldn't be alone and the fact he had said to come alone with only Elliot and Axel indicated that we were going to be outnumbered, but I didn't fucking give a shit. We needed to be careful but I was leaving this shitty warehouse he was hiding in with my family, all of them.

The drive seemed to take an eternity, and as every minute passed I worried what was happening to my little siren.

I'd seen the kind of man Vinnie was and my only hope was that if he really was Lexi's father he wouldn't hurt her or at least he wouldn't kill her.

Pulling up at the dark warehouse, it looked like something from a horror movie as I scanned the grounds looking for any indication that we were walking into a trap.

The place looked deserted.

Taking out the guns, we slowly moved towards the building, covering each other's back.

Quick as lightning, I caught the movement of a shadow to my left. Grasping my gun, I shot into the dark. Hearing the pained groan indicated that I'd hit one of Vinnies guards and he was down.

"AL, TO THE LEFT!" Axel yelled out, but before I had time to turn, Elliot aimed his gun, releasing his bullet into the chest of a guard charging straight at me.

Silence filled the air and it appeared that the coast was clear as we began quietly advancing towards the entrance.

Vinnie knew we were coming but I doubted he knew we were here yet unless he heard the gunshot, so managing to use the element of surprise was a plan that would significantly give us the upper hand.

Sneaking inside, I could hear the sinister voices of Vinnie and his minions.

As we approached closer to where they were situated, I spotted Lexi and Morgan crouched on their knees on the filthy floor, their hands tied behind their backs.

Lexi's lip was split open, covered in dried blood, and the sight of it turned my own blood to pure venom. Someone had put their hands on her and today would be the last day they would ever draw breath.

The warehouse was large, filled with wooden crates which luckily were big enough to conceal us as we split up to watch and see what Vinnie did next.

Elliot stayed behind the crate nearest to me and Axel headed silently to the other side of where the girls were being held.

"On three," my uncle whispered, "this bullet is going in Vinnies head, keep me covered from the guards to the right."

I nodded, glancing over to see three guards watching where Vinnie was standing.

I lifted my gun, steadying my hands and taking aim.

"One..."

My breathing steady, I kept aim mostly at the guard that was closest to Lexi in case he had any funny ideas and tried to grab her.

"Two..."

Sweat beaded on my forehead at the anticipation that this would finally be the end to our problems with Vincenzo De La Hoy.

"Thr..."

"Well, well, well what do we have here?" Vinnies words felt like a lorry crashing into me, as I looked over to see my brother being marched from the crate he was crouching behind by one of Vinnies guards, a gun held to his head.

Elliot pulled back the gun in horror, ceasing his fire.

"You made it Mr Mackenzie, now where would your brother and uncle be?"

He glanced around the room as two more guards crept up behind myself and Elliot, holding loaded guns to our heads.

Our hands went up in surrender as we were pushed from behind the crates to where the girls were kneeling.

Vinnie clutched his gun by his side.

"Alaric!" Lexi called. Her eyes flashed with a look of terror.

I ran to her side, but before I could reach her another gun was pointed in my face.

"Alaric, Elliot, so glad you're here. It's about time we came face to face, don't you think?"

Vinnies cool, calm tone was fucking chilling.

"Rather relaxed for a guy who's gonna fucking die today," I snarled at him.

A murderous laugh thundered from his mouth.

"You take after your father more than you could ever imagine."

My body tensed at the mention of my father.

Elliot had never spoken about my father, besides telling me that he and my mother had died in a car accident when I was a toddler and Axel was a baby, leaving him to raise us. *How the fuck did Vinnie know him?* I didn't even remember him.

"What the fuck do you want Vinnie? More women because you don't have the ones you stole from La Tanière anymore? Is that what this is about? Justice for that sick fuck Darien?" My anger was growing more and more uncontrollable.

"Oh Alaric, is that what you think this is? Because of some cheap whores that I can swipe from anywhere? No, I'm afraid your little women from La Tanière were simply collateral."

I scoffed. "Collateral? So why take them? Why set fire to the Hive? Why..."

"BECAUSE I WANTED *HIM* TO SUFFER!"

He shook his gun in the direction of Elliot as he bellowed the words, his deafening roar echoing from the warehouse walls.

"I wanted him to feel what it was like to lose everything bit by bit, the same way I did. To watch his whole life be destroyed right before his eyes and be totally and utterly fucking powerless to stop it."

His face was frantic, his body tensing and a look of infinite hatred in his one good eye.

I turned to look at my uncle but instead of shock or horror on his face, his expression was defeat, sadness.

"Elliot, what is he talking about?"

Elliot kept his eyes fixed on Vinnie. I looked to Lexi who was huddled with Morgan, trying desperately to soothe her.

My uncle remained silent as I turned my attention back to Vinnie.

"So you wanted your old business partner to suffer for something in the past?! Right so why bring Lexi into your fucked up plan? Why use your own daughter?"

"My daughter?" Vinnie laughed like a mad man. If I wasn't sure he was fucking unhinged before, then I sure as hell was now.

"She's not my daughter."

Lexi froze, I saw the tick in her slender throat as she swallowed.

"What?" Her tiny voice sounded strained and all I wanted to do was hug her, tell her everything was going to be okay.

Vinnie began pacing up and down in front of us.

"See, your *uncle* Elliot here was more than just my partner, he was my best friend. We did everything together, were inseparable, the same in every way, well mostly every way."

He looked towards Elliot who wasn't saying a single word.

"See one thing Elliot didn't really agree on was the way I treated women. He was soft you see, didn't agree when I had to dish out the odd black eye or split lip. In fact he was pretty useful at helping me out after a nasty run in with the Tilsley brothers, when they threatened me after I put their little sister in her place a few times when we dated."

His words sickened me, the sooner this cunt was in a six foot hole the better.

"Now things changed between Elliot and I when we met Sienna. Oh sweet Sienna, she was a beauty. The most incredible raven black hair and deep, deep grey eyes. Now the problem was both Elliot and I loved this woman, yep we were both in love with the same girl."

My head spun as I tried to take in every word Vinnie was saying.

"Elliot had to give up though when Sienna chose me."

"You never deserved her," Elliot yelled. His face began to contort in anger.

"Nevertheless, she chose me and within a few months she was expecting my baby. Imagine my joy when she gave birth to my bouncing baby... boy."

In that moment I swear my heart stopped beating. Vinnie had a son not a daughter.

"But see Sienna turned out to be like every other bitch I'd known, and before my son was even two years old, she had fucked my brother resulting in the birth of her second bastard son, and can you guess who that little problem was?... Yep it was you!" Vinnie turned the gun until it was directed straight into the face of my brother. "Axel Mackenzie, the start of all my problems."

Nausea rolled in my stomach.

"But then that would mean..."

"Yesss, Alaric Mackenzie, MY SON, my only son."

My eyes darted to Elliot who was now looking to the floor, his eyes no longer focused on Vinnie.

What the fuck? This couldn't be true. Elliot was my fucking uncle wasn't he?

Vinnie continued raining down pain on everyone in the room.

"Now my brother was easy enough to take care of, but little Axel here was slightly more difficult to do away with. Sienna the slut fled in the night to the comforting, protective arms of my best friend Elliot, who of course took little persuading to hide her and my son away from me. However he may have been able to protect the bastard child but he failed at protecting *her*, didn't you Elliot?"

Elliot's face paled before he snarled, baring all his teeth. "You murdering bastard," he raged.

Vinnie laughed. "Oh how she cried for you and her children as I made her bleed over and over again."

Elliot lunged forward before two guards were on him, a gun

shoved straight into his temple. He stilled, breathing raggedly, and I could see the agony etched on his face.

"However in retaliation, my so-called friend was waiting for me one night with the Tilsley brothers, ready to let them finish me off, but not before you gave me this scar, hey Elliot?"

Vinnie ran his fingers down the ugly, jagged scar on his face.

"I'll never forget the feel of your blade as you dragged it down my flesh and through my eyeball."

I saw Lexi flinch at the words.

"Then you left, letting the Tilsleys have their fun and by God did they have their fun. However, luckily for me I pulled through and since that day I have made it my mission to make you suffer Elliot Mackenzie, studying your life and your work, and the way you carried on the lie with my son. The lie that you were the grieving uncle, bringing him and his poor little brother up. I mean I guess the grieving was probably right."

His laugh was more evil than ever.

"So you waited all these years to punish me?"

Elliot's voice grew quiet.

"Oh I had other things in life going on. It's amazing how much work is involved in the skin trade, and luckily how much cash. I guess I could've ended you but that was just too easy. No fun at all."

"I'm sorry." Elliot turned to face me, his rage now dissolved into devastation. "I only wanted to protect you. Both of you."

He looked to Axel, who stood like he'd seen a ghost.

"Now I have you back, finally my son."

The words from Vinnies mouth enraged me. My fists clenched by my side.

"I am not, and never will be your son."

Elliot looked lost, the pain and devastation in his face was fucking breaking me and the fact he'd been living with this secret all these years, fuck, it felt like my soul was splitting in two.

"That man is more of a father to me than you could ever be. Blood or not, we are family and I'm going to see to it that you fucking rot."

Vinnie walked towards where Lexi was crouching. My whole body tensed.

"You know, I've seen the way he looks at her. Your brother. Be careful Alaric, when two men love the same woman, hell is unleashed."

I glanced at Axel. "We are nothing like you, the bond we have is unbreakable. Nothing my brother does will ever make me turn against him. He's saved my life once before and I would gladly lay down mine for him. Til the day the stars die, he is my brother."

"You're a fool," Vinnie snickered. "Maybe I should be glad I never raised you."

I smiled at his words. He couldn't break me or my family. I just had to wait for the right second to break him.

CHAPTER FIFTY TWO

Lexi

I think I may have stopped breathing for roughly around ninety percent of the last half an hour.

Pure, excruciating horror graces the face of the love of my life and his brother, and I struggled to decide whether devastation or rage was the more dominant inside Alaric at this precise moment.

All I wanted to do was hold him, but instead I was kneeling before a monster, my hands bound behind my back as I watched Alaric's life unravel in front of my eyes

What about the locket? The question burned in my throat until I could no longer contain it within me.

"Why give me the necklace?... it said *'daddy's girl'* inside. Why give it to me if you're not my father?"

Vinnies face seemed to light up at my words and for the first time since I'd been brought here, I felt a tingling fear. The hairs raised on the back of my neck.

"Ahh yes, I almost forgot, how foolish of me. The locket. Forgive me, that was a little theatrical of me I'll admit." He lodged his gun under his arm, threaded his fingers together and cracked his knuckles. "Watching my dear friend Elliot over the years, I'm sure you can imagine how happy I was for him when he met the lovely lady he grew to have a deep fondness for. What was her name? Chloe wasn't it?"

Elliot paled, his body going visibly stiff.

"Chloe yes that was it, well it was lovely to see such a happy couple and she adored my eleven year old son Alaric and his mistake of a nine year old brother. Then what do you know, soon Elliot and Chloe are welcoming their beautiful baby girl Kayla."

My head spins as I try to focus on Vinnies words, the tension in the room growing thicker with every word being spilled.

"But you see Kayla was ill wasn't she? Yes she was a sickly, little thing, strange really because the lovely doctor you saw told you she couldn't give a definite reason why Kayla was so ill and it must have been truly devastating when she passed away."

A single tear dropped from Elliot's eye. The man before me, the man who had always seemed so unbreakable, was breaking right at this moment.

"You better stop talking about my fucking daughter right now," he whispered.

"Oh but Elliot, there's just something I'm dying to tell you, see the reason little Kayla was so ill was because she'd been exposed to copious amounts of drugs and alcohol while in the womb, leading to devastating effects on her tiny body."

Elliot's eyes narrowed as he focused on what Vinnie was saying.

"Chloe would never even touch a drop of wine while she was pregnant," Elliot hissed.

"Of course not." Vinnie laughed furiously. "But the woman who gave birth to Kayla did, a sixteen year old junkie on the same ward. I think you know her as... Kathryn Power."

What the fuck?! My brain was in pieces. I couldn't make sense of a single thing he was saying.

"It really helps to have a desperate doctor under your thumb, begging you not to tell the world about her little prescription medication habit. It's surprising what a little blackmail can do, even switching two beautiful baby girls, both with one blue eye and one brown eye. What are the chances?"

Vinnie was now hysterically laughing but I couldn't hear a

sound. I gulp down a breath to try and quell the rapid beating of my heart. Blood pumped through my ears and it felt as if time was standing still.

"Elliot Mackenzie, meet your daughter…Alexandra Power."

The whole world stopped on its axis as I looked over at the man who had saved me with his nephews from death's door. The man who had confided in me and treated me with such kindness. A man I had grown up never knowing until now. Elliot Mackenzie, my dad?

I tugged at the ropes, my skin on fire until suddenly I managed to wriggle a hand free. I kept my hands behind my back so as not to alert the guards.

"You're lying," Alaric spat the words towards Vinnie.

"Unfortunately not," taunted Vinnie.

Elliot dropped to his knees as he stared at me.

"I should have known." Tears were now streaming down his face. "You look just like her. The flaming red hair, the flawless skin…"

The words choked and died right there in his throat as his heart shattered and mine followed.

A strangled sob left my mouth and tears were now leaking from both eyes as my grief consumed me.

"Oh Lex." Morgan began to sob alongside me.

"Well now Elliot, you made sure I never knew my child so I made sure you never knew yours. I would say this has been a touching reunion although unfortunately it won't last, not when I kill our little Lexi here and frame you for the murder of the siren of La Tanière. Say your goodbyes."

With that he lifted up his gun pointing it straight at me.

"NOOOOO!" Alaric's voice in the distance.

I squeezed my eyes shut as tightly as possible, my hands no longer behind my back and instinctively going to my face as I prepared for my fate.

Suddenly a hard body slammed into me, pushing me out of the way as the deafening bang seized the air.

Sitting up, Alaric was laid beside me shielding my body, but he wasn't hurt and neither was I. We both looked up in horror to see Elliot clutching his chest, blood pouring from the wound and soaking his shirt in the crimson liquid. His eyes wide and the colour drained from him as he fell to his knees.

CHAPTER FIFTY THREE

Lexi

The high pitched scream filled the whole warehouse and I turned in Morgan's direction to offer her comfort. But it was only when Axel head butted the guard who was standing with the gun against his head, that I realised that it wasn't Morgan who was screaming at all. It was me.

Vinnie turned to point his gun in the direction of Axel, when suddenly Alaric raised from the ground shooting him in the back. He staggered forward before hitting the ground.

Axel turned to the left as Alaric faced the right, firing straight at the remaining guards. One by one they went down like dominos.

The guard that had been knocked down by Axel got to his feet, gun poised and aiming straight at me. I dove to the side before Alaric fired the final shot, ending his life on the spot.

I ran to Elliot's side grabbing his hand. Alaric next to me.

"No, no please Elliot, please stay with me," I begged. I'd never felt so frantic in my entire life. The pain, almost unbearable. Hot tears poured from my eyes.

Axel untied Morgan and the two of them ran to where we were knelt.

Elliot laid out flat on the hard floor.

Alaric ripped off his suit jacket, stuffing it under Elliot's head, as he attempted to apply pressure to the gushing wound.

"Hold on Uncle, we're gonna get you help."

Al threw his phone to Axel who called for an ambulance.

Elliot struggled with his laboured breaths, blood dripping from his lips as he looked at me, pain and sorrow in his eyes.

"I love you." The words cut into me like a thousand knives, twisting and biting at my soul.

"I've only just found you," I cried. "I can't lose you now."

Elliot squeezed my hand, as he began to sob.

"I'm so proud of you Lexi, you're just like your mother. I should have known my own daughter."

"No, how could you have? Vinnie ruined all our lives. I could have had a happy life with you, where I was supposed to be."

Elliot coughed, more blood spraying from his mouth.

"It's going to be okay now," I sobbed. "We're together."

Elliot continued gripping my palm as he looked at Alaric and Axel.

"I'm sorry I lied to you both, but I will never regret raising you to be the men that you have become."

"Elliot be quiet, none of it matters. You were our uncle…fuck, you were our father!"

I could hear the heartache in Alaric's voice as he tried to keep it together.

"He's right unc, hey come on you're gonna be fine. We agreed we'd all get out of here together," said Axel.

Elliot inhales sharply before grasping Alaric's hand and placing my palm within his.

"Take care of each other," he smiled.

"No!" I cried, my voice broken and my breathing uneven.

"It's okay." Elliot's eyes found mine one last time. "It's all going to be alright," and in that moment, it may not have been for long, but I lost the only father figure I'd ever known.

Vinnie coughed and sputtered as he tried to crawl away on his stomach like the snake that he was.

Alaric charged over, grabbing him by the shoulder and forcing him onto his back, pressing the heel of his shoe into Vinnies throat.

Holding his gun, he points the barrel straight between Vinnies eyes.

"You've ruined so many lives." His voice was calm and collected. "Mine, my brothers, Elliot's, Lexi's, my mothers." Al cocked his head to the side, taking in the sight below him.

Vinnie scoffed, "you're right, you're no son of mine."

He spat the words with venom. "You're weak, just like Elliot Mackenzie."

BANG!

The bullet barely touched the sides as it pierced a hole in Vincenzo De La Hoys brain. Silencing him for the very last time.

CHAPTER FIFTY FOUR

Alaric

Sirens wailed as the ambulance arrived at the warehouse.

It didn't take a genius to work out that this had been a hostage situation. So when the police got to the scene, they were more than helpful at making sure that the girls were comfortable and the situation was taken care of. It also helped having men on our books from that side of the law sometimes.

I wrapped my arms around Lexi, pulling her into me as she broke down.

We'd both lost so much tonight, and the road to recovery was going to be a tough one, fuck we had both just discovered our whole lives had been a lie, but we had each other and I would protect my little siren with my life.

Lexis soft, plump lips pressed against mine and all I wanted to do was fuck the grief out of both of us.

"I love you."

The words stopped me in my tracks.

"I came to tell you before the fire." She looked down at the reddened skin on my hands where I'd fought against the flames to get to her. She kissed the sore area gently. "I've loved you from the first moment I saw you."

I smiled, pinching her jaw between my thumb and forefinger and tilting her head up to face me.

"I love you too little siren."

I leaned down to give her another kiss, but this one more passionate as her lips parted, inviting my tongue inside.

We stood like that for what felt like an eternity, wrapped in love and with a promise that whatever pain the future may bring we'd face it together. Just me and her.

EPILOGUE

Six Months Later - Lexi

The house was alive with the sound of love and laughter. A completely different place to the one I'd visited on the night of the Feast of Fire.

I still wasn't used to calling Alaric's incredible house my home, but we'd been living here ever since the fire at the Hive.

Alaric had given Axel full control over the flat. Which seemed to make perfect sense now as I sat with my belly, swollen slightly with Alaric's baby.

We'd only found out that I was pregnant a few weeks ago, much to our surprise. But after nervously telling Alaric and seeing how happy he was, I knew everything was going to be alright.

Today we'd invited our La Tanière family around to the house for a grand reveal and a barbecue in the sun, and I couldn't be more grateful for the people I had around me.

After the events six months ago, life had changed considerably for myself and those around me.

Elliot was given the send off he deserved. His loss was felt greatly by the family at La Tanière and as I stood between Alaric and Axel at his funeral, I was overwhelmed to see the amount of people who arrived. Individuals past and present who Elliot had helped and given a new life to.

I may only have known my father for a short period of time, but his presence would be felt deeply for a long time to come.

The Mackenzie brothers had overseen the rebuilding of the Hive. Working towards building an even better home for the staff who lived there.

After deciding I would need to face the fact that Kathryn Power wasn't my mother and never had been, I worried how this would affect her mentally during her recovery at Havencroft. She was the only mother I had ever known, and the thought of revealing something like that to her had been one of the hardest decisions I'd ever made.

However, tragedy was to follow again when, just before the day I had chosen to explain it all to her, she was taken ill and passed away in hospital shortly afterwards. The doctors explained that the damage to her body, through the years of drug abuse, had become irreversible and just too much for her to cope with anymore.

She was buried in the Blackbridge cemetery next to Kayla Mackenzie. Her biological daughter. I only prayed that she had now found peace, and was reunited with her baby daughter to have another chance at being the mother she so desperately wanted to be.

Picking up my glass of orange juice, I straightened out my floral maxi dress and headed over to where Alaric was standing in the kitchen, pouring out more glasses of champagne for our guests.

I took in the sight of his hard, broad shoulders. Muscles rippled under the relaxed, white T-shirt he was wearing. His light blue distressed jeans hung a little lower than necessary, giving a glimpse of his toned, tight stomach when he reached up into the cupboard.

Heat pooled between my legs. Since being pregnant I had been insatiable and Alaric was only too happy to help me out with that.

I smiled as I watched him chop lemons on the counter that he had fucked me on just the night before.

"Hello Mr Mackenzie," I gave him a wicked smile.

"Little siren, you shouldn't be looking at me like that or you'll be on the end of my belt and you know it would pain me to do that to you while you're carrying my precious cargo."

I laughed as I walked over, my lips barely skimming his and my tongue flicking over his bottom lip.

"Oh I hope that's a fucking promise."

His large hand grasped my tit, the pad of his thumb brushing my sensitive nipple over my dress.

I moaned, pressing myself forward into his touch as his hot breath skimmed my jawline. He pressed flush against my body, the thick, hard ridge of his cock letting me know he was getting as worked up as I was.

"Uh hum."

We froze hearing the sudden presence behind us. Morgan stood in the doorway, arms crossed, tapping her little foot. Alaric released me from his arms.

"Time for that later, firstly everyone would like to know why the hell you've brought us here," Morgan smiled.

Al and I glanced at each other, trying to stifle the amusement.

"Okay, okay, let's do this."

I wrapped my arm around Morgan's shoulders pulling her in closer, Alaric following behind as we headed to the garden where everyone was congregated.

Sim wiggled happily on Axel's lap as he dug his fingers into her hips, taunting her with tickles as she swatted at his hand.

It seemed like forever ago since the day Sim had first spotted Axel in Mals coffee shop. Over the last two months she had been spending more and more time at the house with Alaric and I, and she and Axel had naturally gravitated towards each other.

I'm not sure if it was quite love yet but they were definitely heading in the right direction.

Trinity and Sully were laughing hysterically at something Sully had said on the lawn.

Surprisingly Rio and Sapphire were sitting at the table, deep in conversation, her thigh barely grazing his.

Alaric walked to the small booth that had been set up for La Tanières DJ to play music in the yard. He silenced the tunes.

"Good afternoon everyone, I'm sure you're all wondering why we invited you here…"

I rubbed my small bump in anticipation. I was so excited to finally tell our friends we were going to be parents.

"Well we can now announce that…"

Alaric was cut off by the loud ringing of the doorbell.

He looked over at me in confusion and I shrugged my shoulders, turning towards the door. Alaric following.

I reached the large front door as Al jumped in front of me.

"Wait," he said. "After everything that's happened I'll go first, just in case."

I rolled my eyes, another thing I'd noticed over the last six months was how much more protective Alaric had become. *Even though I had no idea how that could even be possible.*

Al pulled on the door handle, revealing a petite, red headed woman on the other side.

She looked between Alaric and myself in awe, before smiling. Her eyes sparkling and her face gentle and kind.

"Hello Alaric."

I looked up at Al to see his eyebrows raised, a stunned expression on his face as he stared at her.

The woman smiled again. "I know it's been a long time."

Alaric broke his stare, turning to face me.

"Alexandra, I'd like you to meet…Chloe."

ACKNOWLEDGEMENT

I still can't believe I'm writing this, now that my very first novel is finally complete.

It's been a surreal journey and I'd like to firstly thank *you,* the readers for taking a chance on Lexi and Alarics story. I had such an amazing time writing about them and I can't wait for you to meet even more dark and dangerous characters in my novels to come.

Thank you to my husband for being patient with me when I've been writing instead of paying him attention.

To Hasan Housein for all the professional advice, when it came to my writing career.

To all my book loving besties who have supported me and been the best cheerleaders for this book, I adore you all.

And last but not least, to my extremely talented cover designer Cat at TRC designs for the simply stunning cover for Siren. It was even more breathtaking than I could have imagined and for that I am extremely grateful.

ABOUT THE AUTHOR

Michelle Briddock

Michelle Briddock grew up in the glorious South Yorkshire city of Sheffield, before moving down south in hope of a bit more sun... it never happened.

She spends her days writing dark romance and being a slave to her three children, and her evenings arguing with her husband about which Netflix series to binge.

As a little girl, she always loved the Disney villains more than the princesses, which she now channels into all her stories.

Join Michelles world on Instagram for updates and all things bookish.

Printed in Great Britain
by Amazon